The History of Tokyo

CRAFTED BY SKRIUWER

At **Skriuwer**, we're more than just a team—we're a global community of people who love books. In Frisian, "Skriuwer" means "writer," and that's at the heart of what we do: creating and sharing books with readers worldwide. Wherever you are in the world, **Skriuwer** is here to inspire learning.

Frisian is one of the oldest languages in Europe, closely related to English and Dutch, and is spoken by about **500,000 people** in the province of **Friesland** (Fryslân), located in the northern Netherlands. It's the second official language of the Netherlands, but like many minority languages, Frisian faces the challenge of survival in a modern, globalized world.

We're using the money we earn to promote the Frisian language.

For more information, contact : **kontakt@skriuwer.com** (www.skriuwer.com)

Disclaimer:
The images in this book are creative reinterpretations of historical scenes. While every effort was made to accurately capture the essence of the periods depicted, some illustrations may include artistic embellishments or approximations. They are intended to evoke the atmosphere and spirit of the times rather than serve as precise historical records.

TABLE OF CONTENTS

CHAPTER 6: THE IMPACT OF THE TOKUGAWA SHOGUNATE

- *Centralized administration and social order*
- *Closed country (sakoku) policies and internal stability*
- *Samurai governance extending to daily regulations*

CHAPTER 7: THE CLOSED COUNTRY POLICY AND ITS EFFECTS

- *Limited trade with Dutch and Chinese, shaping internal culture*
- *Fear of Christianity leading to strict religious policing*
- *Gradual emergence of Rangaku (Dutch learning) amid isolation*

CHAPTER 8: SHIFTS IN POWER AND FOREIGN INFLUENCE

- *Commodore Perry's arrival igniting political tension*
- *Sonnō jōi movement challenging Tokugawa rule*
- *Boshin War and the fall of the shogunate*

CHAPTER 9: THE OPENING OF JAPAN AND THE END OF THE SHOGUNATE

- *Treaty of Kanagawa and the influx of Western demands*
- *Modernizing efforts clashing with conservative samurai ideals*
- *Peaceful surrender of Edo Castle, paving the way for Meiji reforms*

CHAPTER 10: EDO BECOMES TOKYO

- *Renaming the city and centralizing imperial authority*
- *Initial infrastructure changes: roads, canals, and offices*
- *Samurai and merchant classes adapting to new roles*

CHAPTER 1

The Land Before Tokyo

1.1 Introduction to the Ancient Land

Long before Tokyo became a big city, the land looked very different. There were no tall buildings or busy roads. Instead, much of the area was covered in forests, wetlands, and places where wild animals lived. People who walked across this land thousands of years ago did not have houses made of concrete. They often built simple huts or lived in caves. They gathered plants, hunted animals, and fished in rivers or along the shores of the ocean. The climate was different back then too. Over the centuries, the temperature went up and down, which caused changes in the types of plants and animals that lived here.

This chapter will talk about the region before it was called Edo or Tokyo. We will focus on very old times, from the Jomon period to the Yayoi period and beyond. We will see how early people found ways to live and how their culture changed slowly. These changes would set the foundation for the growth of small villages, which later turned into towns and eventually a powerful city.

We should remember that there was no single group of people who lived here at first. Many small groups moved around, looking for food and good places to settle. Over time, some of these groups learned new skills, like farming. Others might have continued to live by hunting and fishing. The region's geography, which included low-lying land near the sea and higher ground inland, also shaped how people survived.

While we talk about the land before Tokyo, we will also explore important archaeology finds. Archaeologists have dug up old pottery, tools made of stone, and even bones of animals that once roamed the area. These discoveries help us understand what life was like back then. By learning about these early days, we get a clearer picture of how later settlements grew. Even though these ancient times feel far away, they are the roots of a story that leads to the city we now know as Tokyo.

1.2 Early Geography and Climate

The land in the region that would one day be Tokyo was shaped by nature over a very long time. Earthquakes, rivers, and changing sea levels all played a part. The ground near the coast could flood easily, while the inland areas had more stable land. People living in those times had to watch out for natural changes and disasters. Today, we understand that Japan sits on what is called the "Ring of Fire," a place with many volcanoes and earthquakes. In ancient times, people also felt these tremors, but they did not know the scientific reasons behind them.

The sea level near the Tokyo Bay area shifted a lot in prehistory. Sometimes, the shore moved inland, covering land with water. Other times, the shore moved outward, revealing more land for people to explore. This meant that fish and shellfish were either plentiful or scarce, depending on the period. Where people chose to live often depended on how they could collect these resources.

Climate changes also shaped this land. In certain periods, temperatures were cooler, and in other periods, they were warmer. When the climate was warmer, plants like broadleaf trees and bamboo grew more. When it was cooler, different kinds of plants thrived. Early inhabitants used local plants for food, tools, and shelter. For example, they might have taken large tree branches to build simple huts or carved wood into rudimentary cooking tools.

Because the land was unstable at times—due to earthquakes or floods—communities had to adapt quickly. They might have chosen higher ground if flooding was a big risk. Or they might have built their huts near rivers for easy access to fish. Survival in these early days depended on understanding and respecting the land. People learned which areas were safer and which provided the best resources.

1.3 Jomon Period: The First Known Inhabitants

Archaeologists say that the Jomon period is the earliest known culture in Japan that left behind clear artifacts. The Jomon period lasted a long time—from about 14,000 BCE to around 300 BCE. Of course, those dates can shift depending on new research. The word "Jomon" itself means "cord-marked," because the pottery from this time often had rope-like patterns pressed into it.

During the Jomon period, the people were mostly hunter-gatherers. They knew how to make pottery, which is one reason they stand out in world history. Many groups around the world that relied on hunting and gathering did not develop pottery so early. The Jomon people made pots by shaping clay coils and firing them at low temperatures. They often decorated them with rope patterns.

Food sources included nuts, berries, and fish. Shellfish were especially important near the coasts, and we can find huge mounds of shells (called "shell middens") where these ancient people threw away their trash. These shell mounds also reveal bones of fish, deer, wild boar, and other animals. From studying such sites, we can learn a lot about what the Jomon people ate and how they lived.

Tools made of stone were common—arrowheads, knives, and scrapers were used for hunting or cutting. Some tools were polished, showing a level of skill in working with stone. They also created small clay figurines called "dogu." These figurines often had human-like shapes and might have been used in rituals or to pray for good health and safety. No one knows for sure the exact purpose of dogu, but they hint that the Jomon people had spiritual beliefs.

In the Tokyo region, archaeologists have found Jomon sites on elevated ground near rivers or coasts. These were good spots to get seafood and freshwater fish. The Jomon population might not have been very large, but they left behind many remnants of their daily life. Pottery shards and shell middens help us understand the connections they had with nature. They also show that the Jomon people were not just wandering nomads. They settled in certain places for extended periods.

Although we do not have written records from the Jomon people, we can guess that they lived in small communities of families who shared resources. They might have moved around seasonally to find the best fishing or hunting areas. Some groups might have chosen to stay in one place longer if food was plentiful. The daily life of a Jomon person was closely tied to nature's cycles, like the changing seasons and the migration of animals.

1.4 Yayoi Period: The Dawn of Agriculture

Around 300 BCE, a new culture started to appear in Japan. We call this the Yayoi period. This period is marked by the introduction of wet-rice agriculture and new types of tools, often made of bronze and iron. Rice paddies began to pop up in various parts of Japan, including regions not too far from what would later become Tokyo. Rice was a stable, reliable food source, and it could feed larger groups of people than hunting or gathering alone.

The shift to farming changed society. People no longer needed to move around all the time to chase herds or find wild plants. Instead, they settled in villages near their rice fields. This led to a growth in population, because stable food supplies usually allow more children to survive. Villages got bigger, and clear social structures started to develop. There might have been leaders who managed the farming and decided how to share rice among the community.

The Yayoi people brought new pottery styles as well. Their pottery was smoother and simpler than the Jomon rope-pattern style. They also began using metal tools, like iron knives, which were stronger and sharper than stone tools. With metal tools, people could cut down more trees and clear land more efficiently for rice paddies.

In the Kanto region—where Tokyo sits today—some Yayoi communities thrived. The land was suitable for farming in areas where water was easy to control. Villages might have grown around rivers, where people built canals or ditches to bring water to their rice fields. Over time, small markets or trading centers might have emerged, where farmers exchanged rice for fish, salt, or other goods.

Social differences also became more visible. Some people had more wealth, shown by better tools, nicer pottery, or bigger houses. This hints that leaders, perhaps early chiefs, were becoming a central part of village life. They might have organized ceremonies or decided when to plant and harvest crops. This was the beginning of a new kind of society, one that was more structured and less equal than in Jomon times.

While the Yayoi period was a big step forward in technology and farming, it did not erase all of the older ways. Some Jomon groups might have continued hunting and gathering, especially in mountainous areas or places not suitable for rice farming. But overall, the Yayoi culture spread widely, setting the stage for even more changes that would come with the next period in Japanese history.

1.5 The Kofun Period: Burial Mounds and Emerging Power

After the Yayoi period came the Kofun period, which lasted roughly from 250 CE to 538 CE. The word "Kofun" refers to large burial mounds built for important people, likely chiefs or early rulers. These mounds were sometimes shaped like keyholes when viewed from above. They were grand structures, showing that society now had powerful leaders with the ability to organize many people to build these tombs.

During the Kofun period, we see the rise of something close to an early state. People were not just living in small villages. Instead, there were leaders who controlled larger territories. They likely collected taxes, which could have been in the form of rice or goods. They also had armies or warrior groups to protect their land and power.

In the region that would become Tokyo, large Kofun tombs have been found, though most of the biggest ones are in other parts of Japan, like the Kansai region. Still, the presence of smaller kofun in the Kanto area suggests that local leaders were part of the broader power network. They might have had connections with more powerful rulers farther west.

Alongside these social changes, technology advanced further. Iron tools became more common, and better farming techniques spread. Trade routes formed between different regions of Japan. People exchanged rice, iron, salt, and other goods. This trade network helped different regions grow. It also allowed the spread of new ideas, customs, and even religious beliefs.

During the Kofun period, we also see the earliest signs of influences from the Asian mainland. People in the peninsula of Korea and in China had more advanced metalworking skills, writing systems, and new religious beliefs.

Some of these ideas began to trickle into Japan, slowly changing local customs. Over the next centuries, these influences would become stronger, eventually shaping the culture in ways that would be more clearly seen in later periods.

Though the Kofun rulers are shrouded in mystery, we do know that they must have had organized communities. Building large tombs requires many workers and good leadership. The tombs often contained treasures, like swords, mirrors, and jewelry. These items were placed with the deceased leaders, perhaps to show their status or for use in the afterlife. Such practices hint at the beginnings of what would later become the imperial system in Japan.

1.6 Local Tribal Groups and Folk Beliefs

Before a centralized government controlled all of Japan, there were many local tribal groups. Some historians think each region had its own chief who claimed authority over that area. These chiefs might have led local people in rituals to honor gods or spirits. Early folk beliefs likely involved nature worship, where forests, rivers, and mountains were seen as powerful spirits. People believed that if they respected these spirits, they would have good harvests and protection from disasters.

In the region near modern Tokyo, there were small tribal groups who might have relied on both fishing and agriculture. They had their own customs and local shrines. Over time, as the power of large political groups grew, these smaller tribes had to follow new rules or even pay tribute to bigger lords. Still, bits of local traditions remained. Some of the earliest shrines in the Tokyo area may have started as small sacred spots near big trees or rocks.

These folk beliefs mixed with new ideas arriving from abroad. For example, Buddhism came to Japan around the sixth century, and it slowly spread across the country. But even after Buddhism arrived, many local places kept their old worship practices. This mix of beliefs continued for hundreds of years, creating a rich spiritual culture. While we do not have detailed written records of these tribal groups, archaeological sites with offerings or ritual objects give us clues about how they might have worshipped nature gods or ancestral spirits.

Meanwhile, leadership at local levels was shifting. Some chiefs earned recognition from more powerful rulers, possibly receiving titles or gifts in return for loyalty. This relationship between local chieftains and bigger regional rulers laid the groundwork for feudal systems that would come in later centuries. As we look back, we see that the seeds of Tokyo's future were already being planted in these local power structures.

1.7 Daily Life in Prehistoric Times

What was daily life like for the people living in the Tokyo region before it was Tokyo? Let's imagine a small community by a river. The huts might be made from wood and covered with thatched roofs made of straw or reeds. Men and women wake up early to tend the fields or prepare tools. Children might help gather firewood or scare away birds that try to eat the crops. If there is a nearby forest, they might collect berries, nuts, and herbs.

Food would be cooked in clay pots or over an open fire. Rice becomes more important over time, but wild plants, fish, and meat are also part of the diet. People might store extra food in pits or in containers made from natural materials. Since there were no refrigerators, preserving food with salt or by drying it in the sun was common.

Clothing in these early periods was simple. People used fibers from plants or animal skins. In colder weather, they might layer furs or thicker textiles if they were available. Over time, as weaving skills improved, people started wearing clothes made from hemp or other plant fibers. Social gatherings likely took place around the fire or in a communal space, where stories and myths could be shared. Music might have been made using basic drums or flutes carved from bamboo.

Life was not always peaceful. Sometimes, different groups might fight over land or resources. This is shown by the existence of weapons and the remains of fortifications in some archaeological sites. People also had to protect themselves from wild animals, like boars or bears, which roamed the forests. Disease was another worry, because there were no modern medicines. Superstitions and rituals might have been used to ward off illness or bad luck.

But even with these difficulties, many communities found ways to thrive. Over generations, small improvements in farming techniques, housing, and trade helped societies become more stable. Craftspeople learned how to make better tools, and spiritual leaders guided people through ceremonies that kept the community united. These early lessons in cooperation and adaptation would be crucial later, as the region moved toward more centralized forms of rule.

1.8 The Transition to Early Statehood

As centuries passed, different kingdoms and states began to form in various parts of Japan. The Yamato state, centered in the region of modern-day Nara, grew powerful. They sent envoys to China and learned about Chinese writing, political systems, and philosophies like Confucianism. Through these diplomatic connections, they gained new knowledge that helped them strengthen their rule back in Japan.

For local areas near what is now Tokyo, this meant more significant outside influence. Court officials from the Yamato state or other rising powers might visit to ensure loyalty. They might also set up administrative offices or appoint local governors. Though the Tokyo area was not the heart of power at this time, it was still affected by these changing political currents.

Gradually, the idea of a centralized government, linked to an emperor or imperial family, started to spread across Japan. Local chiefs were integrated into this system, sometimes willingly and sometimes through force. As a result, the old tribal lifestyle began to fade. Instead, people had to follow the laws and taxes set by this emerging central authority. While life for farmers and fishermen might not have changed dramatically at first, they could no longer live entirely separate from the broader political structure.

Religious practices also changed as Buddhism gained more followers among the elite. Temples began to appear in different regions. The common people might have visited these temples out of curiosity or because local leaders encouraged them to do so. Over time, Shinto beliefs (based on nature and ancestor worship) blended with Buddhist ideas. This mix would later become a key part of Japanese culture.

1.9 Archaeological Insights

Our main window into these prehistoric and early historic periods comes from archaeology. Since people in the Tokyo region did not always write things down, we learn about their lives by studying what they left behind. Pottery, tools, bones, and old fire pits all reveal clues. For instance, by examining the layers of soil where pottery is found, experts can guess how old it is. They can also see how pottery styles changed over time.

Shell mounds are one of the best sources of information about the Jomon and early Yayoi inhabitants. These heaps of shells and other garbage might not sound exciting, but they are like snapshots of daily life. By analyzing the shells, bones, and other materials, we know what animals were eaten and even what season people collected these foods. Sometimes, human remains are also found, giving us clues about health, diet, and lifespans.

When archaeologists find iron tools in a site that mostly has stone tools, they know there was a shift happening. That shift might mark the arrival of new people or the introduction of a new technology. Changes in pottery style, especially moving from Jomon cord-marked pots to Yayoi smoother pots, also show transitions in culture and daily habits.

Various excavation sites in the Tokyo area have uncovered pit dwellings. These are homes partially dug into the ground, with a wooden framework covered by thatched roofing. The shape and size of these dwellings can tell us about family structures—were they small huts for one family, or larger communal spaces shared by many people? Sometimes, archaeologists find clay figurines or small charms near the entrance, suggesting spiritual beliefs or protective rituals.

As we move closer to the start of recorded history in Japan, we find more advanced items like bronze mirrors, swords, and bells. These might have been used in rituals or as symbols of status. Because these items are linked

to cultures in mainland Asia, we can guess that the Tokyo region was part
of a trade network that stretched beyond Japan's shores. Even if the local
communities were not as large or powerful as those in western Japan, they
were not isolated.

1.10 Setting the Stage for Edo

By the end of these early periods—the Jomon, Yayoi, and Kofun—the land
that would one day be Tokyo had a history of adaptation and change.
People had learned to farm, fish, and trade. They dealt with natural
challenges like earthquakes and floods. They also started forming social
hierarchies and local leadership structures that would later evolve into
feudal domains.

While the region was not yet a major political center, it was far from empty
or undeveloped. Early inhabitants left their marks on the land, shaping it
with rice fields, settlements, and spiritual sites. Over time, roads began to
appear, connecting the Kanto region (where Tokyo is located) to other
parts of Japan. Trade and communication became easier, although travel
was still slow and done mostly by foot or by small boats along the coast.

The next chapter will move us forward in time, where we will see the
establishment of Edo. But it's important to understand that Edo did not
appear out of nowhere. It grew on ground that had been home to people
for thousands of years. These ancient communities laid the groundwork for
the city's culture, economy, and even some of its spiritual traditions. They
passed down skills and knowledge that later generations would build upon.

In this first chapter, we have traveled through many centuries, from the
earliest hunter-gatherers to the beginnings of state formation. We saw how
nature played a huge role in shaping life and how people adapted to the
environment. By the time political power structures started to take hold,
the Tokyo region was already part of a broader network of trade, culture,
and even religion. This sets the stage for the rise of Edo, which will form
the core of Tokyo's early history.

CHAPTER 2

The Rise of Edo

2.1 Introduction to Edo's Beginnings

Before Tokyo was called Tokyo, it was known as Edo. The name Edo, written with characters meaning "bay entrance" or "estuary," referred to the area around the meeting point of the Sumida River and Tokyo Bay. Edo began as a small fishing village. It had fertile land for farming and good access to waterways, which made it a handy spot for those who wanted to control trade and transportation.

In this chapter, we will explore how Edo evolved from a quiet place with a few huts and fields into the seat of power for the Tokugawa shogunate. This transformation did not happen overnight. It took many years, different rulers, and various historical events to shape Edo into a bustling castle town. Once it became the administrative headquarters of powerful warlords, Edo started attracting merchants, artisans, and many other people seeking opportunities.

We should also remember that Japan during these times was ruled by samurai lords, known as daimyo. These daimyo had their own domains, each with its own resources and political structures. The area around Edo fell under the influence of different families over the centuries, but one of the most notable families would be the Tokugawa clan. They would eventually move the center of power from western Japan to Edo.

2.2 Early Medieval Japan: Setting the Scene

To understand how Edo rose to prominence, we need to look at the broader landscape of medieval Japan. After the central imperial court in Kyoto started losing power, local lords and warrior families grew stronger. This led to a period of clan-based rule and frequent conflicts. Many samurai bands fought over land and titles. The emperor still existed, but his influence was limited, especially outside the Kyoto region.

Power shifted from the court nobles to warrior families, such as the Minamoto and Taira clans. Over time, the Minamoto clan gained the upper hand and set up the first shogunate in Kamakura (in the Kanto region, not too far from Edo) around the late 12th century. This government was called the Kamakura shogunate, and it marked a big change in Japanese politics. Samurai rule became the norm, and the emperor's court was mostly symbolic.

During the Kamakura period (1185–1333), the region around Edo was still fairly rural. However, the creation of the shogunate in Kamakura drew more attention to the Kanto area. Trade routes that supplied Kamakura with food and other resources passed near Edo. Some local warlords realized that controlling these routes could bring them wealth. As a result, local strongholds and small forts appeared, possibly near the future Edo location.

Next came the Muromachi period (1336–1573), under the rule of the Ashikaga shogunate. Power structures continued to shift, and the country in many ways was still not united. Different clans vied for control. In the mid to late Muromachi era, Japan faced a period known as the Sengoku period ("Warring States period"), which lasted roughly from the mid-15th century to the early 17th century. This was a time of constant warfare among regional lords, each trying to expand their territory and influence. Edo's growth was slow during this chaotic era, but important changes were happening behind the scenes.

Amid this chaos, the Hojo clan, Uesugi clan, and other families held sway in the Kanto region at different points. Edo was sometimes just another point on the map. It had strategic importance because of its location by the water, but it was not yet a major power center. That would change when one warlord recognized Edo's full potential and decided to build a proper castle town there.

2.3 Ota Dokan and the Early Edo Castle

The first person often credited with establishing Edo as a castle site is Ota Dokan. He was a samurai and a poet who served the Uesugi clan. In 1457, he built a castle in Edo. It was not as large or grand as the castle that would come later under the Tokugawa, but it was a strong fortress for its time. The area around it was mostly marshy, with rivers that could be used for defense and transport.

Ota Dokan was known for his skill in both the military arts and cultural pursuits like poetry. He recognized that Edo Castle could be improved by creating moats that connected with the local rivers, making it harder for enemy forces to attack. He also built shrines and temples to encourage people to settle in the area. Some of these places of worship would last for centuries, becoming important local landmarks.

The castle that Ota Dokan built had wooden walls and watchtowers. It likely had multiple baileys (courtyards or sections) separated by gates. The location was chosen carefully to take advantage of the natural terrain. Even though Edo was small, the presence of a castle made it a local hub. Merchants and artisans came to serve the samurai there. Farmers brought their goods to sell to the castle residents. Over time, small settlements started to form near the castle gates.

Unfortunately for Ota Dokan, his achievements did not guarantee him a peaceful life. He faced political struggles and eventually was killed in 1486. Still, the foundations he laid for Edo Castle were not forgotten. Later lords who took over the region saw the value in the fortifications he had started. Even after power shifted among rival clans, the basic plan of Edo Castle remained in use.

2.4 From a Local Stronghold to a Strategic Asset

During the Sengoku period, many warlords fought for control of the Kanto region. The Hojo clan, based in Odawara, was particularly influential, dominating much of the area. Sometimes they held Edo Castle, sometimes they lost it to another clan. The castle changed hands a few times. Because the region around Edo was not the most fertile farmland in Japan, it was not as wealthy as some other areas. Still, the strategic location made it worth defending.

Some warlords tried to expand Edo Castle, repairing or improving walls and moats. Others might have abandoned it if they had a stronger fortress nearby. By the late 16th century, Japan was undergoing massive unification efforts under powerful figures like Oda Nobunaga, Toyotomi Hideyoshi, and later Tokugawa Ieyasu. These men set out to bring the entire country under one rule, ending the chaos of the Warring States period.

When Toyotomi Hideyoshi rose to power after Oda Nobunaga's death, he forced many local lords to either submit to his authority or be destroyed. One such lord was Tokugawa Ieyasu, who was given control over the Kanto region in the 1590s. As part of this arrangement, Ieyasu took Edo Castle as his new base. This moment was critical in Edo's history. With Ieyasu in charge, Edo would soon become much more than a small fortress town.

2.5 Tokugawa Ieyasu Moves In

Tokugawa Ieyasu was a strategic thinker. He saw that Edo, while not as developed as other places, had enormous potential. It had access to the sea through Edo Bay, and the land around it could be shaped for agriculture. Ieyasu moved into Edo Castle around 1590 and started major building projects to reinforce and expand it. He brought in workers from other parts of Japan to help with construction.

Under Ieyasu, a large moat system was dug to connect with local rivers. This made the castle more secure and helped with transporting supplies. Stone walls were built around the inner parts of the castle, using massive rocks that had to be hauled from distant quarries. This was no small feat. It required detailed planning and a lot of labor.

Ieyasu also invited merchants and artisans to settle near the castle. He promised them security and a chance to prosper. By doing this, he laid the foundation for a bustling town that would offer goods and services not just to samurai, but also to travelers and traders. Over time, roads leading into

Edo improved, and more people came. This was the beginning of Edo's transformation into a major urban center.

When Toyotomi Hideyoshi died, there was a power struggle that led to the Battle of Sekigahara in 1600. Ieyasu emerged victorious, and this paved the way for him to become the shogun in 1603. The shogunate was a military government, meaning real power was held by the shogun, while the emperor in Kyoto served more as a spiritual or symbolic figure. Once Ieyasu became shogun, he made Edo his official seat of power, turning it into the capital of the Tokugawa shogunate.

2.6 Building a Castle Town

A castle town (jokamachi) was a specific type of urban development centered around a lord's castle. In Edo's case, the castle was massive and formed the core of the city. Surrounding it were districts where samurai lived, districts for commoners (including merchants and artisans), and later areas for temples and shrines. The Tokugawa government wanted a well-organized city that could handle the flow of people and goods.

Samurai in service to the Tokugawa lived in barracks or residences called yashiki. These homes varied in size based on the rank of the samurai. High-ranking lords had large estates, while lower-ranking samurai had modest dwellings. These areas had walls, gates, and sometimes moats of their own, creating little neighborhoods that were both living spaces and defensive zones.

Commoners lived in more crowded districts, closer to markets and shops. Streets were often laid out in grids, though not always perfectly aligned. The city grew over time, so some areas followed careful planning, while others were more haphazard. Still, compared to many other cities of the period, Edo's growth was partly planned by the shogunate to ensure good order and security.

In addition, water transportation was crucial. Canals were dug to connect different parts of the city. Goods like rice, fish, and vegetables often arrived by boat. The Sumida River became a lifeline for the city, with boats carrying people and cargo. Bridges started popping up, making it easier for people to travel from one side to the other.

2.7 The Rapid Growth of the Population

As Edo became the shogun's capital, daimyo from all over Japan were required to spend part of the year there under a system called sankin-kotai (alternate attendance). This meant that regional lords had to travel to Edo and maintain a residence there. Their families often stayed in Edo year-round as hostages to ensure loyalty. Because of this, Edo's population soared. Daimyo needed retainers, servants, and bodyguards. Merchants came to sell goods to these wealthy households. Artisans provided everything from swords to fine cloth.

By the mid-17th century, Edo was one of the largest cities in the world. Some estimates suggest it had over a million residents at its peak. This sudden growth created challenges in terms of housing, sanitation, and food supply. The shogunate tried to address these by building new districts and improving roads and water systems. Still, fires were a big danger, since most buildings were made of wood. Large parts of the city burned multiple times during the Edo period.

Despite these problems, people kept coming. The city offered jobs, excitement, and a chance to serve in the shogun's court or in a daimyo's household. Different neighborhoods became known for different trades. One area might be famous for weaving cloth, another for selling fish, and another for blacksmithing. Over time, a real urban culture took root, with festivals, theaters, teahouses, and much more.

2.8 The Social Structure of Edo

In Edo society, people were divided into classes. At the top were the samurai, who served the shogun or the daimyo. Below them were the peasants, who farmed the land, followed by artisans who made things, and merchants who sold them. This was called the "shi-no-ko-sho" system. In theory, each class had its own duties and privileges, and movement between classes was rare.

Samurai had the right to carry swords and were expected to live by the bushido code. However, not all samurai were wealthy. Some were poor and struggled to feed their families. Peasants had the important job of producing food, especially rice, which was used as a form of tax. Artisans and merchants lived in towns and had to follow many rules, such as wearing certain types of clothing or living in specific neighborhoods.

This social structure shaped Edo's physical layout. Samurai often lived closer to the castle. Merchant and artisan districts were located further away, near the rivers and canals that carried goods. There were also special areas for outcasts or people considered "impure," such as butchers and tanners. Strict social codes dictated who could do certain jobs and where they could live.

Though these rules were strict, everyday life in Edo also had moments of fluidity. Samurai sometimes married into merchant families for financial support, and some merchants became quite wealthy. Still, official status was determined by birth and was not easy to change. The class system helped the shogunate maintain control, since it kept everyone in a clearly defined place in society.

2.9 Edo's Cultural Beginnings

With so many people gathering in one place, Edo naturally became a center of cultural development. Kabuki theater, for instance, grew popular among commoners. It featured colorful costumes, dramatic acting, and lively music. Originally, kabuki was an art form that even samurai might enjoy in secret. However, samurai were officially discouraged from attending kabuki because it was seen as a less refined form of entertainment compared to the more traditional Noh theater.

The ukiyo-e art form also blossomed in Edo. Ukiyo-e means "pictures of the floating world," referring to images that captured the everyday life of Edo's pleasure quarters, famous actors, and landscapes. These woodblock prints became a key way for the growing middle class to enjoy art. They were cheaper than paintings and could be made in large numbers. Scenes of the Sumida River, local festivals, and kabuki actors became common subjects.

Literacy also started to spread, at least among the townspeople. Book lending shops appeared, and people could read popular novels or illustrated storybooks called kusazoshi. Even if someone couldn't read well, they might gather with others who could read out loud. Such gatherings often happened in teahouses or someone's home. Education was not just for samurai children. Some commoners received basic schooling in small private academies or temple schools.

In short, Edo was alive with cultural energy. While the city was still under strict samurai rule, it offered a unique blend of official ceremonies, military displays, merchant activities, and artisan creations. Visitors to Edo might have been surprised to see how large the city was and how many forms of entertainment were available.

2.10 Concluding Thoughts on Edo's Rise

By the early 17th century, Edo had turned from a small fishing village with a modest fortress into the capital of a powerful shogunate. This transformation was due in large part to Tokugawa Ieyasu's vision and the policies that required daimyo to maintain residences in Edo. The castle town model provided the structure, and the sankin-kotai system provided a steady flow of people and wealth.

The city was not without its problems. Fires, strict social rules, and the threat of political conflict were always present. Still, Edo continued to grow and adapt. Over time, it developed its own vibrant culture that would leave a lasting impression on Japan's history. From the castle gates to the bustling merchant quarters, Edo was a place of contrasts: strict samurai codes next to lively entertainment districts, wealthy daimyo mansions next to crowded commoner neighborhoods.

In the chapters ahead, we will look more closely at how people lived in this fast-growing city. We will explore how the Tokugawa shogunate controlled the population, maintained order, and dealt with foreign influences. But for now, we can see that the rise of Edo was both rapid and carefully planned. It set the stage for centuries of stability known as the Edo period (1603–1868). This period would shape Japan in countless ways, leaving behind traditions, customs, and a cultural legacy that still impact the country today.

CHAPTER 3

Life in Early Edo

3.1 A Typical Day in Edo

Life in early Edo was busy and full of variety. The city was growing fast, and people woke up early to start their work. Most days began with the sound of footsteps on dirt roads or wooden walkways. Farmers who lived just outside the city walls brought vegetables and grains to sell in town, and fishermen arrived with fresh fish from nearby waters. Merchants opened their shops, displaying goods like rice, cloth, or pottery. Meanwhile, samurai reported to their lords or attended training in swordsmanship or other martial arts.

Commoners usually ate a simple breakfast of rice or millet. Sometimes they had pickled vegetables or miso soup. After eating, they hurried to their jobs or daily chores. Women might have stayed at home to look after children and do housework, or they might have worked in family businesses. Children often helped with small tasks, such as gathering firewood or delivering messages. The city was alive from dawn until nightfall, with people moving about the streets, canals, and bridges.

In the evening, the city gradually quieted down. Families lit lanterns or small oil lamps inside their wooden homes. People gathered around a hearth if the weather was cold. Dinner was usually rice, fish, or vegetable dishes, and sometimes tofu. After dinner, some folks visited bathhouses or listened to storytellers. Others turned in early, resting so they could wake up and do it all over again the next day.

3.2 Samurai Life and Responsibilities

Samurai made up a special class in Edo. They served the shogun or other high-ranking lords called daimyo. Their main duty was to be ready for military service, but during long periods of peace, many samurai found themselves with extra time. They still trained in martial arts, including swordsmanship, archery, and sometimes even the use of firearms. However, when wars were rare, samurai also worked in administrative roles, helping their lords manage land, taxes, and local disputes.

The samurai code, often called *bushido*, emphasized loyalty, honor, and skill. Samurai wore two swords: a long sword (katana) and a shorter one (wakizashi). These swords were symbols of their status, and commoners were not allowed to carry them. While some samurai enjoyed wealth and big houses, not all of them were rich. Lower-ranking samurai sometimes struggled to provide for their families. They received stipends in rice, but the amount could be small. If costs rose, they might have to borrow money from merchants, which caused embarrassment.

In everyday life, samurai often had to meet strict rules of behavior. They were expected to keep a calm and honorable manner in public. However, many also had private interests, like studying poetry, calligraphy, or tea ceremony. Some wrote haiku or practiced flower arrangement to improve their focus and appreciation for beauty. Even though they were warriors, these cultural arts were seen as ways to develop a refined spirit. This blend of martial skill and artistic sense helped define the samurai character in Edo.

3.3 Merchants: The Busy Traders of Edo

Merchants stood at the heart of Edo's economy. They bought and sold goods like rice, fish, silk, paper, and more. Because Edo was the home of the shogun, many daimyo and samurai had to live in the city part-time. This created a constant demand for food, clothing, and household items. Merchants set up shops along busy streets or in special markets. They arranged their goods in neat displays, hoping to attract customers.

Though the social order placed merchants below samurai and farmers, many became quite wealthy. Smart traders understood what people needed and brought those products to Edo. For example, merchants might import fine silk from distant provinces or special seasonings from coastal towns. Wealthy samurai families liked high-quality items, so merchants who catered to them often made good profits. However, they had to be careful not to show off their money too much, because samurai looked down on merchants who acted arrogant.

Merchants also formed guilds, which were groups of people doing the same type of work. These guilds made rules about prices, quality, and fair trade. By working together, merchants protected themselves from unfair competition. They also supported each other in times of need, like during fires or other disasters. Over time, successful merchants helped shape the culture of Edo by sponsoring festivals, theaters, and other forms of entertainment, thus giving the city its lively spirit.

3.4 Artisans and Their Crafts

Artisans were the skilled workers who made items that people in Edo used every day. They included carpenters, blacksmiths, potters, weavers, and many others. These craftspeople often lived and worked in small workshops lined up on narrow streets. Walking through these artisan quarters, one would see and hear all sorts of activities. Carpenters might be sawing wood to build houses or repair temples. Blacksmiths heated metal and hammered it into tools or swords.

A typical artisan workshop was small and family-run. Parents taught their children the family trade, ensuring that skills passed down through generations. Many artisans were proud of their craft and tried to create the best items possible. For instance, some potters specialized in making simple everyday bowls, while others made elegant tea ceremony cups. Over time, certain districts in Edo became famous for specific crafts. If you wanted a beautiful kimono, you would visit the weaving or dyeing district. If you needed high-quality metalwork, you went to the blacksmith's area.

Artisans often relied on merchant patrons or samurai orders to stay in business. They worked hard and lived modestly. Still, their crafts enriched Edo's culture. People from all classes needed their products, whether it was a farm tool or a fancy lacquer box for storing valuables. Even today, Japan is known for its craftsmanship, and much of that tradition traces back to the artisans of places like Edo.

3.5 Women in Early Edo

Women in Edo had a range of roles, though their opportunities were limited compared to men. In samurai families, women were expected to maintain the household, educate children, and manage finances if the husband was away. They also practiced basic self-defense, sometimes learning to handle a short dagger called a *kaiken*. Still, they rarely went to battle. In merchant and artisan families, women often worked alongside their husbands, keeping track of sales, weaving cloth, or preparing items for trade.

Many women also found roles as entertainers or performers. For example, geisha were skilled in music, dance, and conversation. They entertained guests in tea houses and were respected for their cultural talents. There were also women who ran small businesses, like food stalls or lodging houses for travelers. However, strict social rules could limit a woman's freedom. They were expected to obey their fathers, husbands, or sons. Some women found ways to influence family decisions quietly, especially regarding finances or marriages.

For commoner families with farms, women labored in the fields, planted rice, and took care of livestock. In the city, they might have sold vegetables or fish in the market. They played crucial roles in keeping families stable, even if official records often focused more on men. Despite facing many challenges, women in Edo contributed greatly to the city's society and economy through daily work, cultural arts, and family management.

3.6 Childhood in Edo

Childhood in Edo varied by social class, but many children shared certain experiences. Samurai children learned manners, calligraphy, and basic martial arts. Boys might practice with wooden swords, while girls learned proper etiquette for tea ceremonies or household management. In some cases, samurai families hired tutors or sent their sons to special schools. Commoner children, on the other hand, usually helped with family businesses. Boys might run errands for a shop, and girls might help cook or mind younger siblings.

Education was important, but it was often informal. Temple schools called *terakoya* offered basic reading, writing, and arithmetic to commoner children who could pay a small fee. These schools were sometimes run by monks, scholars, or even retired samurai. Children in these schools memorized texts and copied characters on wooden tablets or paper. They also learned moral lessons about respecting parents and elders.

During festivals, children enjoyed special treats like sweet dumplings or candy. They played games in the streets or fields, sometimes with spinning tops or cloth balls. Seasonal events, such as cherry blossom viewing in spring or snow viewing in winter, also delighted youngsters. While children faced responsibilities early in life, they still found ways to have fun and learn about the world around them.

3.7 Food and Cooking in Early Edo

Food in Edo ranged from simple meals to elaborate feasts, depending on one's status and wealth. Rice was the main staple, though poor families sometimes ate more millet or barley because rice could be expensive. Common side dishes included fish, pickled vegetables, tofu, and soup made with miso paste. Soy sauce was widely used to add flavor, and seaweed was also common.

Merchants and artisans might eat warm bowls of soba noodles or grilled fish at small street stalls. These stalls were popular with busy workers who had little time to cook at home. Sweets, such as sweet rice cakes or bean paste desserts, could be found at certain shops. People enjoyed seasonal changes in food. In the spring, bamboo shoots were a treat; in the autumn, chestnuts and sweet potatoes were favorites.

Wealthier samurai and daimyo families could afford special meals with many courses. They used fine plates and bowls, sometimes made of lacquer or porcelain. These meals included different kinds of fish, fresh vegetables, and even rare ingredients like wild boar or special mushrooms. Tea was a key part of Edo life for all classes, though the tea ceremony was especially important among samurai. The tea ceremony focused on harmony and respect, showing the cultural side of dining in Edo.

3.8 Clothing and Fashion

Clothing in Edo was shaped by class and rules set by the government. The most common garment was the kimono, made from fabrics like cotton, hemp, or silk. Wealthier people wore silk kimonos with elaborate patterns. Commoners wore simpler, darker colors to avoid drawing attention. Samurai wore kimonos, too, sometimes with a family crest on the sleeves. Over the kimono, samurai wore a stiff pleated skirt called *hakama*.

During colder months, people layered up, adding thicker robes or jackets. They wore sandals or wooden clogs called *geta* when walking outside. Hats varied from straw hats for farmers to more refined cloth hats for samurai. Women's hairstyles differed by age and status. Married women often wore their hair in a tight bun, while younger women styled their hair in more ornate ways, sometimes adding decorative pins or combs.

The government tried to enforce laws about which colors and fabrics different classes could wear. These were called sumptuary laws and were meant to keep social ranks clear. Still, some wealthier merchants pushed these boundaries, wearing fancy clothes in subtle ways. Fashion was a way for people to express themselves, but it also had to follow tradition and government rules. Despite these restrictions, Edo's streets showed a lively mix of outfits, from plain work kimonos to more colorful attire for special occasions.

3.9 Houses and Neighborhoods

Edo's neighborhoods reflected a city growing in all directions. Most houses were wooden, with paper screens called *shoji* or *fusuma* to separate rooms. Roofs were often tiled in wealthier areas or thatched in poorer districts. Samurai residences, known as *yashiki*, could be quite large, with walls and gates surrounding gardens. Merchant houses were narrower and closer together, often with a shop in the front and living space in the back.

Inside a common home, people sat on straw mats called *tatami*. There was usually a main room for eating and sleeping. At night, they laid out futon bedding on the tatami, then stored it away in the morning. Because houses were made of wood and paper, fires were a huge risk. Neighborhoods had watchmen who patrolled at night with lanterns and wooden clappers, warning people to be careful with flames.

Some districts specialized in certain trades. You might find a street where all the shops sold rice, and another street where shops sold fish. Temples and shrines were sprinkled throughout the city, providing quiet spaces amid the hustle and bustle. There were also pleasure quarters where entertainment like kabuki theater or teahouses could be found. Each neighborhood had its own flavor, but they all added up to the busy tapestry of life in early Edo.

3.10 Religion and Spiritual Beliefs

Religion in Edo was a blend of Shinto, Buddhism, and folk beliefs. Shinto, focused on nature spirits called *kami*, was practiced in shrines. People visited to pray for good fortune, health, or success in work. Buddhist temples were also common and offered rituals for the dead, prayers for the living, and moral guidance. Many families kept altars in their homes to honor ancestors, lighting incense sticks and offering food or flowers.

Samurai families often followed Confucian teachings as well, which emphasized loyalty, respect for elders, and proper social behavior. These teachings shaped how samurai governed and interacted with their lords. Festivals were an important part of religious life. Seasonal matsuri, connected to Shinto shrines, often included colorful parades, music, and street food. People of all classes enjoyed these events, seeing them as both religious and social gatherings.

Though Edo's government was strict about keeping order, they generally allowed people to practice their faiths without much interference, as long as it did not threaten the shogun's power. Christianity, however, was banned after the Tokugawa shogunate became suspicious of foreign influence. Harsh laws punished anyone suspected of being a Christian. Despite that, other forms of worship coexisted relatively peacefully, weaving a rich spiritual tapestry in everyday life.

3.11 Entertainment and Leisure

Edo was famous for its lively entertainment. Theater was a big draw, with kabuki standing out as the most popular. Kabuki actors wore colorful costumes and performed exciting stories about heroes, love affairs, or even comedies. Commoners loved kabuki because it was energetic and easy to enjoy. Samurai were officially discouraged from attending, but some went in disguise or sent servants to bring back the story.

Puppet theater, known as *bunraku*, was also popular. Skilled puppeteers controlled large wooden dolls while narrators told dramatic tales accompanied by shamisen music. Street performers entertained people with juggling, acrobatics, or storytelling. Teahouses provided another form of leisure. People would gather to sip tea, chat, or listen to musical performances. These teahouses varied from simple stands to elegant rooms for special guests.

For those who liked quieter activities, there were reading circles or poetry gatherings. The art of haiku blossomed in Edo, celebrating nature and daily life in just 17 syllables. Even after a hard day's work, many could find some form of entertainment or relaxation. Whether it was watching a street performer, enjoying sweet dumplings, or taking a stroll along the river at sunset, Edo offered countless ways to unwind.

3.12 Festivals and Celebrations

Edo's calendar was filled with festivals, many linked to the seasons or to a specific shrine. During these festivals, the streets came alive with music, dancing, and bright decorations. For instance, in summer, large paper lanterns hung from shops, and teams of people carried portable shrines (*mikoshi*) through neighborhoods. Spectators cheered and clapped as the shrine bearers shouted rhythms to keep themselves moving in unison.

The New Year was one of the biggest celebrations, marked by cleaning the house thoroughly to welcome good luck. Families prepared special foods called *osechi ryori*, neatly packed in colorful boxes. Children received small gifts of money from relatives. The cherry blossom season also inspired gatherings to view the flowers. People sat under blooming trees, sharing food and drinks while admiring the delicate pink petals.

These festivals not only brought joy but also helped bond communities. People worked together to plan events, set up stalls, and manage crowd safety. For a few days, the worries of daily life faded as everyone joined in the fun. Even samurai sometimes relaxed their strict behavior to enjoy the festive atmosphere. By linking religion, seasons, and community spirit, festivals became an essential part of Edo's cultural heart.

3.13 Crime, Punishment, and Law Enforcement

Edo was generally orderly, but with so many people, crime still happened. Petty theft, brawls, and fraud were common issues. More serious crimes included robbery or violence. The Tokugawa shogunate set up a strict legal system to maintain control. Samurai had the right to punish lower-class people on the spot if they felt disrespected, but there were also official courts that handled cases for all classes.

Local officers, known as *machi-bugyo*, oversaw city governance and acted as judges. They worked with police-like groups called *doshin* and *okappiki* to keep the peace. Punishments could be harsh, ranging from fines or public humiliation to forced labor or even death for severe crimes. Prisons were grim places, and torture was sometimes used to extract confessions.

Despite this strict system, commoners appreciated that it kept serious violence relatively low. Samurai were also expected to follow rules. A samurai who acted dishonorably faced severe consequences, possibly including the ritual of *seppuku* (ritual suicide). Law enforcement methods in Edo might seem harsh today, but they were designed to deter wrongdoing and preserve social order in a crowded city.

3.14 Fires and Firefighting

Fires were a constant threat in Edo. Because houses were made mostly of wood and paper, even a small spark could start a large blaze. Crowded neighborhoods also made it easy for fire to spread from one building to the next. Strong winds coming from the bay could push flames quickly through districts, sometimes destroying hundreds of homes in a single day. People referred to fires as "flowers of Edo" because they occurred so often.

To protect against fires, the shogunate organized teams of firefighters called *hikeshidan*. These groups were usually made up of commoners like carpenters or laborers, who were strong and knew how to handle heavy equipment. When a fire broke out, they rushed to the scene carrying ladders, hooks, and buckets. Instead of water hoses (which did not exist in the same way then), they used bucket brigades to splash water on the flames. Sometimes they tore down nearby houses to create a firebreak, stopping the blaze from spreading.

Fires were terrifying, but they also brought communities closer. Neighbors helped each other rebuild, and local authorities often allowed people to stay in temporary shelters. Over time, Edo's firefighting teams became quite organized, and their colorful uniforms and banners became a source of city pride. Still, the danger of fire was a daily worry, shaping how people built and maintained their homes.

3.15 Education and Literacy

Even though the government did not have a modern school system, many people in Edo learned to read, write, and do basic math. Samurai children studied Confucian texts, military strategy, and other skills needed for administration. Commoner children, when they had time and money, could attend temple schools called *terakoya*. These small schools taught reading and writing using simple texts and moral lessons.

Some commoners became quite literate, especially merchants who needed math and record-keeping for their businesses. Books, including novels, poetry collections, and travel guides, circulated among the city's growing reading public. Lending libraries appeared, charging a small fee for borrowing. People also enjoyed *kusazoshi*, which were illustrated storybooks or comic-like pamphlets. These had simple, entertaining tales that were fun to read.

Literacy in Edo helped boost the popularity of theater, poetry, and art. Even if someone could not read perfectly, they might gather with friends or family who would read aloud. This sharing of stories and information made Edo a place where new ideas and trends could spread quickly. By historical standards, Edo had a relatively high literacy rate for a time when most places in the world had far fewer people who could read or write.

3.16 Bath Culture and Cleanliness

Public bathhouses, known as *sento*, were a common sight in Edo. People believed that bathing was good for health and cleanliness. Men and women often bathed separately, though in some small neighborhoods they might share a bath if space was limited. Bathhouses had large wooden tubs of hot water. Customers first rinsed themselves off in a washing area, then soaked in the tub to relax and warm up.

Bathhouses were also social hubs. Neighbors could chat, share news, or talk about daily concerns. Some bathhouses offered small snacks or tea to enjoy after soaking. Because wooden homes could be cold in winter, people looked forward to the comfort of a hot bath. Bath fees were usually cheap enough that most commoners could afford to bathe regularly.

Samurai also used bathhouses, though high-ranking samurai had private baths at home. Cleanliness was linked to spiritual purity in Shinto beliefs, and bathing rituals often accompanied religious ceremonies. With so many bathhouses spread across the city, Edo developed a strong culture of cleanliness, which was somewhat rare in many parts of the world at that time.

3.17 Getting Around the City

Edo did not have cars or trains, so people got around on foot or by simple modes of transport. Some wealthier individuals used palanquins called *kago*, carried by two bearers. These looked like small, enclosed chairs with poles on either side. They offered privacy and comfort on bumpy roads. For longer distances, people could hire horse messengers or join small boats traveling on the rivers and canals.

Bridges were key to crossing the many waterways in Edo. The Nihonbashi Bridge, for instance, was a major landmark, marking the starting point of roads that connected Edo to other parts of Japan. Traveling by boat along the Sumida River or the network of canals was often faster than walking on crowded streets. Goods also moved by boat, making it easier to deliver rice, fish, and other supplies to markets.

Despite not having modern vehicles, Edo functioned surprisingly well. Street vendors, porters, and courier services connected different parts of the city. People learned to live at a walking pace, which helped them observe and enjoy the daily sights and sounds of their neighborhoods.

3.18 Nature in the City

Even though Edo was a large urban center, nature was not entirely removed from daily life. Trees and gardens could be found in samurai estates, temple grounds, and some public areas. Daimyo built beautiful gardens in their residences, often using ponds, rocks, and carefully trimmed pine trees to create calm spaces. Commoners, too, enjoyed small gardens if they could afford them, planting flowers or vegetables behind their shops or homes.

The Sumida River was a natural focal point. People liked taking boat rides to view cherry blossoms in spring or fireworks in summer. These outings became a big part of Edo culture, letting city dwellers connect with nature without leaving town. Fishing along the banks was also common, and children might wade into shallow waters looking for small fish or shellfish.

In autumn, people visited places known for bright red leaves. They might travel a short distance outside the city to see fields of flowers or tall grasses waving in the breeze. For many, these trips were a break from crowded streets and noisy markets. The appreciation for natural beauty deeply influenced Edo's art, poetry, and daily routines, reminding everyone of the changing seasons and the balance between city life and the natural world.

3.19 The Meaning of "Edo Period"

When historians speak of the "Edo period," they usually mean the years from 1603 to 1868, when the Tokugawa shogunate ruled Japan from Edo. This long stretch of peace allowed the city to grow rapidly, leading to advances in culture, education, and trade. Edo society had strict social rules, but it also created new opportunities for merchants, artisans, and commoners to influence art, fashion, and leisure.

During the Edo period, Japan had a "closed country" policy, limiting foreign trade and contact. This policy helped the shogunate maintain control, but it also meant that Edo's culture developed in a unique way, influenced mostly by internal trends rather than global ones. By focusing on internal development, Edo became a place where Japanese traditions like kabuki, ukiyo-e, and haiku flourished.

Over time, these traditions would shape Japan's identity. Even after the shogunate ended and the city was renamed Tokyo, many of the cultural forms born in Edo continued. Today, people in Japan still cherish many practices from that era, such as tea ceremony, kabuki, and festivals. In this sense, the Edo period left a lasting legacy on the country and on the city that would eventually become Tokyo.

3.20 Conclusion: Early Edo Comes Alive

Early Edo was a bustling, vibrant place. Samurai, merchants, artisans, women, and children all played their part in shaping daily life. Woodblock prints celebrated the city's scenes, from the busy fish markets to the grand gates of Edo Castle. Street vendors called out to customers, theater crowds cheered for their favorite actors, and temple bells rang in quiet neighborhoods at sunrise and sunset.

Despite strict social rules and the ever-present dangers of fire, disease, and political conflict, Edo thrived. People found joy in seasonal festivals, warm bathhouses, lively entertainment, and the blossoming of cherry trees along the riverbanks. They worked hard in shops, farms, and samurai residences, building a city culture that was both disciplined and creative.

This look at early Edo life gives us a glimpse of how the city managed to grow into one of the largest urban centers in the world at the time. In the next chapter, we will explore the broader phenomenon of castle towns in Japan, seeing how Edo compared to other places and why its growth was so significant.

CHAPTER 4

The Growth of Castle Towns

4.1 Introduction: What Are Castle Towns?

Castle towns in Japan were urban centers that developed around a feudal lord's castle. During the Edo period, these towns spread across the country. Each daimyo governed a domain, and at the heart of that domain was usually a castle. Around the castle, samurai residences, merchant quarters, and artisan workshops formed a lively community. Edo was the largest and most famous of these, but many others existed, such as Osaka, Nagoya, Kanazawa, and Himeji.

In this chapter, we will look at how castle towns grew, how they were organized, and why they were so important. We will also compare some of the better-known towns to Edo, noting similarities and differences. Castle towns shaped Japanese society by concentrating political power in specific locations and encouraging trade, craftsmanship, and cultural activities. The success of these towns helped unify regions and maintain the authority of the shogunate.

4.2 The Feudal System and Domain Structure

Under the Tokugawa shogunate, Japan was divided into domains, each ruled by a daimyo. These daimyos owed loyalty to the shogun, who granted them the right to govern their land. In return, daimyos collected taxes from the farmers and managed the local population. The taxes often took the form of rice, which was measured in units called *koku*. One koku was roughly the amount of rice needed to feed one person for a year.

The size of a domain was determined by how many koku of rice it produced each year. A daimyo with a big production was more powerful. These lords built castles to defend their territory and to showcase their status. The castle served as the administrative center, where officials worked on planning, taxation, and maintaining order. Samurai served as both warriors and bureaucrats, helping the daimyo run the domain.

Edo was unique because its lord, the shogun, controlled not just a single domain but also the entire country's political structure. However, other daimyos also had strong castle towns. They used similar methods to organize their towns and keep them secure. By studying these towns, we can see how feudal power worked on both local and national levels during the Edo period.

4.3 Planning a Castle Town

Castle towns were generally built with the castle at the center or on higher ground for defense. Around the castle, you would find samurai districts. Samurai needed to be close if the castle was attacked. Next came the merchant and artisan districts, which provided goods and services to the samurai and the daimyo's household. Farther out were the farmers' fields, providing food for everyone.

Some castle towns featured a deliberate layout. Streets were designed to slow down invaders, often winding or curving unexpectedly. High walls, moats, and gates controlled access. This defensive planning was important, as daimyos still worried about rebellions or attacks, even though the country was more or less at peace under Tokugawa rule.

There were also places for temples and shrines, which served both religious and community functions. In some towns, specific neighborhoods formed for certain trades, like a district for swordsmiths or potters. The arrangement of these districts made day-to-day life easier, as people knew exactly where to go for the things they needed. At the same time, the physical design reinforced the daimyo's power, reminding everyone who was in charge.

4.4 Edo as the Ultimate Castle Town

While many castle towns flourished, Edo outshined them all in size and influence. As we saw in earlier chapters, Edo Castle was massive. Surrounding it were layers of moats and walls. The samurai estates in Edo were not just for local retainers but for daimyo from all over Japan who were required to spend time there (the *sankin-kotai* system). This caused Edo to expand rapidly, leading to a larger merchant and artisan population than in other castle towns.

Edo's design mixed careful planning with rapid growth. Some districts were laid out in neat blocks, while others grew more spontaneously. Nevertheless, the castle remained the focal point, both symbolically and physically. Roads spread out from Edo in multiple directions, connecting the city to other domains. As the seat of the shogunate, Edo had resources and prestige beyond what any other castle town could match.

Though Edo was the biggest, it still shared many traits with other castle towns: a strong reliance on rice taxes, a clear social hierarchy, and the presence of specialized neighborhoods for different trades. It also faced similar challenges, like fires, overcrowding, and sanitation problems. Yet Edo's massive scale magnified both the benefits and the problems of castle town living.

4.5 Comparing Edo to Osaka and Nagoya

Osaka was known as the nation's kitchen (*tenka no daidokoro*) because it was a center of commerce and rice trading. While it also had a castle, Osaka's identity leaned more toward trade and finance. Merchants there became very wealthy, controlling the flow of goods. Osaka Castle was impressive, but it was not the primary seat of the shogunate, so political power there was limited compared to Edo.

Nagoya, on the other hand, served as the seat of the Owari branch of the Tokugawa family. Nagoya Castle boasted golden dolphin ornaments on its rooftop, showcasing its grandeur. Like Edo, the samurai district in Nagoya was close to the castle, and merchants and artisans lived in separate quarters. Nagoya grew into a lively city with festivals and markets, but still, it was smaller than Edo.

In both Osaka and Nagoya, we see the same pattern of castle-centered development, with a clear social structure and specialized trades. They also had moats, walls, and districts arranged for defense. However, Edo's role as the shogun's capital made it stand out, drawing in people and resources from every corner of Japan.

4.6 The Sankin-Kotai System and Urban Growth

One of the main reasons castle towns flourished during the Edo period was the *sankin-kotai* system, also known as the alternate attendance policy. Under this rule, each daimyo had to spend part of every other year in Edo. Their families had to live there all the time as a form of "hostage," ensuring the daimyo's loyalty to the shogun. When the daimyo traveled to Edo, they brought large processions of samurai, servants, and baggage. These journeys created a demand for roads, lodging, and supplies, boosting local economies.

Once in Edo, daimyos built residences to house their retinues. The money they spent on housing, food, and leisure flowed into the city's economy. As a result, Edo and other route towns on the way to Edo grew rapidly. Merchants set up shops selling everything from rice to luxury goods. Artisans offered services like clothing repair, carriage building, or sword polishing.

For the daimyo's home domains, the sankin-kotai system meant they had to maintain two places of residence: one in their domain's castle town and one in Edo. This was expensive, but it also encouraged the development of both locations. Castle towns improved roads and facilities to prepare for the daimyo's return. Edo expanded to accommodate the influx of lords and their retinues. In this way, *sankin-kotai* tied the whole country together, linking castle towns in a vast network with Edo at the center.

4.7 Merchants and Artisans in Castle Towns

Merchants and artisans were critical to the growth of every castle town. Samurai needed weapons, armor, and household goods; daimyos required fine crafts and supplies; and commoners needed daily necessities like clothing, pots, and tools. In return, merchants earned rice or silver coins from the samurai, feeding it back into the economy. Guilds helped regulate trades, setting quality standards and fair prices.

In some castle towns, a single craft dominated the local economy. For example, a town might be famous for porcelain, lacquerware, or swords. The daimyo often supported these crafts, using them to enhance the reputation of the domain. Skilled artisans sometimes relocated to specific towns because they were promised protection or special privileges by the ruling lord.

Merchants also traveled between castle towns, buying local goods and selling them elsewhere. Over time, certain trade routes became well-established, connecting coastal areas, mountain passes, and river ports. As commerce thrived, more people moved to these towns, and new neighborhoods sprang up near the castle walls or along major roads. Even smaller castle towns benefited from having a robust commercial and craft sector, giving them a sense of identity and economic stability.

4.8 Samurai Residences and Military Readiness

Castle towns, by definition, had a strong military aspect. Samurai were expected to live in or near the castle, ready to defend it if needed. These samurai quarters formed distinctive neighborhoods of wooden homes, some with gardens and gates. Higher-ranking samurai had larger estates, sometimes featuring storehouses for rice and weapons. Lower-ranking samurai lived in more modest houses, often sharing walls with neighbors.

Though Japan was mostly at peace, the threat of rebellion or outside invasion could not be ignored. Castles were equipped with watchtowers, gates, and thick walls. Moats surrounded the central keep, making it harder for enemies to approach. Samurai in castle towns routinely practiced martial arts, archery, and strategy. They also held tournaments or demonstrations, both to maintain morale and to remind commoners of their authority.

At the same time, not all samurai spent their days training. Many had administrative jobs, serving as tax collectors, record keepers, or local governors. The balance between military duty and civil administration was a key feature of Edo-period castle towns. This arrangement kept a large population of samurai tied closely to the daimyo, ensuring loyalty and a quick response in any crisis.

4.9 Commoners and Castle Town Hierarchies

Castle towns followed the strict social hierarchy of the Edo period: samurai on top, farmers second, artisans third, and merchants last. However, in practice, castle town life often blurred these lines. Wealthy merchants wielded economic power even though their official status was low. Artisans sometimes enjoyed special respect if they produced high-quality goods sought after by samurai.

Farmers usually lived on the outskirts, near their fields, because they needed to be close to the land they worked. However, market days or festivals in the castle town brought them into the city to sell produce and buy supplies. Some farmers aspired to move into the town permanently if they could afford to open a shop or workshop. This created some social mobility, even if it was subtle.

The castle town hierarchy also included outcasts, such as leather tanners or those who dealt with the disposal of dead animals. These people lived in separate districts due to beliefs about impurity. Despite official discrimination, their services were essential for making leather goods or cleaning up the town. In this way, every level of society had a role to play in keeping the castle town functioning.

4.10 Infrastructure: Roads, Moats, and Bridges

A well-developed castle town had a solid infrastructure. Moats defended the castle, while walls or palisades separated different districts. Within these walls, roads connected the castle to samurai quarters, merchant districts, temples, and gates. Many towns also had a main commercial street where shops lined up, attracting visitors. The presence of bridges was important for crossing moats or rivers. Some bridges were guarded or had gates that closed at night.

Because the daimyo needed to travel to Edo regularly, roads leading out of the castle town were also crucial. These roads joined the larger network of highways across Japan, such as the Tokaido or Nakasendo routes. Along these highways, post towns provided lodging and food for travelers. This system of roads and towns allowed goods, ideas, and people to move efficiently, supporting both local and national economies.

Maintaining infrastructure required cooperation among different classes. Samurai oversaw construction projects, while commoners provided labor or materials. Taxes supported large-scale works, like repairing a castle wall or digging a new moat. When everyone pitched in, the castle town remained strong and well-organized, reflecting the power of its ruling lord.

4.11 Castle Town Culture and Arts

Culture in castle towns developed under a mix of samurai values and commoner creativity. Samurai supported refined arts such as tea ceremony, flower arranging, and Noh theater. These arts showed discipline and a love for tradition. Meanwhile, commoners enjoyed more playful forms of entertainment like kabuki, puppet theater, and street performances. In larger towns, both styles might exist side by side, with each class having its favorite venues.

Poetry gatherings, calligraphy lessons, and music ensembles also thrived in castle towns. Merchants and artisans who became wealthy often sponsored cultural events or built private halls for gatherings. Over time, popular arts spread from one town to another via travelers, actors, and traveling musicians. Ukiyo-e prints sometimes depicted scenes from famous castle towns, capturing festivals or local landmarks.

Because the Edo period lasted so long, many of these cultural forms had time to mature. Samurai might learn a musical instrument in their leisure hours, and merchants might participate in a tea ceremony. This cross-class appreciation for the arts brought some unity to castle town life, even though strict social rules still existed.

4.12 Economic Exchange Among Castle Towns

Castle towns did not exist in isolation. They traded with each other, sharing local specialties. For example, a town known for pottery might send bowls and plates to a town famous for producing salt. Edo, as the biggest market, needed all sorts of goods—rice, fish, cloth, building materials, and more. In return, Edo shipped out goods like fine textiles, fashionable items, and cultural products.

Daimyos often encouraged their domains to produce something unique that could be sold elsewhere. This could be a type of ceramic, a special paper, or even a variety of fruit. By creating a notable product, the domain earned extra income and gained fame. Over time, certain castle towns became widely known for particular crafts. As goods traveled, styles and ideas also spread, linking the country through trade and culture.

This network of exchange helped keep peace under Tokugawa rule. When domains depended on each other economically, they had fewer reasons to fight. Rather than seeking conquest, many daimyos focused on improving their local industries and participating in nationwide commerce. That is why the Edo period is sometimes called a golden age of stability, at least for those within the established system.

4.13 Defense and Military Preparedness

Even though Japan was mostly peaceful during the Edo period, castle towns were designed with defense in mind. Castles themselves were layered strongholds, with multiple baileys or courtyards, thick gates, and hidden traps. Some castles featured stone walls that sloped outward, making them harder to climb. Many had a main keep (tenshu) that offered a final defensive position if the outer walls fell.

Beyond the castle, samurai in a castle town regularly practiced drills. They might hold archery tournaments or test new firearms. Keep in mind, firearms had entered Japan in the mid-16th century, so some domains invested in matchlock rifles. However, the Tokugawa shogunate tightly controlled the production and ownership of guns, fearing large-scale revolts.

In reality, most castle towns never faced a major siege after Tokugawa rule began. The mere presence of these fortifications acted as a deterrent. Yet the structures remained important symbols of the daimyo's authority and the shogunate's unified command over the land. They reminded people that, if needed, the samurai class stood ready to fight.

4.14 Social Control in Castle Towns

Castle towns were not just about defense and trade; they were also centers of social control. The daimyo or the shogun set strict rules about where each class could live, what they could wear, and how they should behave. Samurai had to live close to the castle. Merchants and artisans had their own districts. Farmers were supposed to remain in rural areas unless they had special permission.

These rules were enforced by officials who kept detailed records of each neighborhood. Night curfews were common, with gates closing at a certain hour. Anyone caught outside without a proper reason could face punishment. Ceremonies and processes for travel permits were also common. This made it difficult for people to move freely from one domain to another without official approval.

While such controls might seem harsh, they helped maintain a stable society where everyone knew their place. The strict order allowed the daimyo to collect taxes efficiently and kept rebellions to a minimum. At the same time, it limited personal freedom. People found ways to adapt, but the castle town system was clearly designed to benefit the rulers more than the commoners.

4.15 Town Life and Entertainment

Despite social restrictions, castle towns were full of life. There were festivals, markets, and performances that catered to both samurai and commoners. Each town had its own local customs and celebrations linked to the castle or shrines in the area. Traveling entertainers brought new ideas from other domains, while local artisans showcased their talents at regional fairs.

Kabuki troupes, puppet shows, or storytellers might pass through, setting up temporary stages in open spaces. Merchants could sell souvenirs, street food, or toys. Artisans held demonstrations to attract customers. These events created a festive atmosphere that broke the daily routine of hard work and strict rules. Samurai, in more relaxed moments, might attend in disguise or send their families to enjoy the festivities.

Many castle towns also had pleasure quarters, though smaller than Edo's Yoshiwara district. These areas offered teahouses, geisha entertainment, and other amusements. They were often separated from the samurai quarters to maintain a certain level of decorum. Still, people from different classes mingled there, sharing music, dance, and conversation. This mix of order and pleasure gave castle towns a unique rhythm.

4.16 Transportation and the Role of Post Towns

Because daimyos had to travel to Edo under the sankin-kotai policy, the roads connecting castle towns became more important. Along these highways, the government established post towns at regular intervals. These were places where travelers could rest, eat, and hire porters or horses. Inns in post towns competed to offer the best service, hoping to attract wealthy daimyo processions or samurai messengers.

For commoners, traveling often required special permits. But some merchants and artisans traveled frequently to deliver goods or attend trade fairs. Post towns made it possible for them to journey safely, as they could find shelter and supplies. Local officials also kept records of who came and went, ensuring that no one plotted against the shogun or daimyo.

Over time, the network of highways and post towns helped unify Japan's economy. Castle towns could send goods to Edo or to neighboring domains more easily. Information also moved faster, whether it was political news, market prices, or cultural trends. In this sense, the growth of castle towns and the improvement of roads went hand in hand, forging a stronger national identity.

4.17 Castle Towns and Foreign Influence

During most of the Edo period, Japan had a "closed country" policy, limiting foreign contact. The Dutch and Chinese were allowed to trade at Nagasaki, but that was far from Edo, and the activity was heavily monitored. However, some cultural and technological ideas still seeped into Japan. Daimyos who were curious about Western science might secretly acquire books or instruments. Occasionally, new knowledge about medicine or astronomy made its way to castle towns.

Still, the shogunate was wary of foreign influence. Christian missionaries were banned, and any sign of Christian worship was harshly punished. Castle towns remained largely focused on domestic issues, with little direct exposure to the outside world. This isolation helped preserve traditional arts but also meant that Japan lagged behind in some forms of technology and knowledge.

Despite this official isolation, the curiosity about the outside world existed. Some samurai and scholars studied "Dutch learning" (Rangaku), which included Western medicine and science. They passed this knowledge along in small circles. As time went on, these new ideas slowly influenced castle town thinking, laying groundwork for changes that would come in the late 19th century.

4.18 Decline of Castle Towns

Toward the end of the Edo period, various problems arose. Some daimyos faced heavy debts due to the cost of sankin-kotai and the need to maintain samurai households. Merchants grew in power, sometimes overshadowing the samurai economically. Natural disasters, crop failures, and famines also hit certain domains hard, leading to peasant uprisings.

As foreign ships began to appear off Japan's coasts in the mid-19th century, the shogunate's policy of isolation started to crumble. Certain castle towns tried to modernize, but the lack of international trade experience made it difficult. Meanwhile, discontent samurai in some domains called for reform or the overthrow of the shogunate. All these pressures led to the eventual fall of the Tokugawa regime in 1868.

After the Meiji Restoration, Japan's new government abolished the domain system, creating prefectures. Many castles were dismantled or repurposed. Samurai lost their stipends, and the strict social classes dissolved. Castle towns had to adapt to a new era, where the focus shifted to modernization, railways, and factories. Some towns managed to transform into modern cities, while others declined.

4.19 Legacy of Castle Towns

Despite their decline, castle towns left a rich legacy. The urban layouts, with streets curving around where moats and walls once stood, can still be seen in some cities today. Castles themselves, if preserved or rebuilt, attract tourists who want to see Japan's feudal past. Traditional crafts that once thrived in these towns continue in modern workshops, passed down through generations.

Culturally, castle towns shaped many Japanese arts, from theater to ceramics. The interplay between samurai culture and commoner creativity gave rise to new forms of entertainment, clothing styles, and social practices. The roads and highways that linked castle towns laid the groundwork for Japan's future transportation networks. In this way, the history of castle towns is not just a story of old walls and feudal lords; it's also a story of community building, artistic growth, and the transition into modern times.

4.20 Conclusion: The Significance of Castle Towns

Castle towns were the backbone of Edo-period Japan. They balanced defense, administration, and commerce in carefully planned spaces. Samurai protected them, artisans and merchants kept them stocked with goods, and farmers fed them. Though Edo was the largest, many smaller towns played crucial roles in regional economies and culture. The sankin-kotai system tied them all to Edo, forming a web of mutual reliance.

These towns fostered vibrant cultural scenes, combining elite arts with commoner entertainment. They also enforced strict social order, which allowed the Tokugawa shogunate to rule peacefully for over two centuries. While the arrival of modernity eventually changed or dismantled many of them, their impact remains visible today in city layouts, cultural festivals, and long-standing traditions.

Understanding the growth of castle towns helps us see how Edo itself thrived. In the next chapters, we will continue our journey through Tokyo's history, examining the Tokugawa shogunate's impact, the closed country policy, and the changes that set the stage for the end of feudal Japan. But for now, remember that Edo's story is deeply connected to a network of castle towns that once stretched across the land.

CHAPTER 5

Everyday People and Culture

5.1 The Heart of the Common People

When we think of Edo, we often imagine samurai in armor or grand daimyo processions. But the true energy of the city came from everyday people: merchants, artisans, laborers, and families who worked hard to keep life moving. These people, sometimes called *chonin* (townspeople), lived in wooden houses crowded together in busy districts. They sold goods, made clothing, cooked meals, and raised children. Their daily routines might seem simple at first, but they built a vibrant culture that influenced the entire city.

Daily life for these commoners involved early mornings and late nights. Many rose before sunrise to open shops or start craft work. Artisans labored at spinning wheels or in small forges, and merchants prepared their stalls. Children helped by fetching water or running small errands. Through these tasks, the young learned the family trade, ensuring that skills passed down generation after generation.

Edo's common people were not only workers—they were also creative and social. After a hard day, they would visit local teahouses, watch street performers, or meet friends in small gathering spots. Over time, this sense of community shaped a lively culture, with festivals, special customs, and unique forms of entertainment. Even though strict rules governed Edo society, everyday people found ways to enjoy life and celebrate their city.

5.2 The Rise of the "Floating World"

One term often linked to Edo's common culture is "ukiyo," sometimes translated as the "floating world." It described the pleasure districts, theaters, and teahouses where people sought enjoyment away from daily worries. Many were attracted to the floating world because it offered an escape from strict social rules. Inside these lively zones, laughter, music, and storytelling filled the air.

Merchants who became wealthy joined in, spending money on plays, geisha performances, or fine dinners. Artisans also found customers eager for elegant clothing or stylish hairpins. People from different walks of life mingled, though samurai were officially expected to stay away. Some samurai did visit these areas secretly, removing identifying crests or leaving their swords behind to avoid attention.

One product of this floating world was ukiyo-e—woodblock prints that showed scenes of kabuki actors, famous courtesans, and landscapes. These prints became popular not just among the rich but also among middle-class townspeople who collected them for decoration or for pure pleasure. Over time, ukiyo-e prints depicted more than entertainment. They also showed street life, festivals, and everyday people. This art form remains a key symbol of Edo's cultural spirit.

5.3 The Role of Festivals and Seasonal Events

For many commoners, festivals (matsuri) were the highlights of the year. Each neighborhood had its own shrine or temple, and residents worked together to plan celebrations. During these events, the strict class lines softened a bit. Everyone joined in parades, carrying portable shrines (*mikoshi*) or playing drums and flutes. Brightly colored banners and lanterns lined the streets, and children ran around in excitement.

Seasonal festivals connected people to nature's cycles. In spring, cherry blossom viewing parties brought families and friends to the riverside or nearby hills to appreciate the fleeting beauty of the blossoms. In summer, fireworks lit up the sky above the Sumida River. Autumn harvest festivals thanked the gods for crops, and winter gatherings helped people stay cheerful in the cold. These seasonal rhythms formed a shared calendar that tied the city's residents together.

At festival stalls, vendors sold snacks like candied fruit, grilled squid, or sweet rice cakes. Others offered simple games where children could win small toys. Dancers or storytellers performed near the shrine gates, entertaining visitors for hours. Even the poorest families tried to save a little money to buy festival treats. During these vibrant days, daily stress eased, and the city felt like one big community celebrating life.

5.4 Women's Lives and Contributions

Although Edo's society was male-dominated, women played important roles both at home and in local business. Many wives of merchants helped run the family store, keeping track of money, handling negotiations, and greeting customers. In artisan families, women and children worked alongside the master artisan, preparing materials or finishing detailed tasks. Their contributions were often unrecognized by outsiders but were vital for the success of the household.

Women also passed along cultural traditions. Through daily interactions, they taught children social customs, proper speech, and household duties. Some women learned refined arts like calligraphy, flower arranging, or tea ceremony. However, these pursuits required spare time and money, so they were more common in wealthier families. For most commoner women, free time was scarce, but they found small moments to enjoy conversation with neighbors or share folk songs.

There were also women entertainers, like geisha, who developed exceptional skills in music, dance, and storytelling. Geisha were not simply performers of beauty; they studied for years to master instruments such as the shamisen and learned the art of conversation. They performed at banquets and teahouses, bringing a touch of elegance to Edo's nightlife. Even though they lived in a world with strict rules, geisha had a unique position, showcasing high-level cultural arts to paying guests.

5.5 Children and Education

Childhood in Edo was shaped by family, work, and occasional play. Many children from merchant or artisan families started helping with chores at a young age. Boys might run deliveries or watch the shop, while girls did tasks like sorting thread or helping with cooking. Despite this early involvement in adult responsibilities, children also played with spinning tops, balls made of cloth, and simple dolls. Street corners or small courtyards turned into makeshift playgrounds.

Formal education for commoners took place in temple schools called *terakoya*. Teachers showed students basic reading, writing, and arithmetic. Lessons used simple books with moral teachings, often printed with woodblocks. Students practiced copying characters on wooden tablets or paper, learning proper brush strokes. Because the cost was not too high, many commoner children attended these schools, at least for a few years. This helped Edo's literacy rates grow, allowing people to read popular storybooks or notices.

Samurai children had their own form of schooling, focusing on Confucian classics, writing, and sword practice. Boys learned martial arts, while girls studied etiquette and household management. Even though the classes differed for samurai and commoners, both groups learned values like respect for elders, honesty, and dedication to family. As children grew older, they gradually stepped into adult roles, ensuring that Edo's traditions and knowledge continued.

5.6 Food Culture and Dining

The common people of Edo enjoyed a wide range of simple yet tasty foods. Rice was a staple, but it could be expensive, so many families mixed it with barley or millet. Seasonal vegetables like daikon radish, eggplant, and bamboo shoots added variety. Fish and seafood were common due to Edo's coastal location, with dried fish or seaweed being easy to store and cook.

Street food stalls thrived, offering quick meals to workers and travelers. Soba noodles in hot broth, grilled eel (*unagi*), and fried tofu pouches (*inari sushi*) were popular choices. These stalls allowed busy artisans or shopkeepers to grab a bite without needing to cook at home. Small teahouses served green tea and light snacks, providing a place to rest and chat.

For special occasions, families prepared more elaborate meals. They might buy sweet bean paste desserts, fancy pickles, or even rare fruits if they had extra money. Wealthier merchants sometimes hosted banquets featuring a dozen small dishes, showcasing fresh fish, simmered vegetables, and delicately flavored soups. But for many commoners, a hearty bowl of rice and miso soup was enough to power them through the day.

5.7 Entertainment Beyond the Pleasure Quarters

Not everyone could afford to visit theaters or teahouses in the main pleasure districts, so local neighborhoods developed their own forms of fun. Street performers, or traveling troupes, often entertained crowds with acrobatics, juggling, or comic skits. Children gathered wide-eyed, and adults tossed coins into a small box as thanks. It was an easy, cheap way to enjoy music and laughter.

Another popular pastime was sumo wrestling. Though today it's a large-scale sport, in Edo it began as a form of performance connected to shrine events. Temporary sumo rings were set up in open spaces, and people came to watch strong wrestlers push and grapple. Over time, sumo became more organized, with top wrestlers gaining fame and fan support. Even lower-class citizens might dream of success in the ring, showing that talent could cross social barriers.

Storytelling was another cherished amusement. In some neighborhoods, a performer called a *rakugo* storyteller would sit on a small stage, spinning funny or dramatic tales with just a paper fan and a cloth as props. Skilled storytellers could make people laugh or gasp by changing their voice and facial expressions. These performances spread moral lessons or just silly humor, helping Edo residents relax after a day's hard work.

5.8 Personal Grooming and Fashion Trends

Edo's commoners might not have worn the grand silk robes of samurai lords, but they still had a sense of style. Cotton kimonos dyed in indigo were popular for everyday wear. The government enforced laws about which classes could wear silk or specific colors, so most people stuck to simpler patterns. However, creative artisans found ways to make bold designs using tie-dye or resist-dye techniques, giving outfits a subtle flair without breaking rules.

Hairstyles were important in showing status and identity. Men often shaved the tops of their heads and gathered the remaining hair into a small topknot, a style known as the *chonmage*. Women's hairstyles varied by age and social position. Younger women styled their hair in elaborate coils or buns, sometimes decorated with combs or ornamental pins. Older women preferred simpler updos. Visiting a hairdresser regularly could be expensive, so many women learned to style hair at home, helping each other keep up with trends.

Bathhouses were central to personal grooming. People of all social classes enjoyed soaking in hot water to relax and clean off the day's dirt. These public baths also served as places to meet neighbors and catch up on local gossip. Because houses were made of wood and paper, having a personal bath at home was rare and risky. So, the public bathhouse became a routine stop, often visited in the evenings before dinner or bedtime.

5.9 Travel and Pilgrimages

Even though the shogunate set rules that limited travel, commoners still found reasons to journey beyond Edo. Some people took part in religious pilgrimages to famous shrines or temples, like the Ise Grand Shrine. Pilgrimages were both spiritual and social events. Groups of neighbors formed travel clubs, pooling money and planning routes. Along the way, they stayed at post towns, ate local specialties, and bought souvenirs.

Travel guides and maps—though not always detailed—were sometimes printed on woodblocks, helping travelers plan. However, official checkpoints (called *sekisho*) along major roads checked travelers' documents. To pass these checkpoints, pilgrims or merchants needed travel permits or had to claim a religious purpose. Once they reached the shrine or temple, they offered prayers and small donations. Then they enjoyed the local sights, returning home with stories of distant places.

For many Edo commoners, travel was a once-in-a-lifetime adventure. They brought back tales of different dialects, unusual foods, and strange customs. These stories spread new ideas and fashions, shaping Edo's culture. Even the act of planning a trip became part of the fun, as families saved money for months or even years. Through these journeys, Edo residents learned that their city was just one part of a larger and diverse Japan.

5.10 The Spirit of Edo's Common Culture

What made Edo's everyday culture so special was how it balanced strict rules with moments of freedom and creativity. Government laws about clothing, travel, and social rank shaped life, but people found ways to flourish within those limits. Artisans developed new dye patterns, merchants sponsored local festivals, women ran businesses, and children learned reading and writing at temple schools. Communities worked together to prepare for festivals, handle fires, or rebuild after disasters.

Commoners also showed adaptability. Whenever a policy changed or a new fashion arrived, they adjusted their lifestyles to keep up. This flexibility helped Edo stay lively and open to fresh ideas, even during a time when Japan was mostly closed to foreign countries. The shared experiences of daily labor, bathing, eating noodles at a street stall, and enjoying festivals tied people together with a sense of belonging.

As we move into the next chapter, we will see how the Tokugawa shogunate's power and policies shaped Edo's entire society. While the commoners built a rich cultural life, it was the shogunate that provided the overall framework—sometimes supportive, sometimes restrictive—that allowed Edo to thrive for more than two centuries. In many ways, the simple joys and communal spirit of Edo's people stand as a lasting reminder of how culture can bloom, even under rigid social structures.

CHAPTER 6

The Impact of the Tokugawa Shogunate

6.1 Introduction to the Tokugawa Government

The Tokugawa shogunate, also called the Edo bakufu, was the military government that ruled Japan from 1603 to 1868. Tokugawa Ieyasu founded this system after winning power at the Battle of Sekigahara. Once he became shogun, he set up a government in Edo, making the city the center of political control. Over time, the Tokugawa family passed the title of shogun from one generation to the next, maintaining power through a combination of alliances, strict policies, and a well-structured administration.

At its core, the Tokugawa government was about keeping order. They worked to unify a land that had been torn by civil wars and local conflicts. Through careful management of the daimyo (powerful feudal lords) and the samurai class, the shogunate built a stable society. This stability allowed commerce, arts, and culture to grow. However, it also limited personal freedom, prevented social mobility, and kept Japan mostly isolated from the outside world.

In this chapter, we will explore how the Tokugawa shogunate shaped everyday life, economy, and culture in Edo and beyond. We will also see the structure behind the scenes: the officials who handled taxes, roads, foreign affairs, and policing. This view helps us understand why Edo developed the way it did, turning into a bustling city with unique customs and challenges.

6.2 The Bakuhan System: Balancing Central and Local Power

The Tokugawa shogunate used a system often called "bakuhan," combining "bakufu" (the shogun's central government) with "han" (the domains of the daimyo). The shogunate governed major issues like foreign policy, national roads, and large-scale trade. Meanwhile, each daimyo controlled local matters within their own domain, collecting taxes and keeping order. This balance ensured that the daimyo remained somewhat independent but still loyal to the shogun.

To maintain this loyalty, the shogunate had several methods. One was the *sankin-kotai* system (alternate attendance), where daimyo had to spend part of the year in Edo, leaving their families behind as "guests" (effectively hostages). Another was limiting the construction of new castles, preventing daimyo from fortifying themselves too strongly. Finally, the shogunate watched domain finances closely. If a daimyo accumulated too much power or wealth, the shogunate might force them to spend more on public works or even reduce their domain's size.

This system created a sort of "pyramid of power," with the shogun at the top, followed by powerful daimyo, lesser daimyo, and then the samurai, peasants, artisans, and merchants. While each domain had its own culture and traditions, they all recognized the Tokugawa's supreme rule. This unity brought peace after centuries of warfare, letting the country focus on internal improvements and cultural development.

6.3 Administrative Roles and Officials

Below the shogun were high-ranking officials called *roju* (senior councilors) who advised the shogun on major decisions. They handled issues like appointing daimyo to certain lands, managing large construction projects, and setting important policies. Below them were *wakadoshiyori* (junior councilors) who assisted in day-to-day governance.

In Edo itself, several magistrates (known as *bugyo*) oversaw different aspects of city life. The *machi-bugyo* looked after commoners' affairs, including disputes, taxes, and policing. The *kanjo-bugyo* handled financial matters, monitoring the flow of rice, coins, and trade. For foreign relations, there were special offices in Nagasaki and other ports to oversee the limited contact with China and the Netherlands.

Samurai who did not hold high office often worked in smaller administrative roles within the shogunate or their daimyo's domain. They might be tax collectors, inspectors, or guard captains. These administrative tasks provided samurai with a sense of duty and a regular income (usually paid in rice). This large network of officials made sure the shogunate's rules reached every corner of the country, keeping the system stable for over 250 years.

6.4 Laws and Social Control

One key way the Tokugawa shogunate preserved peace was through strict laws and social control. They required everyone to stay within their social class: samurai, peasants, artisans, and merchants. Samurai had privileges such as wearing two swords, but they were also forbidden from doing "lower" work like farming or trade. Peasants had to stay in villages, growing rice. Artisans produced goods in towns, while merchants handled buying and selling. Changing classes was extremely difficult.

Sumptuary laws controlled how people dressed and displayed wealth. Samurai had rules about wearing formal garments in certain settings. Merchants could not wear flashy silk kimonos, at least not openly. Peasants were expected to dress in plain cotton. By keeping a clear visual difference between classes, the shogunate discouraged social mixing that might lead to unrest or rebellion.

People also needed official permission to travel between domains. At checkpoints, guards inspected travel passes to ensure no criminals or unauthorized persons were sneaking around. The shogunate even used a neighborhood spy system called *goningumi*, grouping households together to watch each other and report suspicious activity. Though these rules might seem harsh, they did reduce crime and maintain order, which was a top priority for the Tokugawa rulers.

6.5 Economic Impact: Rice, Taxes, and Trade

The Tokugawa economy rested on rice production. Daimyo taxed their peasants in rice, measured by *koku*. Each daimyo's wealth and status depended on how many koku they controlled. The shogunate also took a portion of domain rice or demanded tributes. Samurai were paid in rice stipends, which they then converted into money through merchants. This created a cycle where rice flowed into Edo, fueling the city's massive population.

Merchants became important players in this system. They stored rice, sold it in markets, and traded it for goods. Over time, big rice brokers and moneylenders in cities like Edo and Osaka grew wealthy, sometimes lending to samurai who struggled to make ends meet. Because merchants were officially ranked lowest in society, but controlled so much wealth, tensions sometimes arose. Samurai resented owing money to those they considered beneath them.

Beyond rice, the Tokugawa shogunate promoted local industries to make each domain self-sufficient. For example, some domains became famous for pottery or sake, while others produced cotton or lumber. Inter-domain trade developed as merchants carried these goods along major roads. The policy of alternate attendance also spurred the economy, since daimyo and their retinues spent heavily on lodging, food, and gifts when traveling to Edo. This demand kept roads busy and markets thriving.

6.6 Infrastructure and City Building

Because daimyo traveled often to Edo, the shogunate invested in roads and post stations. The most famous roads were the Tokaido, Nakasendo, and

Koshu Kaido, each lined with towns offering inns and stables for weary travelers. These roads also made it easier for the government to send messengers or troops to different domains if problems arose.

Inside Edo, the shogunate managed large building projects. They expanded Edo Castle, dug canals for transportation, and constructed bridges over the Sumida River. They also enforced rules for how neighborhoods were laid out. Certain wards were designated for samurai mansions, while others were set aside for commoners. This kept classes physically separate, reducing conflict. Fires were a constant worry, so the shogunate organized firefighting teams and set regulations on how houses should be built to lower the risk of large-scale blazes.

Other major cities, like Osaka and Nagoya, also benefited from improved infrastructure. Osaka's castle protected an important commercial hub, and Nagoya's castle anchored the Owari domain. Though each city was unique, they all reflected the Tokugawa approach: build strong centers of power, connect them with well-guarded roads, and keep a close eye on who traveled where.

6.7 Isolation from the Outside World

One of the most famous Tokugawa policies was sakoku, or the "closed country" policy. From the 1630s onward, Japan strictly limited contact with foreigners. They expelled Christian missionaries, fearing that foreign religion and influence could weaken the shogunate. Trade with European nations was restricted to a small Dutch trading post in Nagasaki. Chinese merchants could also trade there, but direct contact with other nations was mostly cut off.

This policy stemmed from the Tokugawa desire to control all aspects of society. Foreign ideas, technology, or religions could inspire rebellion or challenge samurai traditions. By isolating the country, the shogunate hoped to maintain power and stability. Over time, a field called "Dutch learning" (Rangaku) developed among curious scholars who studied the Western sciences through limited Dutch texts. But these scholars had to be careful not to appear disloyal.

While sakoku protected Japan's internal stability, it also meant the country missed out on some technological and cultural developments elsewhere in the world. Shipbuilding, navigation, and modern weaponry advanced in Europe and Asia, while Japan remained in a more traditional mode. Eventually, this gap would become a serious problem, but during most of the Edo period, isolation seemed to work, and everyday life continued without major foreign threats.

6.8 Effects on Social Classes

The Tokugawa shogunate's rigid class system had both positive and negative effects. On one hand, people knew their roles in society. Samurai served as protectors and administrators, peasants produced food, artisans crafted goods, and merchants handled trade. This clear structure reduced the chaos of earlier centuries. On the other hand, it locked people into statuses they often could not escape. A peasant with an inventive mind had few chances to rise unless they gained rare patronage from a lord.

Samurai faced their own challenges. During the long peace, many had no battles to fight. Their stipends stayed the same even as prices rose, forcing some to borrow money from wealthy merchants or take side jobs as teachers. This created tension: samurai were supposed to be above money matters, yet they needed funds to maintain a respectable lifestyle. Over time, the image of the proud, sword-carrying warrior contrasted with the financial reality many faced.

Merchants, at the bottom officially, used their skills and connections to gain power. Some built large businesses in rice trading, textiles, or banking. They quietly influenced daimyo by lending them money or supplying them with luxury goods. However, they had to show humility in public, dressing modestly and not boasting about their wealth. The shogunate sometimes cracked down on merchants who appeared too rich or tried to ignore sumptuary laws.

6.9 Influence on Arts and Learning

Even though the shogunate tried to control society, it unwittingly allowed arts and learning to flourish. Peace and stability gave people the time and resources to pursue creativity. The samurai class developed refined arts like tea ceremony, Noh theater, and calligraphy, often supported by daimyo who sought cultural prestige. Commoners brought kabuki theater, ukiyo-e prints, and haiku poetry to new heights, as we saw in earlier chapters.

Confucianism became the core philosophy for samurai education. It taught loyalty to superiors, proper behavior, and moral living. Scholars who studied Confucian texts also wrote commentaries on government and ethics, influencing how officials viewed their roles. Some thinkers proposed reforms to address economic or social problems, though the shogunate often silenced any ideas that seemed too radical.

In temple schools for commoners, basic literacy spread, enabling more people to read storybooks and share ideas. Although the government preferred to keep people in their place, it could not stop the spread of knowledge entirely. Over time, these growing skills in reading and writing contributed to a more informed society. People began to question old ways, paving the way for big changes in the 19th century.

6.10 Lasting Legacy on Edo and Beyond

By the mid-1800s, the Tokugawa shogunate faced rising problems. Foreign ships appeared off the coasts, demanding trade and diplomatic relations. Some domains, especially in western Japan, grew restless and critical of the shogunate's leadership. Economic troubles, crop failures, and debt made everyday life harder for many people. These strains built up, eventually causing the fall of the Tokugawa regime in 1868, when power returned to the emperor during the Meiji Restoration.

Still, the Tokugawa shogunate left a deep mark on Edo and the whole country. Its policies shaped the city's layout, social classes, economy, and cultural life. The long peace allowed arts, crafts, and literature to flourish. Roads, post stations, and city planning improved connections across Japan. Even though the system was strict, it gave rise to unique forms of entertainment, from kabuki to sumo wrestling.

When the Edo period ended, people began calling the city Tokyo and rushed to modernize. But many Edo-period customs and traditions continued for years—some survive to this day. Festivals, woodblock prints, traditional crafts, and the spirit of neighborhood cooperation all trace back to the Tokugawa impact. In looking at how the shogunate governed, we also see how ordinary people lived, adapted, and created. This balance between power and daily life defines Edo's long chapter in Japan's history.

As we move on, later chapters will explore how the "closed country" policy finally broke down and how Edo became Tokyo. But we should keep in mind the strong foundations set by the Tokugawa. Their system was far from perfect, but it gave birth to a city and culture that remain famous worldwide. The story of Tokyo cannot be told without understanding the deep and lasting influence of the Tokugawa shogunate.

CHAPTER 7

The Closed Country Policy and Its Effects

7.1 Introduction to Sakoku

During the Edo period, the Tokugawa shogunate created a policy often known as *sakoku*, which means "closed country." This policy severely limited Japan's contact with the outside world for more than two centuries. Although it was not a complete end to trade—some foreign ships were still allowed under strict rules—*sakoku* cut off most ordinary people from direct foreign influence. In this chapter, we will explore how and why the shogunate put these limits in place, what life was like under these rules, and the long-term effects that shaped Edo and the rest of the country.

The idea behind *sakoku* was to protect Japan from threats the shogunate believed could destabilize society. Christian missionaries, European merchants, and new foreign ideas seemed like dangers to Tokugawa authority. By regulating any contact with foreign countries, the shogunate hoped to prevent uprisings or the spread of beliefs that might challenge traditional structures. While these policies helped maintain internal peace, they also cut Japan off from technological and cultural developments in the wider world. Only a few carefully controlled "windows" remained open, mostly in Nagasaki, where Dutch and Chinese traders were permitted limited access.

Though this policy focused on foreign relations, it also deeply influenced Edo's internal life. People living in Edo had little direct knowledge of places beyond Japan's shores. Over time, a small community of scholars became interested in Dutch books and scientific instruments, sparking what was called *Rangaku* (Dutch learning). But for the vast majority, daily life continued without much thought of foreign lands. Only in later decades, when foreign ships began appearing more often, did the *sakoku* system begin to crack, leading to major upheaval in Edo and across Japan.

7.2 Reasons Behind the Closed Country Policy

The Tokugawa rulers had several reasons for sealing off Japan from most foreign contact. One major concern was the spread of Christianity. Missionaries had arrived in Japan during the late 16th century, converting some local lords and commoners. The shogunate worried that Christian converts might place loyalty to the Pope or European kings above their loyalty to the shogun. They feared that this new faith could inspire internal conflicts or even pave the way for European colonial powers to interfere in Japan's affairs.

Another reason was political unity. By limiting foreign influence, the shogunate could keep Japan's feudal domains more dependent on the central government. If daimyo (feudal lords) had easy contact with foreign nations, they might buy advanced weapons or form alliances outside Tokugawa control. The shogunate's strict rules on shipbuilding, travel, and foreign trade prevented rival domains from gaining too much independent power.

Finally, *sakoku* helped the shogunate maintain a certain social and economic balance. They wanted to preserve the class system—samurai, farmers, artisans, merchants—and keep production focused on rice and traditional crafts. Rapid introduction of new technologies or foreign goods might disrupt local markets. By controlling what came into the country, the government aimed to protect its own authority and avoid social unrest. Although this policy was extreme by modern standards, it made sense in the context of a government seeking long-term stability after centuries of civil war.

7.3 Limited Points of Foreign Contact

Despite the official isolation, Japan did not entirely stop interacting with foreign nations. The shogunate allowed certain narrow channels for trade and information:

1. **Nagasaki and Dejima**: Perhaps the most famous "window" was the artificial island of Dejima in Nagasaki Harbor. Originally built for

Portuguese traders, Dejima later became the sole trading post for the Dutch after Christianity was banned and the Portuguese were expelled. Dutch merchants on Dejima could not travel freely in Japan, and each year they made a controlled trip to Edo to present gifts to the shogun. Chinese traders were also allowed in Nagasaki but faced their own set of strict regulations.

2. **Tsushima Domain**: Located between Japan and the Korean Peninsula, Tsushima facilitated limited trade and diplomatic exchanges with Korea. The So family, who ruled Tsushima, handled official communication and trade shipments in ways approved by the shogunate.

3. **Ryukyu Kingdom**: In the far south, the Ryukyu Islands (modern Okinawa) maintained a semi-independent status but were under the influence of both Japan (specifically the Satsuma Domain) and China. As a result, they served as another gateway for cultural and commercial exchange, though under tight restrictions.

These small points of contact allowed Japan to obtain some foreign goods such as medicines, books, and scientific instruments. They also enabled the Dutch to bring limited knowledge of Western science, technology, and astronomy. However, for the average resident of Edo, foreigners remained distant figures. Travelers from overseas were rarely seen on city streets, and foreign products were expensive or unavailable. In this environment, Edo's culture grew mostly on its own terms, unaffected by direct European or Asian trends.

7.4 Life Under Isolation

To understand the everyday impact of *sakoku*, we need to see how it shaped people's views of the world. Since travel outside Japan was illegal for almost everyone, many people in Edo had little idea what lay beyond their own country. Tales of foreign lands came through folk stories, rumors, or the few accounts shared by the Dutch interpreters in Nagasaki. As a result, foreign cultures took on a sense of mystery. Some imagined exotic places filled with strange creatures or wondrous inventions. Others viewed foreigners with suspicion, seeing them as barbarians or potential invaders.

The strict control of information meant that Edo's publishing industry, while vibrant, rarely included accurate depictions of foreign lands. Most books focused on local topics—history, romance, religion, or how-to manuals for arts and crafts. Maps of Japan existed in detail, but maps of the outside world were either outdated or purely speculative. This insular viewpoint contributed to a unique cultural identity. Edo residents found their entertainment, education, and sense of wonder within Japan's borders, celebrating local festivals, landscapes, and traditions.

Still, isolation did not mean a complete lack of curiosity. Some samurai, scholars, and doctors managed to get hold of Dutch medical texts or scientific materials. They studied human anatomy, astronomy, and engineering techniques that had advanced in Europe. This field of Dutch learning (*Rangaku*) slowly expanded, proving that even under strict isolation, a certain thirst for new knowledge could not be entirely extinguished.

7.5 Policing the Borders and Seas

The Tokugawa shogunate made great efforts to enforce *sakoku*. They passed laws forbidding Japanese people from building large ships capable of long-distance travel. Coastal vessels had to be built with specific designs that limited open-sea navigation. Any Japanese person who tried to leave the country without permission faced severe punishment, and those who managed to leave were often banned from returning.

Similarly, foreign ships that drifted near Japan's shores were turned away or, if they landed illegally, their crews might be arrested. Over time, laws were introduced that commanded local authorities to attack foreign ships that approached without official permission. This was sometimes called the "No second thought" decree, reflecting the policy that Japanese coastal defenses should not wait for instructions but act immediately.

These measures largely succeeded in keeping foreign powers at bay for many years. However, as global maritime powers like Britain, Russia, and the United States grew stronger in the 18th and 19th centuries, Japanese isolation became harder to maintain. Some foreign vessels, looking for trade or resources, began appearing off the coasts more frequently. Edo officials grew increasingly anxious, realizing that Japan lacked modern ships or weapons to keep out determined foreign navies indefinitely.

7.6 Economic and Cultural Effects of Isolation

Economically, *sakoku* meant Japan had to rely mainly on its own resources and industries. While this encouraged self-sufficiency, it also limited access to foreign technology or goods that could have boosted productivity. For instance, Western cannons and firearms improved rapidly during the 18th century, but Japan's weaponry mostly stayed the same, following older styles. Artisan techniques advanced, but not always with the new tools and methods found overseas.

Culturally, isolation allowed Edo-period arts to flourish in a uniquely Japanese style. Kabuki theater, ukiyo-e prints, haiku poetry, and traditional crafts all developed with little outside influence. Some historians argue that this led to a "golden age" of Japanese traditional culture, preserving forms of art that might have changed more radically if foreign trends had poured in. The result was a rich cultural landscape that continues to fascinate people worldwide.

However, *sakoku* also had downsides. Scholars who wanted to explore foreign knowledge had to do so in secret or face government suspicion. While some domains experimented with Western-style cannons or ships, many felt it was safer to follow the shogunate's lead and stay insulated. This inward focus delayed Japan's modernization. When foreign powers did arrive with advanced technology in the mid-19th century, Japan struggled to catch up quickly.

7.7 Christianity and Religious Tensions

One of the biggest factors motivating *sakoku* was the threat of Christianity. The Tokugawa government had witnessed how Christian lords in the 16th century formed alliances with European powers. The most famous rebellion linked to Christian influence was the Shimabara Rebellion (1637–1638), where a large group of mostly Christian peasants rose against heavy taxes and harsh treatment by a local lord. The rebellion ended in a bloody defeat, and it convinced the shogunate that Christianity was a serious threat to stability.

After crushing the revolt, officials intensified persecution of Christians, requiring people to prove they were not Christian by stepping on images of Jesus or the Virgin Mary—a practice called *fumi-e*. Any suspected Christians faced torture or execution. These strict rules forced surviving Christians to practice in secret or abandon their faith. In Edo, the government kept close records of everyone's religious affiliation, typically expecting them to be affiliated with a Buddhist temple.

Over time, fear of Christian influence became one of the key justifications for isolating Japan from the West. Even minor signs of Christian symbols were treated as evidence of treason. Although these measures were harsh, they reflected the shogunate's determination to eliminate any ideology that could undermine its authority. This approach also fueled the idea among commoners that foreigners were dangerous, reinforcing the isolationist mindset.

7.8 Dutch Learning (Rangaku)

Despite the ban on most foreign contact, a handful of Japanese scholars pursued Western knowledge through Dutch sources. Medical texts were among the most prized, as European anatomy and surgery had made significant progress. Japanese doctors who learned from these texts made improvements in diagnosis, surgery, and the study of diseases. Mathematics and astronomy also benefited from Dutch writings, leading to more accurate calendars and star charts.

Over time, these scholars formed a small but influential circle in Edo and other cities. They translated Dutch books, experimented with Western scientific instruments like telescopes or microscopes, and conducted dissections to learn about the human body. Some of them published their findings in Japanese, spreading new ideas to a broader audience of curious samurai and artisans.

For the shogunate, *Rangaku* was a double-edged sword. On one hand, advanced knowledge could help the government manage issues like epidemics or improve mapping and surveying. On the other hand, too much foreign influence risked challenging traditional teachings. Officials kept a close watch on *Rangaku* scholars, allowing some research while suppressing anything that seemed too politically sensitive. This careful balance lasted until the mid-19th century, when an influx of foreign ships forced Japan to reconsider its isolationist stance.

7.9 Daily Life in Edo Under Sakoku

For the average person in Edo, daily life might not have felt dramatically impacted by the *sakoku* policy, at least in the short term. People still woke up early, worked in shops or workshops, took their evening baths, and enjoyed festivals. The city's population grew, and merchants found steady demand from the samurai and daimyo who lived in or visited Edo. Crime remained relatively low, thanks to the shogunate's strict policing.

Still, the policy shaped the city's mindset. With few foreigners around, Edo residents saw themselves as part of a unique and self-contained world. This perspective encouraged a focus on local traditions, styles, and amusements. The result was a boom in cultural activities—kabuki theaters thrived, ukiyo-e artists captured urban life in woodblock prints, and everyday amusements blossomed. People's horizons were limited mainly to Japan's islands, yet they found endless variety within their own culture.

Some curiosity about the outside world existed. Rumors would spread if a strange foreign ship was sighted off the coast, or if a returning castaway told stories of faraway lands. Most Edo residents, however, had little reason to question the shogunate's isolation policies. They trusted that the government was keeping them safe, and life under the *sakoku* system felt stable and predictable for generations.

7.10 Challenges and Cracks in the Policy

As the 18th century advanced into the 19th, cracks in *sakoku* became more visible. Foreign whaling ships and merchant vessels, especially from Russia, Britain, and America, began to roam the Pacific. Some landed in Japan out of necessity—seeking water, food, or shelter from storms. When Edo officials told them to leave, tensions sometimes flared. Several incidents showed that Japan lacked the modern cannons or coastal fortifications to repel a serious foreign intrusion.

Meanwhile, some daimyo and scholars worried that Japan was falling behind in technology and military power. They pointed to China's struggles against Western powers, noting that isolation had not saved the Chinese from defeat in the Opium Wars. A debate grew within Japan: should the country stay closed and risk being overwhelmed by foreign navies one day, or open up carefully to learn from Western science and weaponry?

The shogunate attempted minor reforms, like allowing certain translations of Western texts or building a few Western-style cannons. But these half-measures were not enough to modernize quickly. Pressure mounted as foreign ships kept appearing along the coasts. Eventually, this pressure would boil over when American Commodore Matthew Perry arrived in 1853 with steam-powered warships, demanding that Japan open its ports.

7.11 Growing Discontent Among Domains

Internally, *sakoku* also contributed to growing discontent among some domains. While the Tokugawa shogunate enforced peace, certain lords in southwestern Japan—like those in Satsuma or Choshu—wanted a freer hand to deal with foreign threats or explore new trade opportunities. They resented the shogunate's tight control and suspected that isolation made the country weak. These lords began building up their own arsenals and studying Western military technology in secret.

Moreover, economic troubles struck many domains. Crop failures, famines, and rising debts led peasants to rebel in smaller uprisings. Merchants gained more wealth, but they had little official power. Samurai stipends lost value when the price of rice fluctuated. All these issues made people question the wisdom of a system that kept Japan closed off, reliant on old methods, and led by a shogunate that seemed slow to respond to new dangers.

As dissatisfaction spread, the concept of "revering the emperor and expelling the barbarians" (Sonno Joi) took root among some samurai and scholars. They argued that loyalty should shift from the shogun back to the emperor in Kyoto, and that foreigners should be driven out to protect

Japanese purity. Ironically, while *sakoku* originally aimed to prevent foreign conflicts, it ended up fueling a crisis as more Japanese people realized that the world outside had changed and Japan risked falling behind.

7.12 The Arrival of Foreign Ships

The first strong test of the *sakoku* policy came in the early 19th century with increasing visits from Russian traders in the north. Then in 1844, a Dutch king sent a message encouraging Japan to open trade, which the shogunate ignored. More alarming were the British naval successes in China, which showed that Western nations had powerful steamships and advanced weapons. Japan's coastal defenses were outdated, mostly reliant on traditional cannons.

In 1853, Commodore Perry sailed into Edo Bay (modern Tokyo Bay) with American "black ships." The sight of steam-powered vessels shocked the Japanese. Perry delivered a letter from the U.S. president, demanding that Japan open its ports for trade and the safe harboring of shipwrecked sailors. The shogunate, lacking the means to resist, stalled for time. A year later, Perry returned, and in 1854, Japan signed the Treaty of Kanagawa, marking the first step toward ending *sakoku*.

This treaty did not immediately flood Japan with foreigners, but it broke the isolation. Soon, Britain, Russia, France, and others made similar demands, forcing Japan to sign unequal treaties. Edo residents became aware that their country could not simply turn away these foreign powers. News of these events spread quickly, causing fear and confusion in the city. People realized the world was larger and more advanced than they had imagined. The slow unraveling of *sakoku* had begun, setting the stage for massive changes in Edo's political and social order.

7.13 Consequences for Edo

The end of isolation had immediate effects on Edo:

1. **Foreign Presence**: Although foreigners mainly lived in treaty ports like Yokohama (south of Edo), some made trips to the city. Samurai and commoners alike were astonished to see Westerners in odd

clothing, speaking strange languages, and using modern devices. Curiosity and suspicion often mixed in these encounters.

2. **Economic Shifts**: Foreign trade agreements led to new markets for silk, tea, and other Japanese goods. However, the influx of cheap foreign products disrupted local industries. Merchants who once thrived under a closed economy had to adapt. Inflation rose as gold and silver left the country in large amounts.

3. **Political Tension**: Samurai loyalists who believed in expelling foreigners grew angry at the shogunate's weakness. They felt betrayed by leaders who had failed to protect Japan's independence. Edo became a center of plotting and debate, with some groups advocating to restore the emperor's power.

These factors would eventually stir rebellion, prompting the collapse of the Tokugawa regime and the birth of a new era under Emperor Meiji. As we will see in coming chapters, the fall of *sakoku* was both dramatic and inevitable, propelled by forces beyond the old system's control.

7.14 Cultural Legacy of Sakoku

While *sakoku* ended in the mid-19th century, it left a lasting cultural legacy. The centuries of relative isolation fostered highly distinctive Japanese arts and traditions. The classic image of Edo-era fashion, architecture, and entertainment grew out of a society that was forced to look inward for inspiration. This led to developments like:

- **Kabuki Theater**: Flourishing under minimal foreign influence, kabuki became a uniquely Japanese performing art, with dramatic makeup, stylized acting, and vibrant costumes.
- **Ukiyo-e Prints**: Artists like Hokusai and Hiroshige produced woodblock prints focusing on local scenery and daily life, creating iconic images that later fascinated Western collectors in the late 19th century.
- **Refined Ceremonies**: Tea ceremony, flower arranging, and other practices reached new heights of elegance in a stable, self-contained society.

At the same time, *sakoku* slowed Japan's technological progress. Once it reopened, the Meiji government raced to catch up with Western powers, adopting railways, telegraphs, modern armies, and new forms of industry. Much of the old Edo charm was overshadowed by modernization. Still, the arts and customs born during the closed country era remained cherished parts of Japan's identity, becoming symbols of "traditional Japan" in the modern world.

7.15 Conclusion: A System Under Pressure

The *sakoku* policy defined the Edo period in many ways, allowing the Tokugawa shogunate to maintain power and unity for over two centuries. It created a unique cultural environment in which Edo thrived as a city focused on internal growth, local arts, and a sense of self-reliance. But as the world changed, Japan's isolation became a growing problem. Foreign ships, stronger militaries, and new ideas knocked at the door, demanding entry.

For the common people, *sakoku* meant familiarity and stability. They lived their daily routines with little fear of outside invasion, trusting in the shogunate's order. For scholars and progressive samurai, however, isolation was a barrier preventing Japan from learning about new technology or forming beneficial ties abroad. In the end, these two views collided when Western powers forced their way in. The next chapter will examine how power shifted in Edo as these pressures mounted, leading to the final days of the Tokugawa rule and the dawn of a new era for the city we now call Tokyo.

CHAPTER 8

Shifts in Power and Foreign Influence

8.1 Growing Tensions in the Late Edo Period

By the mid-19th century, the pressures on the Tokugawa shogunate had become immense. Economic struggles, natural disasters, and the threat of foreign powers weighed heavily on Edo. Within the city, factions formed among the samurai. Some believed the shogunate should reform and modernize, working with foreign nations to strengthen Japan. Others, especially younger samurai in certain domains, saw foreign presence as an insult and called for direct action to expel them.

This period of unrest was marked by political assassinations, secret alliances, and fierce debates. The shogunate tried to appease foreign demands while keeping control, but each concession to Western powers made them look weak. Meanwhile, merchants and craftsmen in Edo faced new competition from imported goods. Samurai stipends lost value, and peasants in many domains starved due to poor harvests or heavy taxes. All these issues fed a sense of crisis that no one could ignore.

At the center of this storm was Edo itself, a city of more than a million people packed into narrow streets and districts. Rumors traveled fast, carrying news of domain uprisings or foreign ships. The old social order, once held firmly in place by Tokugawa rule, began to shift. In this chapter, we will see how these tensions led to key events like the appearance of new political groups, violent clashes, and ultimately the downfall of the shogunate.

8.2 The Arrival of Western Diplomats

The Treaty of Kanagawa in 1854 was just the first in a series of agreements that allowed Western nations more access to Japan. Soon after, Britain,

Russia, France, and the Netherlands negotiated similar treaties. These were typically known as "unequal treaties" because they granted foreign powers special rights—like extra-territoriality (foreigners being tried by their own country's laws) and low import taxes—while Japan received few benefits in return.

Western diplomats set up legations (official residences) in Edo and other treaty ports like Yokohama. Some even traveled around the country, escorted by shogunate officials. Commoners in Edo had never seen Westerners up close, and they were shocked by their clothing, height, and strange customs. Meanwhile, the foreigners complained that the Japanese were slow to allow them free movement and that the living conditions in Edo were cramped and unsanitary.

This new foreign presence revealed Japan's technical and military weaknesses. Western ships could navigate Japan's waters with ease, and Western guns far outmatched Japan's older weaponry. Some forward-thinking daimyo and samurai proposed rapid modernization, hoping to build modern warships and adopt Western military drills. But others—especially hot-blooded young samurai—attacked foreigners or threatened them, believing that such violence would force them to leave.

8.3 The Sonnō Jōi Movement

A key movement that emerged was *Sonnō Jōi*, which means "Revere the Emperor, Expel the Barbarians." This slogan captured the anger many samurai felt toward the shogunate for allowing foreign ships and merchants to enter Japan. They argued that true authority lay with the emperor in Kyoto, not the shogun in Edo. They also believed that Japan's strength came from keeping out foreigners who could corrupt Japanese values or colonize the country.

Many supporters of *Sonnō Jōi* came from southwestern domains like Choshu and Satsuma, which had strong samurai traditions and were geographically closer to the trade routes through the East China Sea. These domains secretly acquired Western weapons to prepare for a possible war against foreign ships—or against the shogunate itself. Clashes erupted when Choshu forces fired on foreign vessels in the Shimonoseki Strait. In return, Western navies shelled Choshu's coastal defenses, proving how powerful modern warships were.

In Edo, *Sonnō Jōi* supporters carried out assassinations of shogunate officials who seemed too friendly to foreign interests. They also targeted foreigners themselves, attacking them on the streets. This violence, however, did not drive away foreign nations. Instead, it increased foreign pressure, as Western governments demanded that the shogunate punish the attackers and pay large fines. The turmoil undermined the shogunate's authority, pushing Japan closer to open conflict.

8.4 Reform Attempts by the Shogunate

Recognizing the danger, the shogunate tried to reform. Some high-ranking officials thought Japan needed to learn from Western technology to defend itself. They built new coastal batteries, purchased foreign ships, and invited Western experts to teach modern naval strategies. Edo's shipyards began constructing vessels that blended Japanese and Western designs. The shogunate also sent a small group of students abroad to learn foreign languages, engineering, and medicine.

These efforts were a major departure from the isolationist mindset of earlier decades. However, they happened too late to restore public confidence fully. Many samurai viewed the new programs as half-hearted, while foreign powers continued to demand more concessions. Economic problems also persisted. The cost of buying foreign ships and weapons, along with heavy fines imposed by foreign governments after violent incidents, strained the already shaky finances of the shogunate.

Within Edo, some improvements did appear. The city saw the introduction of gas lamps in certain districts and the construction of a few modern-style buildings. Western fashions intrigued curious onlookers, and a handful of shops sold imported goods to wealthier samurai or merchants. Yet these glimpses of modernity clashed with the city's older traditions, creating an uneasy mix of excitement, fear, and resentment.

8.5 The Role of the Imperial Court in Kyoto

As the shogunate struggled, the emperor in Kyoto gained new attention. For centuries, the emperor's court had existed mostly as a ceremonial institution, overshadowed by the shogun's military government in Edo. But in the mid-19th century, supporters of *Sonnō Jōi* rallied around the emperor. They claimed that the shogunate had lost the "mandate to govern" by failing to repel foreign intruders.

The court itself became a political battlefield. Some nobles in Kyoto supported the Tokugawa, urging compromise with the West. Others backed the *Sonnō Jōi* cause, calling for the removal of the shogunate and a revival of imperial rule. Gradually, leaders from powerful domains like Choshu and Satsuma formed alliances with key court nobles. They promised to defend the emperor and drive out foreigners, a stance that won them public support in many parts of the country.

This shift was crucial because it gave the anti-shogunate forces a unifying symbol: loyalty to the emperor. Even people who were not sure how to deal with foreigners could rally behind the idea of restoring imperial authority. Edo, once the center of power, now faced a challenge from Kyoto, where new alliances were taking shape. The stage was set for a confrontation that would decide Japan's future.

8.6 Samurai Discontent and Violence in Edo

In Edo itself, samurai discontent grew stronger with each new foreign treaty. Young samurai from various domains stayed in the city, sometimes without official permission. They formed secret societies, exchanging ideas about how to save Japan from foreign domination. Some practiced radical acts, such as attacking officials deemed traitors or raiding foreign settlements.

The environment in Edo became tense and fearful. Ordinary people worried about random violence, while foreigners and pro-shogunate officials lived under constant threat. The shogunate created special police units to track down and arrest radical samurai, leading to street chases and sword fights. Many of these violent samurai were from lower-ranking families who felt they had little to lose and saw heroic acts as a way to restore their honor or gain fame.

At the same time, commerce in Edo was changing. The presence of foreign goods and currency caused fluctuation in prices. Wealthy merchants found opportunities to trade new items, but also risked losing business if local products became less competitive. Many commoners struggled with inflation and wondered if the old days of strict isolation had actually been better for their livelihoods. The city's future felt uncertain to almost everyone, from peasants to high-ranking officials.

8.7 Choshu and Satsuma: The Breaking Point

Two domains in particular, Choshu and Satsuma, stood at the center of the coming revolution. Both had modernized their armies by purchasing Western rifles and cannons. Initially, Choshu tried to keep foreigners away by force, firing on passing ships. When foreign navies retaliated and inflicted heavy damage, Choshu leaders realized they needed to modernize even more. Satsuma similarly fought a short conflict with Britain after some of its samurai killed a British merchant, and British warships bombarded Kagoshima in response.

These experiences taught both domains that they could not win against Western powers with outdated weapons alone. Instead, they shifted focus to toppling the Tokugawa shogunate, believing that a new, strong central government—centered on the emperor—could unite Japan and negotiate from a position of strength. In secret, Choshu and Satsuma formed an alliance in 1866, vowing to take down the shogunate.

For Edo, this spelled doom. If powerful domains openly rebelled, the shogunate's authority would crumble. In 1867, the reigning shogun, Tokugawa Yoshinobu, tried to save the situation by returning political power to the emperor. He hoped this gesture would maintain Tokugawa influence in a new imperial government. But events moved too quickly. Forces from Choshu and Satsuma advanced toward Kyoto, determined to make a clean break with Tokugawa rule.

8.8 The Meiji Restoration and the End of the Shogunate

The decisive moment came in 1868, when supporters of the emperor declared the restoration of imperial rule—known to history as the Meiji Restoration. They formed a new government under Emperor Meiji, effectively ending the Tokugawa shogunate. Tokugawa loyalists fought back, leading to a short but intense civil conflict called the Boshin War. Key battles took place in and around Edo (soon to be renamed Tokyo), as the new imperial army, modernized with Western-style rifles and artillery, confronted the shogunate's outdated forces.

Edo surrendered to imperial troops in 1868 without a major urban battle. The city changed hands peacefully, avoiding mass destruction. Shortly afterward, the new government renamed Edo as Tokyo, meaning "Eastern Capital." This name change symbolized the city's transformation into the center of a modernizing Japan, under direct imperial rule rather than a military government run by the Tokugawa.

Thus ended over 260 years of Tokugawa rule. For many Edo residents, the change was sudden and disorienting. Samurai had to adapt to a world where carrying swords and receiving rice stipends would soon be abolished. Merchants faced a flood of new opportunities and risks as the new government opened Japan fully to global trade. Laborers and artisans saw the arrival of Western entrepreneurs and technology. The city's entire structure, shaped by centuries of feudal governance, began to evolve quickly into a modern capital.

8.9 Foreign Influence Grows

With the fall of the shogunate, foreign nations gained even more influence. The new Meiji government recognized the need to renegotiate the "unequal treaties," but first it had to strengthen Japan through rapid modernization. Western advisors were invited to teach in various fields—military science, engineering, law, and education. Young Japanese were sent abroad to learn and bring back new knowledge.

Tokyo (former Edo) became the hub of this transformation. Western-style buildings appeared, modeled after architecture in Europe or America. Gas lighting and telegraph lines spread, and horse-drawn carriages rattled over newly paved roads. Newspapers in Western formats circulated, introducing global news to city dwellers. Fashion also changed, with some officials wearing Western suits and hats instead of kimonos.

For many, these changes were exciting and promised a bright future. Others worried about losing Japanese identity. They feared that opening to the world meant copying foreign ways too eagerly. Debates raged in newspapers and public gatherings: How much of Western culture should Japan adopt, and how quickly? These questions would shape Tokyo's development for the next several decades.

8.10 Samurai Displacement and Social Upheaval

One of the most dramatic changes in this new era was the displacement of the samurai class. Under the Meiji government, the feudal domains were abolished, replaced by prefectures. Samurai stipends were gradually converted into bonds, then eliminated. Samurai also lost the exclusive right to wear swords. Many who had once lived in Edo found themselves jobless in the modern economy. Some joined the new imperial army or police force. Others tried business, farming, or teaching. A few became discontented and rebelled, as seen in the Satsuma Rebellion of 1877.

For commoners, life also shifted. The end of rigid class distinctions meant they could pursue new occupations or move more freely. Still, modernization brought new taxes, conscription into the army, and unfamiliar laws. In Tokyo, neighborhoods changed as older samurai estates were sold or demolished to make way for modern roads, factories, and government buildings. Artisans adapted or lost their livelihoods if demand for traditional crafts declined. Merchants found new business opportunities in imported goods and industrial production.

In just a few years, Tokyo's population rose even more as people from rural areas flocked to the city in search of work. The result was overcrowded districts, rising rents, and a mix of old Edo customs and modern Western ideas. The city's skyline began to transform, with taller brick structures and Western-style civic buildings standing alongside wooden houses and temples.

8.11 Cultural Exchange: From Edo to Tokyo

The transition from Edo to Tokyo also meant a shift in cultural outlook. Many traditional forms of entertainment persisted—kabuki, sumo, and festivals—but they competed with new forms like Western music halls and public exhibitions of scientific wonders. Schools opened that taught foreign languages and subjects like physics and chemistry. The government encouraged citizens to learn from Western nations, hoping to build a strong, respected country that could stand on equal footing with global powers.

At the same time, certain Edo traditions became nostalgic symbols of a vanishing era. Ukiyo-e prints that once depicted everyday life in the pleasure quarters started focusing on historical or romanticized themes of old Japan. Former samurai families sought to preserve tea ceremony, flower arranging, and other refined arts as cherished cultural legacies. Intellectuals argued over how to balance Japanese identity with the need for modernization.

This cultural exchange was visible on the streets. Some men wore Western suits with their hair cropped short, while others still wore kimonos with topknots. Women's fashion began to blend East and West, with some adopting Western hairstyles and dresses, though traditional kimono remained the main style for daily wear. Over time, these hybrids became common sights, reflecting Tokyo's unique blend of old and new.

8.12 Impact on Everyday Life

Though political change happens at the top, everyday life is often where the most immediate effects are felt. In the years following the Meiji Restoration, Tokyo's residents experienced:

1. **Infrastructure Upgrades**: Brick buildings, modern roads, and telegraph lines improved communication and commerce. Street lamps lit up certain districts, extending nightlife and making the city safer after dark.

2. **New Employment**: Modern industries like spinning mills, shipyards, and printing presses offered jobs. People who once lived under feudal constraints could now explore different careers.
3. **Education Reforms**: The government established a system of public schools to teach literacy and Western subjects. Children learned arithmetic, science, and geography, alongside moral studies rooted in Confucian ideals.
4. **Healthcare Advances**: Western medicine gradually replaced older methods. Public health measures, such as vaccination campaigns, started to take hold, though they faced some resistance from traditional healers.
5. **Fashion and Food Changes**: Western-style clothing shops appeared, and restaurants began serving dishes like beef stew (inspired by European cooking). Rice remained a staple, but new ingredients and recipes entered Tokyo's culinary scene.

These changes did not spread evenly. Wealthy families and government officials embraced them quickly, while poorer neighborhoods adapted more slowly, lacking the money or desire to switch to unfamiliar ways. Over time, the gap between the modern districts and older districts became more noticeable.

8.13 Foreign Communities in Tokyo

As Japan opened up, more foreigners moved to Tokyo. Diplomats, merchants, teachers, and engineers arrived, bringing their languages and customs. Some settled in special areas, forming small Western-style enclaves with brick houses and Western shops. They introduced sports like baseball, which Japanese students soon picked up with enthusiasm. They also built churches for Christian worship and opened schools that taught in English or other European languages.

This foreign presence could cause friction. Some Tokyo residents resented foreigners who seemed to walk around with a sense of privilege, especially since the unequal treaties gave them special legal status. Others were curious, learning English or French and seeking ways to cooperate in business. Over time, many foreign experts left once their contracts ended, but others stayed, marrying Japanese spouses and contributing to the city's evolving culture.

In the late 19th century, the Meiji government worked hard to revise the unequal treaties. To do this, they had to modernize the legal system, adopt Western-style courts, and show that Japan could be a reliable international partner. By the end of the century, they succeeded, and Japan regained full control over its tariffs and legal affairs. Tokyo continued to grow as an international city, though it kept much of its traditional charm.

8.14 Farewell to the Old Edo

Looking back, the transition from Edo to Tokyo was swift and transformative. The centuries-old samurai system ended abruptly, and the once-mighty Tokugawa shogunate vanished. In a matter of years, the city that had been so tightly controlled by feudal rules opened up to new ideas, technologies, and global currents. Streets that once echoed with the clatter of wooden geta sandals now heard the rumble of horse-drawn trams, and soon, steam locomotives.

Many older residents felt nostalgia for the stability and familiarity of Edo times, even if that era had also been strict and limiting. Younger generations, on the other hand, saw endless possibilities in the Meiji period. They wanted to build a strong, modern nation to stand alongside the Western powers that had once forced open Japan's doors. This energy fueled rapid industrialization, the growth of national newspapers, the establishment of universities, and a wave of cultural creativity.

In the next chapters, we will dive deeper into how life changed in Tokyo after the Meiji Restoration. We will examine the cultural, social, and educational reforms that reshaped the city. But it's important to remember this turning point: the shift in power from the Tokugawa shogunate to the emperor's government forever altered Tokyo's destiny, carrying it away from its feudal past and toward an ambitious, modern future.

CHAPTER 9

The Opening of Japan and the End of the Shogunate

9.1 Setting the Stage for Change

By the mid-19th century, Edo had grown into a large city under Tokugawa rule. Even so, troubles were piling up. The government faced natural disasters, rising debts, and unrest among samurai and commoners. Although Japan had followed the *sakoku* (closed country) policy for over two centuries, foreign ships had started appearing off the coasts more frequently. Many people in Edo sensed that a big change was coming.

Inside the city, folks still woke each morning to open shops or practice their trades. But whispers about strange foreign boats and new treaties made them anxious. Samurai from distant domains quietly roamed Edo's streets, some meeting in teahouses or secret gatherings to discuss what should be done about the Tokugawa shogunate, which they felt was losing its grip. Others stayed loyal to the shogun, believing that only a strong central rule could protect Japan from foreign powers. Tensions simmered, and no one knew exactly how events would unfold.

In this chapter, we will look closely at the final steps that led to the end of the shogunate. We will see how foreign influence, internal disagreements, and the rise of new political ideas all came together, forcing Edo—and the rest of Japan—to leave its old ways behind.

9.2 Early Warnings of Foreign Pressure

Even before Commodore Perry's ships arrived in 1853, there were signs that isolation would not last forever. Russian traders had ventured near Japan's northern islands, seeking furs and trade goods. British and American whaling ships traveled across the Pacific, sometimes landing on Japanese shores to get fresh water or repair damage. Each encounter tested the Tokugawa policy that demanded foreigners leave immediately.

The shogunate tried to issue strict orders: no foreign ship should be allowed to stay, and local officials were told to drive them away if necessary. But these officials often lacked modern cannons or large warships. In some cases, they simply gave the stranded sailors food and water, then told them to leave. That worked for a while when encounters were small in number. Yet as years passed, more and more ships appeared.

Anxiety spread among the samurai who governed coastal regions. They worried about falling behind in military technology. Some domains began small-scale experiments with Western-style firearms, hoping to be ready for a larger threat. But the Tokugawa government was slow to approve such measures, clinging to the notion that strict isolation and old defenses would still keep Japan safe.

9.3 Commodore Perry's Arrival

In 1853, everything changed when four black-hulled American warships, under the command of Commodore Matthew Perry, steamed into Edo Bay (modern Tokyo Bay). Unlike earlier foreign vessels that had mostly been small or damaged ships seeking aid, Perry's squadron was a show of force. The black smoke pouring from the ships' funnels and the heavy cannons on their decks made it clear that the Americans were serious about opening Japan to trade.

The Tokugawa officials in Edo were caught off guard. They had never encountered steam-powered warships before. Local people, seeing the thick smoke from a distance, feared something supernatural. Perry presented a letter from the U.S. president, demanding that Japan allow American ships to refuel and resupply, and also open up for limited trade. Then Perry left, saying he would return in a year to hear Japan's answer.

This event sparked a huge debate in Edo. Some top advisors believed Japan should open negotiations, fearing war if they refused. Others insisted that Japan must refuse any foreign demands and prepare to fight. But the country lacked the modern guns and ships needed for a full-scale conflict with America. Daimyo across the land sent messages to the shogunate, offering opinions or asking for guidance. The once-powerful government seemed unsure, revealing cracks in its authority.

9.4 The Treaty of Kanagawa

When Perry returned in 1854 with an even larger squadron, the Tokugawa shogunate decided it could not risk battle. They signed the Treaty of Kanagawa, which allowed American ships to stop at two ports (Shimoda and Hakodate) for supplies. It also promised fair treatment for shipwrecked American sailors. While it did not open Edo to full-scale foreign trade, it ended centuries of strict isolation.

This treaty caused a stir throughout Japan. People in Edo felt shock, anger, or relief—depending on their views. Some were outraged that the shogunate gave in to foreign demands, seeing this as a shameful loss of face. Others believed it was a practical move to avoid a disastrous war. Daimyo in southwestern regions, such as Satsuma and Choshu, who had strong samurai traditions, began criticizing Edo's leadership. They argued that the shogunate had betrayed Japan by allowing foreigners a foothold on Japanese soil.

The Treaty of Kanagawa soon led to similar agreements with Britain, Russia, and other Western powers. These treaties were often called "unequal" because they gave foreigners favorable trading rights and legal exemptions. Many Japanese felt their government had been bullied. Within Edo, the mood grew tense. Samurai from various domains gathered, some determined to push the foreigners out by force, others aiming to modernize to compete with Western technology.

9.5 The Struggle to Modernize

Realizing how far behind Japan had fallen in terms of military might, the shogunate scrambled to buy cannons, rifles, and steamships from abroad. They also hired foreign experts to teach modern shipbuilding, gunnery, and navigation. This was a big departure from the old ways. Just a short time earlier, people could be punished for studying too much about foreign countries. Now, the government paid Western advisers to train samurai in new techniques.

In Edo, small shipyards began making steam-powered vessels under foreign guidance. Samurai students studied Dutch, English, or French, hoping to translate new military manuals. The government built coastal defenses, placing new cannons in strategic spots along Edo Bay. But these efforts were rushed and costly. Merchants demanded higher payments, inflation rose, and many people felt uncertain about the sudden changes.

Meanwhile, dissatisfaction spread among lower-ranking samurai. For years, they had endured low stipends and high expenses. They believed the shogunate was weak and corrupt, unable to protect Japan's honor. Some joined secret groups that supported the *sonnō jōi* slogan: "Revere the Emperor, Expel the Barbarians." They plotted violent attacks against foreigners, Tokugawa officials, and anyone else seen as a traitor.

9.6 Rise of the Sonnō Jōi Movement

The call to "Revere the Emperor, Expel the Barbarians" grew stronger with every new treaty that gave Western powers more privileges. Many samurai blamed the shogun for not standing firm. In their view, the emperor in Kyoto, who had been largely ceremonial under Tokugawa rule, should be the true leader of Japan. Loyalists in domains like Choshu and Satsuma began to rally around the imperial court, forming alliances with court nobles who also distrusted the shogunate.

These loyalist samurai believed that Japan should drive out foreign influence altogether, returning to a pure state under imperial rule. They despised the Western clothes and gadgets that were starting to appear in Edo. They felt that studying foreign languages and sciences was a betrayal of Japanese tradition. Some took matters into their own hands, assassinating shogunate officials who promoted modernization or foreign trade.

In Edo, violence escalated. Foreigners living in treaty towns faced attacks. Samurai loyalists burned down buildings or struck at perceived traitors in nighttime raids. The city's long-standing sense of order felt shaky, as the old policing methods struggled to contain the new wave of political violence. Commoners stayed indoors after dark, worried about being caught in the crossfire.

9.7 Attempts at Reform

In the face of growing chaos, the Tokugawa government tried to reform. They made changes to the council that advised the shogun, including some forward-thinking officials who wanted to negotiate better deals with foreign powers. They also tried to improve the military structure, creating a new kind of force that combined modern rifles with traditional samurai discipline.

The shogunate opened schools in Edo to teach Western science and languages, hoping to train a new generation of samurai who could understand the foreigners' world. They took small steps to improve roads, build telegraph lines, and even set up the first gas-lit street lamps. But these reforms happened too slowly to calm the anger of the *sonnō jōi* factions. At the same time, many of the older Tokugawa supporters felt uneasy about changing centuries of tradition so quickly.

Money problems added to the trouble. Buying foreign ships and weapons was expensive, and domain lords (daimyo) had to pay higher taxes. Some domains went deep into debt. Farmers resented new taxes, and occasional famines led to peasant uprisings. In Edo, prices rose, making it hard for lower-ranking samurai and commoners to afford daily necessities. All these difficulties weakened the once-strong Tokugawa hold on power.

9.8 Tensions Between Shogun and Emperor

For centuries, the emperor lived in Kyoto, playing a ceremonial role while the shogun held real power in Edo. But as foreign pressures grew, many political figures began looking to the emperor for guidance. In 1863, Emperor Komei issued an "order to expel barbarians," reflecting the *sonnō jōi* sentiment. The shogunate found itself in a bind: it could not realistically force foreign ships out with Japan's outdated weaponry, yet failing to follow the emperor's command angered loyalists.

Some shogunate officials traveled to Kyoto, trying to negotiate with the imperial court. They hoped to find a middle ground—maybe modernize enough to defend Japan, but avoid open conflict with the West. However, the *sonnō jōi* activists saw these talks as betrayal. They believed the Tokugawa were stalling and showing weakness. Clashes broke out in the region between Kyoto and Edo, as domain armies loyal to different sides skirmished. These were signs that the old balance of power was crumbling.

The emperor, swayed by anti-Tokugawa nobles, began supporting domains that openly challenged the shogunate. Meanwhile, the shogun tried to maintain a presence in Kyoto, sending troops to keep control. This struggle heightened the rivalry between the Tokugawa's Edo-based government and the emperor's court in Kyoto, with pro-imperial domains waiting for the right moment to strike.

9.9 The Choshu-Satsuma Alliance

Two powerful domains—Choshu and Satsuma—emerged as key players in the anti-shogunate movement. Initially, these two domains had different strategies for dealing with foreigners. Choshu had tried to fire on Western ships in the Shimonoseki Strait and suffered bombardment in return. Satsuma had clashed with the British over the killing of a British merchant. Both domains realized that Western military might was too strong to overcome without modern weapons and better training.

Over time, leaders in Choshu and Satsuma decided that the main obstacle was not the foreigners alone but the Tokugawa government. If Japan united under the emperor, they believed, the country could modernize faster and stand up to the West. Secretly, Choshu and Satsuma put aside their past rivalries and formed an alliance in 1866. They imported Western guns and built modern ships. They also gained support from influential court nobles in Kyoto who favored imperial restoration.

Word of this alliance spread through Edo. Some saw it as a dangerous conspiracy to topple the shogunate, while others hailed it as Japan's best hope. Either way, it made the Tokugawa regime look vulnerable. Young samurai from all over Japan flocked to join the cause. The old system, with the shogun at the top, began to appear outdated and fragile.

9.10 Final Years of Tokugawa Rule

In 1866, Tokugawa Iemochi, the young shogun, died of illness, leaving his successor, Tokugawa Yoshinobu, to face the crisis. Yoshinobu was more open to modernization than many of his predecessors. He tried to reorganize the government, creating a council that included daimyo from major domains. He wanted to form a new coalition that could handle foreign relations and keep peace within Japan.

For a moment, it seemed like a workable plan. But Satsuma and Choshu leaders distrusted Yoshinobu, believing he only wanted to protect Tokugawa power. Meanwhile, violence continued. In Edo, radical samurai carried out attacks on officials who seemed too close to foreign interests. Outside Edo, smaller uprisings flared, and roads became dangerous for travelers. Merchants grumbled about unstable markets, and commoners feared high taxes and random violence.

Faced with these obstacles, Yoshinobu took a drastic step in late 1867. He announced that he would return power to the emperor, effectively resigning as shogun. He hoped to preserve some Tokugawa influence by joining a new government centered around the imperial court. However, the anti-shogunate forces saw this move as too little, too late. They wanted a complete break from Tokugawa control.

9.11 The Fall of Edo

In early 1868, the imperial court in Kyoto declared that it was taking charge of the country. The young Emperor Meiji ascended to the throne, backed by the Choshu-Satsuma alliance. They demanded that Yoshinobu give up Edo and all Tokugawa authority. Fearing a full-scale war, some leaders tried to negotiate a peaceful handover. Yet fighting broke out in certain areas, including near Kyoto and along roads that linked to Edo.

The Boshin War began, pitting the newly formed imperial army against Tokugawa loyalists. Although many Tokugawa samurai fought bravely, the modernized forces of Satsuma and Choshu—equipped with rifles, cannons, and some foreign advisors—had the edge. They advanced toward Edo, capturing important strongholds. Many samurai in the city realized they could not hold out for long.

Finally, high-ranking officials on both sides agreed to surrender Edo peacefully to avoid massive bloodshed. On May 3, 1868, imperial forces entered Edo Castle without a major battle. The castle gates opened, and the city changed hands. This event marked the symbolic end of Tokugawa rule. The city, once the seat of the shogunate, was about to enter a new phase under direct imperial authority.

9.12 Consequences of the Shogunate's Fall

With Edo under imperial control, the Tokugawa shogunate effectively ceased to exist. Some loyal Tokugawa samurai retreated north, hoping to continue resistance, but their efforts were short-lived. The Boshin War ended in mid-1869 with imperial victory. The emperor's government then punished Tokugawa allies in various ways but showed leniency to some, trying to unify the country rather than prolong conflict.

For ordinary people in Edo, the sudden change brought uncertainty. Many wondered if the new imperial government would be better or worse. Samurai worried about losing their stipends and status in a rapidly modernizing society. Merchants hoped the new government might bring stable trade deals and better markets, but they also feared new taxes or rules. Artisans waited to see if old Edo traditions would survive under imperial rule.

In a sign of the times, Edo was renamed Tokyo, meaning "Eastern Capital," reflecting the fact that the emperor planned to move there. This name change was both practical and symbolic: it showed that power would no longer rest in Kyoto alone. The city would become the hub of a modernizing nation, open to ideas from the West. Though the final transformation lay ahead, the end of the shogunate was a major turning point in Japan's history.

9.13 Reflections on the Opening of Japan

Looking back at these events, it becomes clear that the end of isolation and the collapse of the Tokugawa shogunate were closely connected. Foreign ships arrived with demands Japan could not ignore. The strain of trying to modernize quickly, plus internal rivalries and the rise of *sonnō jōi* sentiment, pushed the old system to its limits. Many in Edo saw foreign influence as the immediate threat, but the deeper issue was that the Tokugawa government had lost the trust of the people, including many samurai.

Some historians argue that if the Tokugawa had opened up earlier and reformed more boldly, they might have stayed in power. Others believe that the feudal structure was too rigid to adapt. Either way, once Commodore Perry anchored in Edo Bay, the days of complete isolation were numbered.

9.14 The Legacy of the Shogunate's End

The final years of the shogunate remain a dramatic chapter in Edo's story. They show how quickly a system can unravel when faced with new technology, outside pressure, and internal dissent. They also remind us that while isolation gave Japan peace for centuries, it could not last forever in a world growing more connected by steamships and global trade.

In Edo, life changed slowly at first. Many city dwellers continued their daily routines even after imperial soldiers took over. But the seeds of major transformation had been planted. The city's name would soon officially become Tokyo, and new buildings, new institutions, and new social rules would follow. Samurai traditions, once the backbone of society, began to fade. Western styles of clothing and thinking seeped into everyday life.

Yet many Edo customs did not vanish overnight. Festivals, kabuki theater, sumo wrestling, and popular arts persisted, bridging the gap between the old era and the new. In the next chapter, we will see how Edo truly became Tokyo—how the city's identity shifted under the Meiji government and how people adapted to the biggest changes they had ever faced. But for now, we have reached the end of the Tokugawa shogunate, a monumental shift that closed one door and opened another in Japanese history.

CHAPTER 10

Edo Becomes Tokyo

10.1 A Moment of Transition

In 1868, Edo came under direct imperial control after the peaceful surrender to the new government. Soon after, the city was renamed "Tokyo," which means "Eastern Capital." This change signaled that the emperor—traditionally based in Kyoto—would make Tokyo the seat of political power. For people living in Edo, this might have felt like a sudden shift, but in truth, it was part of a much larger series of changes that had been building for years.

While many people continued to call the city "Edo" out of habit, official documents and signs began to use "Tokyo." Samurai who once served the Tokugawa wondered about their future, as the new imperial government introduced reforms at a quick pace. Merchants, artisans, and farmers watched carefully, hoping the end of feudal restrictions would lead to new freedoms. At the same time, they feared sudden social upheavals that might ruin their livelihoods.

In this chapter, we will explore the process of Edo transforming into Tokyo. We will look at how the city's leadership, social classes, and daily life adjusted under the early Meiji government. Although we will not dive deeply into modern times, we will see the roots of change that made Tokyo very different from the feudal capital it once was.

10.2 The Imperial Court Moves East

When the Boshin War ended, Emperor Meiji traveled to Tokyo for the first time. He was still a teenager, but he symbolized a new era. In late 1868, the emperor made Tokyo his official residence. Imperial court officials, nobles, and various attendants followed him. They set up new offices in and around Edo Castle (now often called Tokyo Castle or simply the Imperial Palace).

This move was both practical and symbolic. Tokyo was bigger than Kyoto, had better access to coastal trade, and was already a major urban center. By making Tokyo the imperial seat, the government showed that the old power structure—based in Kyoto with samurai lords scattered around—was over. A centralized state would now guide Japan from the "Eastern Capital," pushing rapid reforms to catch up with Western powers.

Local people noticed immediate changes around the old castle district. Former Tokugawa offices turned into imperial bureaus. Some samurai who had served the Tokugawa left to seek new jobs or returned to their home domains. Others stayed, hoping to find work with the Meiji government. The roads around the castle saw unusual processions, mixing elements of courtly tradition with Western-influenced uniforms or vehicles.

10.3 Samurai Without a Shogun

One of the biggest shocks in the early Meiji period was the sudden end of the samurai class as it had been known. Under Tokugawa rule, samurai answered to their daimyo, who in turn served the shogun. After the Meiji Restoration, domains were gradually abolished and turned into prefectures under direct imperial rule. Daimyo lost their old powers, and samurai no longer received rice stipends. In Tokyo, thousands of samurai found themselves without their usual income or social role.

Some joined the new national army, which was beginning to adopt Western-style training and organization. Others became police officers, teachers, or local officials. A few tried to open small businesses, though they often lacked the skills for commerce. Many struggled financially and felt deep frustration that their centuries-old status had vanished in a few short years. This frustration led to several samurai uprisings in other parts of Japan, though Tokyo itself stayed mostly calm.

For everyday city life, the decline of the samurai class meant fewer armed men walking around in formal outfits. Over time, many samurai gave up wearing two swords, especially after a law in 1876 banned carrying swords in public (except in rare cases). Traditional samurai homes near the castle were sold or rented to new residents, turning old samurai neighborhoods into more mixed districts. As a result, Tokyo's social landscape began to look very different from Edo's rigid caste divisions.

10.4 The Changing Role of Merchants and Artisans

Under the old Tokugawa system, merchants were considered the lowest class (even though many were wealthy), and artisans were slightly above merchants. However, in the new Meiji era, the government recognized the importance of commerce and manufacturing for building a strong nation. Policies were introduced to encourage trade, factories, and innovation—though these efforts were still modest at first.

Suddenly, merchants who had been restricted by class rules found more freedom to invest, trade, and expand. Artisan guilds that once operated under feudal oversight could adapt to new opportunities. Some artisans began producing goods for Western-style markets, such as silk products, clothing, or items that would sell abroad. Western visitors in Tokyo often bought traditional crafts as souvenirs, fueling a small export market.

Despite these openings, not everyone prospered. Rapid changes meant that older methods or items might become outdated. For instance, certain swordsmiths struggled since the demand for samurai swords declined. Many artisans had to retool their skills or close up shop. Even so, for the first time, there was no official barrier preventing a merchant from rising in wealth and influence, as long as he could seize the new economic chances.

10.5 Early Steps in Modernization

One of the Meiji government's key goals was to strengthen Japan by adopting selected Western technology and ideas. Even before the Meiji era, some Tokugawa officials had tried to modernize the city's defenses, but now the effort expanded to many areas of daily life. In Tokyo, this meant:

- **Road Improvements**: The government began to widen major roads and introduce new surfaces, although most streets remained unpaved for years.

- **Communication**: Telegraph lines were installed between Tokyo and Yokohama, allowing faster communication with the outside world.
- **Lighting**: Gas lamps lit certain districts at night, surprising residents used to oil lamps and wooden lanterns.
- **Education**: Western-style schools were founded, some by foreign teachers who taught subjects like arithmetic, science, and geography. Samurai children and commoner children could, in theory, attend.
- **Clothing Changes**: Some officials wore Western suits, top hats, or military uniforms based on European models. People stared, wondering if these outfits were merely a passing fancy or a sign of the future.

These changes were mostly visible in the areas near the old castle or along main thoroughfares. Many neighborhoods remained much as they had been, with wooden houses, narrow alleys, and traditional markets. The pace of modernization was uneven, and some older residents resisted, calling the new ways strange or un-Japanese. But the overall direction pointed toward a city that was gradually shedding its purely Edo identity.

10.6 New Government Buildings and Public Spaces

As Tokyo became the imperial capital, the Meiji government needed new offices. They began repurposing Tokugawa administration buildings and samurai mansions, turning them into ministries for finance, the military, education, and more. Western architects were invited to design some structures in stone or brick, a departure from Edo's mostly wooden style. For the first time, Tokyo saw multi-story buildings that did not rely on traditional carpentry alone.

The government also created public parks, partly to mirror European cities. Ueno Park, for instance, was established on the grounds of a former temple. It became a place where people could stroll, see cherry blossoms, or visit the city's first museum. This was a new concept: a green space meant for everyone's enjoyment, not just for a temple or a daimyo's private garden.

These developments didn't happen overnight. Many residents were not sure why the government was spending money on parks or large Western-style buildings. Yet officials believed that showing "modern" facilities would prove to foreign visitors that Japan was no longer a backward nation. It also aimed to inspire the Japanese people to feel pride in a changing city that could stand alongside European capitals.

10.7 Reforming the Class System

During the Edo period, everyone was classified as samurai, farmer, artisan, or merchant, with a few more categories at the fringes. The Meiji government declared that all subjects were now simply "commoners" under the emperor, though a new nobility system was introduced for former daimyo and high-ranking court officials. This meant, at least on paper, that old barriers were gone. A person from a merchant family could pursue military or official careers. Former samurai could become businessmen or farmers.

In daily life, these reforms took time to sink in. People were used to thinking in terms of old social ranks. Some families kept wearing clothing styles that matched their former status, even if the law no longer demanded it. Others embraced the new freedom, moving to different neighborhoods or changing occupations. Over time, Tokyo became more fluid, with people mixing more than before.

One area that changed slowly was marriage. Families still often arranged marriages based on factors like wealth, connections, or old social standing. However, the idea that class boundaries no longer mattered began to influence younger people. By the 1870s and 1880s, it was more common to see marriages between former samurai and merchant families, though it was not always welcomed by older relatives.

10.8 Education and the Rise of Schools

The new government believed that education was key to creating a strong, modern nation. They looked to Western countries where basic schooling was more widespread. The government introduced policies to build elementary schools across Japan, including Tokyo. At first, these schools taught reading, writing, and math with a mix of traditional Japanese methods and Western textbooks. More advanced schools added foreign languages, science, and history of other nations.

In Tokyo, some of the earliest Western-style schools were small and privately run. Missionaries set up Christian-based schools, foreign experts opened language academies, and former samurai started schools focusing on Western sciences. The government also sent promising students abroad to study engineering, medicine, or military tactics. When these students returned, they often became teachers or government officials, accelerating the spread of new knowledge.

Commoners who could afford the fees sent their children to these schools, hoping it would lead to better jobs. Poor families sometimes hesitated, since they needed children to help at home or in the fields. Over time, however, the idea of attending school became more accepted. By the 1870s, official notices encouraged all children in Tokyo to get at least a basic education, though not everyone did. This growing school system planted the seeds of a more literate and informed society, quite different from Edo's old system where only samurai and some wealthy townspeople had formal schooling.

10.9 Changes in Dress, Food, and Leisure

As Tokyo adapted, everyday customs began to shift. Some high-ranking officials wore Western suits, adopting items like bowler hats or frock coats. Military officers wore uniforms modeled after French or Prussian styles. Over time, these looks trickled down to the broader population, although most commoners stuck with kimonos for daily wear. Clothing shops started carrying imported fabrics and Western accessories, introducing new color choices and patterns.

Food also changed. Western restaurants appeared, serving dishes like beef stew or bread, which had not been common in Edo. Many Japanese were wary at first—eating beef went against older customs for some. Still, curiosity grew, and over time, these foods became part of Tokyo's diverse dining scene. Meanwhile, street vendors continued selling traditional snacks like dango (rice dumplings) and takoyaki (octopus balls), ensuring that not all Edo flavors vanished.

Leisure activities evolved, too. Kabuki and sumo remained popular, but new forms of entertainment emerged. Some theaters began experimenting with Western plays or music. People visited photography studios to get portraits, a novelty that fascinated many. Public exhibitions showcased new technologies, from steam engines to telegraph machines, drawing crowds eager to see the marvels of the modern world.

10.10 Maintaining Old Festivals and Beliefs

Despite rapid changes, Tokyo did not abandon its heritage. Many festivals from the Edo era continued, now celebrated under imperial rule rather than shogunate rule. Shrines and temples still held seasonal events, and people in different neighborhoods maintained their own local celebrations. For instance, summer festivals along the Sumida River carried on with fireworks displays, just as in Edo times.

Religious practices also persisted. Buddhism and Shinto maintained strong followings, even though the Meiji government tried to separate Shinto from Buddhism as part of its nation-building strategy. People continued to visit shrines for blessings, pray at family altars, and observe customs passed down through generations. The city's new identity did not erase beliefs that had anchored residents for centuries.

This blend of old and new shaped Tokyo's character. While Western ideas and technology advanced in government circles, much of the population still lived in wooden houses, used traditional bathhouses, and wore kimonos daily. The city became a patchwork of different eras, with a samurai swordsmith's shop next door to a printing press that produced Western-style newspapers.

10.11 City Planning in Early Tokyo

In the early Meiji period, city planning was more of a series of ad hoc decisions than a grand design. Officials widened roads near important government buildings and constructed a few stone bridges. They also tried to reduce fire hazards by introducing new building standards in select districts. But large areas of Tokyo still had narrow streets and crowded wooden homes, much like the Edo era.

Private companies formed to provide services like horse-drawn carriages or small ferries. Entrepreneurs tried to start banks and factories, with varying success. Over time, certain districts, especially near the castle, became administrative hubs with bigger, more modern buildings. Other areas became commercial zones where shops sold everything from rice to imported clocks. Outlying neighborhoods stayed quiet and rural, supplying the city with vegetables or lumber.

Occasionally, fires swept through, destroying old neighborhoods and giving local leaders a chance to rebuild with slightly wider roads or better materials. But many city dwellers lacked the funds or desire to tear down traditional homes. As a result, the transformation of Tokyo happened in small steps, rarely following one clear plan.

10.12 Foreign Settlers and Diplomats

With the signing of new treaties, foreigners could reside in Tokyo, though many still preferred Yokohama as the main treaty port. Diplomats from countries like the United States, Britain, France, and Germany set up legations. They brought staff, families, and foreign lifestyles, which intrigued local residents. Some Westerners taught English or military science, while others opened businesses selling imported goods.

These foreign communities introduced sports like baseball and tennis, which Japanese observers found unusual at first. Some Japanese youth, especially those from samurai families looking for new roles, embraced these activities to learn about Western culture. Over time, certain local newspapers began carrying articles about events in Europe or America, introducing Tokyo readers to a broader view of the world.

Yet there were also moments of tension. Some conservatives disliked seeing foreigners move freely in the city. They feared losing Japanese customs or land to foreigners. Occasional street arguments or small riots occurred, though less frequently than during the late Edo turmoil. The Meiji government worked hard to maintain order, believing that peaceful coexistence with foreign diplomats was crucial for renegotiating unfair treaties.

10.13 The Emperor's Role in Daily Life

Under Tokugawa rule, the emperor was far away in Kyoto and played little part in Edo's everyday affairs. Now, the emperor lived in Tokyo, and his presence was felt more often. Soldiers guarded the palace gates, and announcements of imperial ceremonies circulated in local bulletins. Court officials sometimes traveled in formal processions through the streets, reminding people that the city was now the home of the imperial family.

The government also promoted the idea that loyalty to the emperor was a central duty of all Japanese. School textbooks praised the emperor's wisdom, and public celebrations marked important imperial events. This focus on the emperor was new for many commoners, who had not previously felt a personal connection to the throne. At times, officials even encouraged people to adopt Western ways—such as short hairstyles or modern clothing—by linking these changes to the emperor's wishes for national progress.

Still, the emperor was somewhat distant. Everyday life for most city dwellers did not involve direct contact with the court. Many families worried more about earning a living than about imperial edicts. Nevertheless, having the emperor in the city shaped Tokyo's sense of being the heart of a new Japan, one that was moving away from feudal rule and toward a united, modern state.

10.14 Communication and News

During the Edo period, news traveled through word of mouth, official notices, and woodblock-printed sheets. In early Tokyo, these methods expanded. Telegraph lines connected Tokyo to Yokohama, speeding up communication with foreign ships and even sending messages overseas via undersea cables. This was a marvel at the time, allowing near-instant reports of global events—though most commoners had no direct access to telegraphs.

Newspapers sprang up, printing local and foreign news in simple Japanese mixed with some Western terms. These papers covered court events, government proclamations, and even features on Western inventions. While literacy was not universal, the expanding school system meant more people could read. Street-corner newsreaders also called out headlines to gather crowds, charging small fees to read full articles to those who could not read themselves.

All this made Tokyo a center for information exchange. People learned about steamships arriving in Yokohama, foreign dignitaries visiting the city, or laws passed by the new government. In this atmosphere, informed debate blossomed. Some residents welcomed the changes; others grumbled that too much Western influence would harm Japanese traditions.

10.15 Challenges and Growing Pains

Transitioning from Edo to Tokyo was not smooth. The Meiji government faced huge tasks:

1. **Financial Pressures**: Modernizing the army, building roads, and sending students abroad cost a lot of money. Inflation and new taxes stirred discontent.
2. **Samurai Discontent**: Many samurai felt betrayed by the loss of their stipends and status, leading to uprisings in other regions, though Tokyo largely remained under government control.
3. **Health and Sanitation**: Tokyo's cramped neighborhoods and poor water drainage caused disease outbreaks. The new government tried to introduce better sanitation practices, but results were slow.
4. **Clashing Values**: Conflicts arose between those who embraced Western ideals—such as scientific thinking or Christian faith—and those who valued the traditional codes of Edo.

Still, each obstacle also pushed the city to adapt. Over time, sewers were improved in some districts, samurai found new roles or left for the countryside, and entrepreneurs started businesses that catered to modern tastes. The government's determination to make Tokyo a showpiece of progress drove many of these efforts.

10.16 Cultural Continuity

Even in a time of upheaval, the city's older customs did not vanish instantly. Traditional arts such as kabuki theater, ukiyo-e prints, and tea ceremony continued, though some forms evolved to suit new audiences. Kabuki actors, for instance, experimented with Western stage techniques or special effects to stay relevant. Printmakers created images of steam trains, telegraph poles, or foreigners in Western dress—reflecting the curious mix of old and new.

Festivals were also as lively as ever. People still carried portable shrines through the streets, ate festival foods, and enjoyed the music of drums and flutes. Shops that sold traditional sweets or handmade goods continued to attract customers, preserving a taste of Edo in a rapidly modernizing environment.

For many residents, this blend felt natural. They could visit a new public park in the morning, watch a sumo match in the afternoon, and finish the day with a bowl of noodles in a lantern-lit street. The city's evolution was real, but it layered on top of older rhythms that had shaped Edo for centuries.

10.17 Toward a New Era

By the early 1870s, Tokyo's identity as Japan's leading city was clear. Rail lines began to connect it with other regions, though that development lay just beyond the first years of Meiji rule. Diplomatic missions from Tokyo traveled abroad to learn from Western governments, returning with ideas about constitutions, legal systems, and industrial growth. Newspapers in the city buzzed with talk of building a modern nation that could stand equal with the West.

The government introduced more reforms each year. Laws changed to unify measurements, currency, and administrative rules across the country. Education spread further, encouraging more families to send their children to school. People debated everything from hairstyles and clothing to how to preserve "Japanese spirit" while adopting "Western knowledge." Tensions flared, but the overall direction was set: Tokyo would lead Japan's transformation.

For those who remembered Edo's quiet canals and nights lit by paper lanterns, the changes could be overwhelming. But for younger generations, new opportunities beckoned. They saw the chance to become government officials, military officers, engineers, or entrepreneurs in a city brimming with possibilities.

10.18 Life at the Edge of Two Worlds

In many ways, early Tokyo stood at the edge of two worlds: the old feudal system and the modern global network. Residents had to learn new ways of thinking, living, and working. The once-powerful samurai class found itself merged into a broader public, while merchants and commoners suddenly had fewer legal barriers to success.

Some historians describe this period as a time of "trial and error." The government tried new policies, sometimes backtracking if they failed. City dwellers tested Western fashions, maybe returning to kimonos if they felt uncomfortable. Schools adopted textbooks from Europe or America, then replaced them with Japanese-authored books when they became available. The city's growth was not a straight line but a series of steps, some forward and some sideways.

Through it all, Tokyo retained a core identity passed down from Edo: a love for festivals, a knack for commerce, and a blend of refined arts with everyday fun. This continuity provided a cultural anchor that steadied people amid sweeping reforms.

10.19 Summing Up Edo's Transformation

By the end of the 1860s and into the early 1870s, Edo had become Tokyo in both name and spirit. The emperor resided there, Western influences touched daily life, and feudal restrictions faded away. Samurai found new paths, merchants gained fresh freedoms, and the city opened up to the outside world more than ever before.

Yet, Tokyo had not reached full modernity. Most streets were still unpaved, and wooden houses still dominated. Electricity was not yet common, and the city's water and sewage systems lagged behind European standards. The greatest changes—heavy industry, large-scale infrastructure, and wide boulevards—were still to come. But the seeds were planted. Tokyo was no longer just the seat of a shogun; it was the capital of a nation that aimed to learn from the world while preserving its own roots.

In future periods (beyond the scope of our pre-modern focus), Tokyo would grow even more, developing railways, adopting a constitution, and hosting foreign embassies on a bigger scale. For now, we leave it as a city in transition—a place where the echoes of Edo still lingered, but the winds of change blew stronger each day.

10.20 Conclusion: Edo's Legacy in Tokyo

Edo left a deep imprint on the city that became Tokyo. The old roads, canals, and neighborhoods provided the skeleton for modern districts. The cultural traditions of festivals, theater, and family-run shops endured, even as Western ideas arrived. The disciplined spirit of the samurai found new life in public service, schools, and the police. Meanwhile, merchants and artisans—once tightly controlled—sought their fortunes in a more open economy.

When we think of Tokyo today, with its towering buildings and modern technology, we might forget that it was once Edo, a city bound by samurai codes and closed to most foreign contact. The transformation took place through a series of events that toppled the Tokugawa shogunate and brought the emperor to the forefront. Along the way, Edo's residents balanced old ways with new pressures, forging a path that would make Tokyo the center of Japan's journey into the modern world.

The story of how Edo became Tokyo reminds us that cities are living entities, shaped by the people who call them home. The end of the shogunate did not erase Edo's heritage. Instead, that heritage blended with fresh ideas, forming a unique capital that stood on the threshold of an era filled with promise and challenge. Even as we conclude this historical overview, Edo's spirit remains an essential part of Tokyo's identity, bridging centuries of tradition with the desires of a rapidly changing age.

CHAPTER 11

Life in the Early Meiji Era

11.1 Introduction to Early Meiji Tokyo

In 1868, Edo became Tokyo, ushering in the Meiji era—a time of rapid change. While the Tokugawa shogunate had collapsed, many traditions still shaped daily life. People did not abandon everything overnight. Instead, they mixed old customs with new ideas. At the same time, the government introduced reforms to modernize the city. Officials believed Japan had to learn from Western nations to become strong and independent. This led to changes in education, work, clothing, and social structures.

During these early Meiji years (roughly the 1870s into the early 1880s), Tokyo was in a state of both excitement and uncertainty. Former samurai faced new rules about carrying swords and earning a living. Merchants and artisans explored new markets, sometimes adopting Western methods. Commoners wondered how these reforms would affect their families and neighborhoods. In this chapter, we will look at what everyday life was like in early Meiji Tokyo. We'll see how people adjusted to fresh opportunities and challenges, all while trying to preserve the heart of the old Edo.

11.2 The Emperor's Growing Presence

One of the biggest differences from Edo times was the emperor's physical presence in Tokyo. Emperor Meiji took up residence in the former Edo Castle, now known as the Imperial Palace. This created a visible shift in authority. While people seldom saw the emperor in person—his court was still somewhat distant—his influence spread in various ways.

Ceremonies and Public Appearances

Government officials arranged parades or events where the emperor made short appearances. Citizens might gather along the roads, eager for a glimpse of the imperial procession. These were rare occasions, but they carried deep meaning. People saw modern uniforms, Western-style carriages, and a new sense of national unity centered on the emperor.

Imperial Decrees

Notices posted on street corners announced imperial decisions. Topics ranged from new school rules to encouragements for people to adopt Western ideas like short hairstyles. Some welcomed these edicts, viewing them as progress. Others felt uneasy, missing the days when the shogun quietly governed from behind the scenes, leaving daily life mostly unchanged. Now, the emperor's name regularly appeared in official documents, and loyalty to him was stressed in schools and public speeches.

Spiritual Connection

In older times, people knew the emperor mainly as a distant figure in Kyoto. Under the Meiji government, loyalty to the emperor became a cornerstone of Japan's national identity. Tokyo residents found themselves part of a grand narrative about building a modern state under the emperor's guidance. This did not erase local traditions, but it added a layer of national pride that had not been so strong before.

11.3 Changing Neighborhoods and Housing

During the early Meiji era, Tokyo's neighborhoods began to evolve. Some changes were subtle, while others visibly transformed the cityscape.

Former Samurai Districts

When the samurai lost their stipends, many had to leave large residences near the old castle. The Meiji government took over some of these properties, using them for new ministries or foreign embassies. Other compounds were sold to private buyers who divided them into smaller lots, creating narrower streets lined with modest homes or workshops. In this way, previously exclusive areas became more mixed, blending families from different backgrounds.

Western-Style Buildings

Certain districts saw the rise of brick or stone buildings with glass windows, imported roof tiles, and in some cases, basic gas lighting. These structures housed new government offices, banks, or small industries. Although still few in number, they stood out from the wooden houses typical of Edo. People often stopped to stare, trying to figure out if these foreign-inspired designs would truly last in Japan's climate.

Crowded Streets and Sanitation

Tokyo's population grew as people arrived from the countryside, hoping to find work in the modernizing capital. Many settled in cheap, cramped lodging houses. These areas lacked good drainage, so mud and waste built up in the narrow alleys. The government attempted to improve sanitation by building drains or requiring residents to clear trash more regularly, but these efforts advanced slowly. As a result, early Meiji Tokyo still faced problems with disease outbreaks like cholera.

11.4 Daily Work and New Occupations

For much of Tokyo's population, daily work life was a mix of old and new.

Samurai Transitioning to Other Jobs

Some former samurai took positions in the new police force or joined the national army, which adopted Western uniforms and drills. Others sought roles in local administration or teaching, using their literacy skills. A few entrepreneurial samurai started small businesses, though many lacked experience in trade. This led to failures and financial stress, creating resentment toward the rapid societal changes.

Merchants and Artisans

Merchants found new chances to supply Western goods—like cloth, hats, or tools—to the budding government offices and foreign visitors. They also began exporting traditional Japanese products, such as silk and tea, to overseas markets. Artisans sometimes adjusted their crafts to appeal to foreign tastes, modifying designs or materials. Those who adapted saw profits grow; others who clung to older styles risked losing customers.

Laborers and Factory Workers

Gradually, small factories emerged. These early industrial centers produced items like textiles, paper, or glass. Laborers, often from poor families, worked long hours for low pay, using imported machines they barely understood at first. The concept of factory work was new and sometimes clashed with traditional rhythms of life. Owners and managers encouraged punctuality and set production targets, ideas that felt strict to workers used to more flexible schedules.

11.5 Education Reforms and Everyday Schooling

The Meiji government believed education was key to Japan's strength. It aimed to create loyal citizens who understood modern subjects. So, Tokyo became a testing ground for new schooling methods.

Government Schools

The government opened elementary schools, some in repurposed temples, others in new buildings. These schools taught basic reading, writing, arithmetic, plus moral lessons emphasizing loyalty to the emperor. They also introduced some Western subjects, like simple science or geography. Children wore a mix of kimonos and Western-style clothes, depending on what their families could afford.

Private Academies

Some samurai who had studied Confucian classics set up small academies. They blended traditional lessons in Chinese literature with new subjects such as Western geography or mathematics. In other cases, foreign missionaries founded schools teaching Christianity, English, and modern science. These private institutions appealed to families who wanted their children to learn skills that might lead to better jobs.

Challenges and Resistance

Not all families embraced these reforms. School fees could strain household budgets, especially for poorer families who needed children to work. Some parents worried that too much Western learning might corrupt traditional values. They preferred the old temple schools where children learned moral stories and basic writing. Over time, however, official pressure and the promise of better job prospects encouraged more families to enroll their children in the new schools.

11.6 Clothing, Food, and Daily Customs

Everyday life in early Meiji Tokyo showed a growing blend of local and foreign influences.

Clothing

While many older citizens continued wearing kimonos, younger men in government roles or business began to adopt Western suits and hats. Samurai swords were increasingly rare, especially after 1876, when carrying swords in public was mostly banned. Women, for the most part, stuck to traditional dress at home. However, a few upper-class women, particularly wives of officials, tried Western gowns at official receptions—sparking both admiration and gossip.

Food

Western-style restaurants, though limited, appeared near foreign legations. They served dishes like beef curry (an adaptation of British stew), bread, and sometimes beer. Most people ate rice and miso soup at home, supplementing with fish or vegetables. Yet the idea of eating beef gradually spread, breaking older taboos against consuming four-legged animals. Over time, dishes like gyu-nabe (beef hot pot) and European-influenced curries gained popularity among curious diners.

Leisure and Pastimes

Traditional pursuits like kabuki theater, rakugo storytelling, and sumo wrestling remained popular. However, new pastimes emerged. Some wealthy families introduced Western card games or billiards. A few foreigners in Tokyo taught locals sports like baseball, which intrigued young men from samurai backgrounds looking for new forms of discipline. These changes did not replace established amusements but added fresh choices to the city's leisure scene.

11.7 Public Safety and Policing

As Tokyo's population grew, so did concerns about crime and disorder. The new government created a modernized police force, influenced by European models.

Police Stations

Small police boxes (koban) appeared in major districts. Inside, a few officers kept watch, took reports, and walked assigned beats to discourage theft or street brawls. They wore uniforms—sometimes a mix of Western jackets with swords or batons. This was quite different from Edo, where city patrols were often neighborhood-based and less formal.

Crime and Punishment

Punishments changed under the Meiji reforms. Public executions, once a part of Edo's strict justice system, became rarer. Western ideas about prisons and rehabilitation influenced new laws. Some criminals were sent to modern prisons that attempted to separate them by crime type, though conditions were still harsh by today's standards. The government also tried to gather better records of births, deaths, and residences, aiming to track suspects more effectively.

Neighborhood Responsibilities

Old traditions of neighborhood watch did not disappear completely. Local elders and volunteers still kept an eye on suspicious activity. Fires remained a constant threat, so firefighting teams continued to operate, some adopting Western pumps while clinging to the proud spirit of Edo's old firefighter brigades. This combination of new and old systems helped Tokyo maintain some order during its rapid changes.

11.8 Communication Breakthroughs

Information flow in early Meiji Tokyo was faster than it ever had been in Edo times.

Newspapers and Printing

The government encouraged newspaper publication, hoping to spread official announcements and foster an informed citizenry. Private newspapers also emerged, covering local events, foreign affairs, and even criticizing government decisions—though censorship still existed. Improved printing methods, often learned from Western presses, made it easier to produce affordable reading material. Many of these newspapers were sold by street vendors who shouted headlines to passersby.

Postal Services

A national postal system developed, introducing standardized postage stamps and regular mail routes. In Tokyo, postal workers wearing distinctive uniforms carried letters and packages across the city. This made communication more reliable and connected Tokyo with other regions. While literacy rates were rising, not everyone could write. Still, people made use of letter-writing services, paying scribes or helpful neighbors to put thoughts on paper.

Telegraph Lines

Telegraph stations in Tokyo linked the city to Yokohama and beyond, facilitating near-instant messages. Government offices, foreign embassies, and some large businesses used telegraphs to coordinate activities. Most ordinary folks had little direct contact with telegraph technology, but they heard stories of how a simple wire could transmit words across great distances in seconds. This added to the sense that Tokyo was entering a modern age.

11.9 Religious and Spiritual Shifts

Religion in early Meiji Tokyo changed in subtle ways, guided by new policies and social currents.

Shinto and State Policy
The government tried to elevate Shinto as a national faith tied to the emperor's divine heritage. Temples that once combined Buddhism and Shinto were sometimes forced to separate these practices. Shrines gained official status, with some recognized as "imperial shrines." Local festivals continued, but the government often used these events to promote unity under the emperor, blending old customs with new patriotic themes.

Buddhism
Although Buddhism remained popular, it lost some of the privileges it had under Tokugawa patronage. Monasteries saw land confiscations, and Buddhist priests were pushed to adapt. Some temples turned to offering new community services, like education or childcare, to stay relevant. Urban residents still visited temples for funerals or memorial rites, maintaining deep cultural ties to Buddhist ceremonies.

New Faiths and Missionaries
Christian missionaries, once banned, now had the freedom to preach. They set up churches, schools, and medical clinics. A few Japanese converts spread Christian ideas, sometimes facing skepticism from neighbors. The overall number of Christians stayed small, but their presence fueled debates about tradition versus foreign influence. Other new religions also sprang up in the city, mixing Shinto, Buddhist, and Christian elements in creative ways, reflecting Tokyo's evolving spiritual scene.

11.10 Women's Roles in Early Meiji

Women's lives in early Meiji Tokyo mirrored the broader shifts in society. While official reforms did not drastically elevate women's status, small openings emerged.

Family Life
A woman's main role remained in the household. She managed finances if

her husband had a government or business job, raised children, and prepared meals. Extended families often lived together, so older women passed down traditions like kimono making or ceremonial tea preparation. Samurai wives who lost stipends adjusted by taking on small income-generating tasks—like sewing or cooking for paying boarders.

Education for Girls

The government's new school system included provisions for girls. They studied reading, writing, and moral lessons. However, many families still prioritized boys' education, so attendance by girls was lower. Over time, a few girls' schools appeared in Tokyo, teaching not only academic subjects but also "home science," etiquette, and some Western accomplishments like piano. These schools were mostly for upper-class families who could afford the fees.

Work Outside the Home

Women in lower-income households often worked as domestics, laundry women, or street vendors. Some found jobs in textile mills, winding thread or operating simple machines. Conditions could be tough: long hours, low pay, and cramped dormitories. Still, these jobs provided much-needed wages. A few pioneering women from elite families took an interest in public affairs—publishing articles or organizing small social groups—but this was very rare. Most women remained confined to traditional roles, even as Tokyo modernized around them.

11.11 Transportation Changes

Early Meiji Tokyo saw new forms of movement, though not yet the large-scale rail systems that would come later.

Rikisha (Rickshaw)

One notable introduction was the human-pulled rickshaw. Adapted from foreign carriage designs, it became a popular way to travel short distances in the city. Pullers, usually strong men from the countryside, transported passengers along Tokyo's uneven streets. Rickshaws replaced many traditional palanquins and provided faster, cheaper rides for those who could afford it. However, they also raised concerns about the physical strain on pullers and the potential for accidents.

Horse-Drawn Carts

For goods and cargo, horse-drawn carts became more common. Merchants used them to move larger loads of rice, vegetables, or manufactured items. Some city roads were widened to accommodate these carts, although traffic jams still occurred in congested districts. Loud calls and bells warned pedestrians to clear the way.

River and Canal Boats

Water transport persisted. Barges and small boats carried supplies along the Sumida River or through surviving Edo-era canals. Despite the push toward modernization, these waterways stayed vital for daily commerce. Fishermen also continued to ply the bay's waters, selling fresh fish in markets. The government considered building more modern docks, but progress was slow, so small wooden piers and boat landings remained a common sight.

11.12 Health and Hygiene

The Meiji government wanted to improve public health, but many Edo-era habits lingered.

Public Bathhouses

Sento (public bathhouses) still thrived, where people soaked in hot water after washing themselves. Bathhouses provided a social space to chat and unwind. However, with the rise in population density, the risk of spreading diseases like cholera grew if the water supply was contaminated. Officials tried to educate owners about cleaner standards, yet old habits were slow to change.

Street Cleanliness

Tokyo's streets were often muddy or dusty, depending on the season. Rain turned dirt roads into sludge, making it easier for germs to spread. The government sent workers to clear trash and introduced fines for dumping waste, but enforcement was spotty. Some districts took pride in volunteer clean-up days, while others lagged behind.

Modern Medicine
Western-trained doctors began practicing in Tokyo, applying methods
learned from foreign textbooks. They introduced vaccines for smallpox and
tried to handle cholera outbreaks with quarantine measures. Many locals
stuck with traditional herbalists or folk remedies, at least until they saw
results from modern medicine. Over time, the presence of Western-style
hospitals and clinics increased, though limited by cost and distance.

11.13 Challenges for the Government

Trying to modernize Tokyo tested the Meiji government's organization and
budget.

Finances
Modernizing roads, building schools, and setting up a new military required
huge sums of money. Tax reforms shifted from rice-based payments to
monetary taxes. Farmers in the outskirts of Tokyo grumbled about heavier
burdens, leading to protests. Inside the city, merchants worried about new
fees or regulations cutting into profits. The government walked a tightrope,
needing funds while trying not to spark rebellion.

Social Tensions
Samurai uprisings in other regions (like the famous Satsuma Rebellion)
showed that not everyone accepted the new order. In Tokyo, many former
samurai quietly coped by finding alternative careers or living off meager
savings. Still, simmering resentment toward wealthy merchants or foreign
advisors sometimes surfaced in the form of small protests. The city police
cracked down on open dissent, but rebellious thoughts lingered in secret.

Managing Foreign Relations
Foreign embassies in Tokyo lobbied for their nations' interests, pushing for
better trade terms or legal protections. The Meiji government negotiated
treaties, aiming to regain full control over tariffs and law courts. Some
Japanese felt humiliated by "unequal treaties" that favored foreigners. The
government promised that modernization would help Japan negotiate fairer
deals. This fueled the push for more roads, better industry, and a stronger
army, all of which cost money and demanded organizational skill.

11.14 Social Gatherings and Cultural Exchanges

Despite the tensions, the early Meiji era also brought cross-cultural interactions.

Banquets and Balls

High-ranking officials sometimes hosted Western-style banquets or dances, inviting foreign diplomats, Japanese nobles, and business leaders. Guests wore mixed attire—some in Western formal suits or gowns, others in refined kimonos. These events were meant to impress foreigners and showcase Japan's willingness to learn modern customs. Many Japanese attendees found them awkward, unsure of Western dining etiquette.

Artistic Fusions

Japanese artists and craftsmen, curious about Western techniques, experimented with perspective in painting or adopted oil paints. Woodblock printmakers produced images of steam trains and telegraph poles, blending local styles with modern subjects. Conversely, foreign residents in Tokyo collected ukiyo-e prints or admired kabuki performances. Thus, a small but vibrant cultural exchange happened, mostly among the educated or wealthier classes.

Language Studies

English language schools gained popularity as more Japanese believed English was essential for diplomacy and business. Some foreign teachers ran private classes, where samurai or merchant sons learned grammar and conversation. Meanwhile, a few foreigners studied Japanese calligraphy or martial arts, intrigued by the local culture. These exchanges built personal friendships and paved the way for deeper mutual understanding, even if only on a small scale.

11.15 Family Life and Marriage

Changes in the city also affected how families formed and functioned.

Marriage Practices

Arranged marriages remained standard, but a few families embraced "love matches," influenced by Western romantic ideas. Such matches were often met with skepticism or disapproval from elders. Still, younger couples in Tokyo's evolving society found the concept appealing, especially if they had some education that exposed them to foreign literature.

Household Structure

Extended families living under one roof was still common. The eldest son inherited property, while other sons might seek different jobs in the city. Daughters married into other families or, if the family had means, could focus on formal education. Some progressive families allowed daughters more say in their future, though this was not widespread.

Child Rearing

School attendance for children increased. Even in traditional homes, parents recognized reading and writing as valuable skills. Education was still shaped by moral lessons that stressed loyalty to the emperor and respect for elders. Outside of school, children played in cramped streets or courtyards, sometimes trying out new games introduced by foreigners. The overall structure of family life was slower to change than public institutions, but subtle shifts began taking root.

11.16 Festivals and Seasonal Events

Tokyo's festivals, carried over from Edo days, remained a source of joy and community.

Spring Celebrations

People flocked to see cherry blossoms at spots like Ueno Park, a newly designated public space. Families picnicked under the trees, mixing modern packed lunches with traditional rice balls. Vendors sold sweets and trinkets, and occasionally someone wearing a Western hat would pass by, causing laughter or curiosity.

Summer Festivals

Districts carried portable shrines (*mikoshi*) through the streets. Drums and flutes accompanied these processions, which could last for hours. Fireworks displays along the Sumida River continued to enchant crowds. Government notices requested caution with open flames due to the risk of fires in tightly packed neighborhoods, but the festive atmosphere seldom dimmed.

Autumn and Winter

Harvest fairs, though modest in an urban setting, still took place. Winter brought year-end markets selling goods for the New Year, a vital time for cleaning homes and settling debts. Traditional Kagami-mochi (stacked rice cakes) appeared in store displays, symbolizing good fortune. Families mingled older customs with newly available Western ornaments, reflecting a growing cultural blend.

11.17 The Role of Entertainment Districts

While major political and social changes took center stage, Tokyo's entertainment quarters maintained a lively spirit.

Kabuki and Theater

Kabuki remained a favorite among commoners and even some upper-class spectators. However, to appeal to new audiences, some theater troupes experimented with Western stage effects or updated storylines. Actors sometimes wore partial Western costumes or set scenes in modern backdrops. Traditionalists complained about losing the pure form of kabuki, while others found these experiments exciting.

Tea Houses and Geisha

Geisha culture continued, with skilled performers entertaining guests through music, dance, and conversation. Some geisha adapted to new trends, learning Western instruments like the violin or piano. Tea houses themselves might hang foreign-style chandeliers or keep a few Western chairs for curious visitors. For the most part, though, these establishments held onto the refined ambiance of old Edo.

Yukaku (Pleasure Quarters)

The pleasure quarters, such as the famous Yoshiwara, adjusted to the new era. A few courtesans adopted Western-inspired hairstyles or clothing to attract fashionable clients. However, the quarters also faced scrutiny from reformers who saw them as backward or immoral. The government, while not banning them outright, enforced stricter regulations. Brothels had to follow sanitary rules and pay taxes. Over time, some aspects of these districts became more discreet, aligning with the government's push for a "civilized" image.

11.18 Early Labor Movements and Unrest

Though labor unions were not fully established yet, signs of worker discontent appeared.

Factory Conditions
In the small factories producing textiles or ceramics, workers often toiled for long hours. Young women, especially from rural backgrounds, formed a large part of the workforce. They lived in crowded dormitories and had few rights to complain. Some argued that factory life resembled older feudal constraints, just in a modern setting.

Artisan Protests
Certain artisan guilds felt threatened by imported goods or new manufacturing techniques. They sometimes petitioned the local government, asking for protective measures or tax breaks. While big reforms were unlikely, these early protests signaled a new awareness that workers and craftsmen could voice collective grievances.

Merchants' Pleas
Merchants in older trades sometimes wrote letters to officials, complaining about sudden competition from foreign businesses. They asked for clearer rules or for the government to support local industries. Many realized, however, that the government's priority was modernization, which often meant welcoming foreign technology and investment.

11.19 Hopes and Anxieties in Daily Life

For many Tokyo residents, the early Meiji period brought a mix of optimism and worry.

Optimism for the Future
Some believed wholeheartedly in the government's claim that learning from the West would make Japan strong. They saw new schools, roads, and communications as proof of progress. Samurai families who found stable jobs in administration or the military felt proud to serve the modernizing nation. Younger people in particular were excited by new fashions, foreign languages, and the promise of social mobility.

Nostalgia for Edo

Older generations missed the familiar rhythms of Edo. They lamented the loss of samurai tradition and worried about moral decline, citing Western behaviors as too free or materialistic. Street chatter sometimes criticized the rush to change, wondering if Japan might lose its identity in the process.

Day-to-Day Struggles

Meanwhile, common folks continued to face daily hardships: rising prices, uncertain job markets, and new taxes. When disease outbreaks or natural disasters struck, the modern government could not always provide swift relief. The mixture of new policies and old problems often led to small-scale grumbling or local riots, quickly subdued by the police.

11.20 Conclusion: An Evolving City

Life in early Meiji Tokyo combined change and continuity. Samurai rule was gone, and foreign ideas entered daily routines. Neighborhoods began to shift, and new institutions appeared, from modern schools to government offices. Yet the city also held onto festivals, bathhouses, traditional shops, and centuries-old customs that shaped how families and communities behaved.

Tokyo was not yet the fully modern metropolis it would become. It was a patchwork of modern innovations and lingering Edo ways. Residents navigated these transformations in different ways, some embracing the possibilities, others longing for the stability of the past. In the next chapter, we will look more deeply into the cultural and social changes that further molded the character of Tokyo during this same early Meiji period, focusing on arts, traditions, and the evolving sense of identity that tied people to the city's long history.

CHAPTER 12

Cultural and Social Changes

12.1 Introduction: The Pulse of a Changing Society

The early Meiji period was not only about political shifts and modernization in a technical sense—it was also a time of deep cultural and social transformation. Tokyo's people found themselves caught between old and new ways of thinking, dressing, creating art, and interacting with one another. The city's vibrant culture, rooted in Edo traditions, evolved in response to new influences from the West and from the government's push for reform.

In this chapter, we will explore how arts, literature, social gatherings, and cultural expressions changed during the early Meiji era. We will see how some traditions were preserved almost intact, while others adapted or even disappeared under the weight of progress. By looking at these cultural and social aspects, we gain insight into the spirit that guided Tokyo residents as they navigated uncertain times.

12.2 Literary Shifts and New Ideas

One of the most telling signs of social change in early Meiji Tokyo was the transformation of literature and printed materials.

Woodblock Prints (Ukiyo-e) Transition

Ukiyo-e, famous during Edo times for depicting kabuki actors or everyday street scenes, began to incorporate modern themes. Artists printed images of steamships, foreign buildings, and even officials in Western suits. Some saw this as a loss of the classic ukiyo-e style, while others praised it for staying relevant. In either case, the genre showed how Tokyo's visual culture adjusted to the new era.

Newspapers and Magazines

As we mentioned in the previous chapter, newspapers boomed. They carried serialized stories—often mixing traditional storytelling with Western elements like detective plots or romantic subplots. By the early 1870s, a few magazines appeared, targeting educated readers eager for essays on philosophy, science, and global affairs. These periodicals exposed people to novel ideas, including democracy, individual rights, and even critiques of the government, though censorship remained a constant threat.

Literary Salons

A small group of literati—former samurai, scholars, or students—gathered in coffee shops or private homes to read foreign texts in translation. Some discussed Western philosophies, like those of Rousseau or Mill, along with Confucian classics. This mingling produced new intellectual currents, pushing people to question long-held beliefs about social hierarchy or governance. Such discussions were still niche, but they sowed seeds for later movements championing greater personal freedoms.

12.3 The Changing Face of Theater and Performance

Edo had always been famous for its lively theater scene, especially kabuki. Now, modern influences began to reshape these performances.

Kabuki Adaptations

Some kabuki troupes experimented with sets that mimicked Western interiors. Actors occasionally wore Western garments on stage if the story involved foreigners or modern settings. Critics argued whether these changes enriched kabuki or diluted its essence. Meanwhile, traditional kabuki plays—set in samurai times—remained popular, especially among older audiences. This split reflected the broader tension in Tokyo's culture: balancing tradition with innovation.

New Western-Inspired Plays

A few playwrights tried their hand at Western-style drama, introducing scripts that focused on everyday family conflicts or social issues rather than samurai tales. These plays had simpler sets and placed more emphasis on dialogue than on kabuki's dramatic gestures. While they never dethroned kabuki, they gained a small following among young intellectuals and curious townspeople. The government sometimes supported these efforts, seeing them as part of "civilization and enlightenment."

Geisha and Music

Music performances also changed. Some geisha, known for their skills on the shamisen and in traditional singing, tried Western instruments like the piano or violin. They performed hybrid compositions at special events, surprising audiences with unfamiliar melodies. Not everyone enjoyed these experiments; some left mid-performance, grumbling about "noise." Nonetheless, these cross-cultural fusions signaled a new artistic openness in Tokyo.

12.4 Education for the Arts

As part of the modernization drive, the government and private sponsors set up schools for arts and crafts, hoping to blend Western techniques with Japanese traditions.

Art Schools

Some official art schools taught Western-style painting, emphasizing perspective, shading, and oil-based colors. Young artists learned from foreign instructors or Japanese who had studied abroad. They sketched modern cityscapes, foreign buildings, and new forms of still-life. While many appreciated these novel skills, purists believed it clashed with the simpler lines and muted tones of traditional Japanese painting.

Technical and Craft Institutes

Traditional crafts like pottery, lacquerware, and metalwork saw the introduction of new tools and chemical processes. Institutes provided short courses to help artisans adapt. Those who succeeded found opportunities to export their goods, as foreigners admired Japanese craftsmanship. Others stuck to older methods, appealing to local customers who valued heritage. This led to a dual market: one side for modern exports, the other for traditional domestic demand.

Music and Dance Academies
A handful of academies for Western music and dance appeared, led by foreign teachers or Japanese returnees from Europe. Students learned instruments like the violin or studied ballet steps. Although small in number, these institutions hinted that Tokyo might one day boast an even wider range of artistic expressions. The vast majority, however, stuck to classical Japanese dance or kabuki-style movements.

12.5 Polite Society and New Etiquette

As Tokyo adopted Western-style uniforms, buildings, and ceremonies, the concept of etiquette also evolved, especially among the upper classes.

Formal Events
Government officials hosted Western-style balls where guests danced waltzes or quadrilles. People wore Western evening clothes, including gloves and bow ties for men, corsets and gowns for women. Such attire was expensive and often uncomfortable. Some Japanese women found the idea of revealing their shoulders scandalous, while men complained about stiff collars and the heat.

Public Manners
At the same time, the government encouraged "civilized" behavior in the streets, such as refraining from loud yelling or spitting. Newspaper articles scolded men for relieving themselves in public alleys, an old Edo custom. The shift was slow, and not everyone followed these new manners. Yet the message was clear: if Japan wanted to be seen as modern, daily habits had to improve in line with Western norms—at least in the eyes of government reformers.

Tea Ceremonies and Social Calls
Traditional tea ceremonies continued, but some wealthy families tried to merge them with Western receptions, serving black tea or coffee in porcelain cups. Younger women from influential households might visit each other for afternoon tea, mimicking English customs read about in magazines. These gatherings blended carefully arranged flowers and tatami mats with small Western cakes or biscuits. Observers joked that these events were half Edo, half Europe.

12.6 The Growth of Volunteer Groups and Societies

Early Meiji Tokyo saw the rise of new organizations, from study circles to charitable societies.

Intellectual Societies

Scholars and students formed groups to discuss political reforms or Western literature. Some societies published journals, spreading ideas about democracy, human rights, or modernization. The government kept a close eye on such groups, especially if they criticized official policies too openly. Still, these gatherings fostered debate and helped shape future leaders who would steer Japan's modernization.

Women's Associations

While women's rights were limited, a few educated women in Tokyo started small clubs focusing on issues like literacy, sewing skills, and child care. They met in private homes to exchange ideas, read each other's writings, or plan ways to help poor families. These groups rarely challenged the social norms outright, but they planted seeds for the idea that women could organize and contribute beyond domestic spheres.

Relief and Charity

Some foreign missionaries and Japanese converts established orphanages or relief programs for the poor. Traditional mutual-aid networks also adapted to modern city life. For example, neighborhood associations sometimes partnered with charities to distribute food during times of crisis. This blend of old communal spirit and new organizational models highlighted Tokyo's evolving approach to social welfare.

12.7 Western Visitors and Their Impressions

Foreign travelers and diplomats who came to Tokyo often wrote about their experiences, influencing how the rest of the world viewed Japan.

Curiosity and Misunderstanding

 Many Western visitors were struck by how quickly the Japanese seemed to adopt new customs. They noted rickshaws, the spread of telegraphs, and the presence of Western fashions in government offices. At the same time, they sometimes misunderstood local traditions—like removing shoes before entering a building—or found old Edo customs puzzling. Travel accounts in Western newspapers and books shaped international perceptions of Tokyo as a city in transition.

Demand for Japanese Culture Abroad

Conversely, foreigners fell in love with Japanese art, especially woodblock prints, ceramics, and textiles. Some visitors shipped crates of these items home, fueling an "Oriental" craze in Europe and America. This demand encouraged more production for export, helping certain Tokyo artisans thrive. It also boosted pride among Japanese who realized their traditional crafts were admired overseas, contradicting the idea that only Western goods were valuable.

Guest Lectures and Exchanges
A few foreign educators and engineers delivered lectures in newly built public halls, discussing topics like railroads, telegraph systems, or modern law. Young samurai-turned-students asked many questions, eager to learn. These events drew small but enthusiastic crowds, further blending foreign knowledge with local ambitions. Over time, some visitors returned home praising Japan's potential, while others warned that beneath the surface, Japan still had far to go to catch up with Western powers.

12.8 The Emergence of National Pride

As Japan opened to the world, a sense of national identity began to grow, partly shaped by Tokyo's new cultural atmosphere.

Patriotic Writings
Newspapers and magazines featured articles about Japan's unique history, praising the samurai spirit or the aesthetic beauty of old Edo. Writers urged readers to feel proud of Japanese culture while embracing modernization. The government also supported texts that glorified ancient myths linked to the imperial family, reinforcing loyalty to the emperor.

Symbols and Ceremonies
Flags and emblems gained significance. The rising sun flag became more visible during official events, symbolizing Japan's unity. Military parades showcased modern uniforms, but used traditional music or references to samurai valor. Schoolchildren learned patriotic songs that combined Western musical scales with Japanese lyrics about the emperor and the nation's future.

Balancing East and West
Within Tokyo, intellectuals debated how to keep Japanese "soul" intact while adopting Western "know-how." Some believed it was crucial to preserve bushido ethics—loyalty, honor, discipline—even though the samurai class no longer held the same power. Others argued that Japan needed a complete overhaul, including democracy and personal freedoms. This tension produced a lively but sometimes confusing blend of old pride and new aspirations.

12.9 Family Crests and Changing Status

Although the social hierarchy had been abolished in a legal sense, many families still held onto symbols of their past.

Use of Family Crests

Samurai families continued to display their kamon (family crests) on formal clothing, sliding doors, or personal belongings. Even after losing their stipends, they took pride in these emblems, which linked them to a distinguished lineage. Wealthy merchant families also created or adopted crests, showing off their newfound status in society. So while class lines were supposedly erased, these markers of identity persisted.

Marriages Across Classes

Increasingly, marriages happened between families once separated by class. A merchant's daughter might wed a former samurai who had a decent job in a ministry. These unions were not always smooth; differences in etiquette or expectations caused tension. However, with arranged marriages still common, parents often saw the benefit of uniting wealth (merchants) and prestige (ex-samurai).

Maintaining Face in Public

Even though the government said everyone was now a commoner (except the newly formed nobility or kazoku), people cared about how they were perceived. Ex-samurai sometimes wore their swords in private gatherings (despite the ban) to maintain a sense of heritage. Former merchants who grew rich built fancy houses that mimicked samurai estates. A quiet social dance continued beneath the banner of equality.

12.10 Leisure, Public Parks, and Sports

Tokyo's push for modernization included new concepts of public leisure, inspired partly by Western parks and sports.

Ueno Park and Other Green Spaces

Once temple grounds, Ueno Park became one of the first public parks. Families strolled there, and artists painted scenes of lotus ponds or lined pathways. Western-style benches appeared. Vendors sold snacks or souvenirs. The government sometimes held public ceremonies in the park, blending nature, civic pride, and a sense of progress.

New Sports

Foreign residents introduced baseball, gymnastics, and cricket. Japanese youths, particularly from former samurai families, enjoyed the discipline and teamwork of baseball. They formed clubs, played matches, and found the sport a refreshing alternative to older martial arts. Spectators gathered out of curiosity, and local papers reported game scores. While still a niche pastime, baseball hinted at bigger changes in physical education and recreation.

Traditional Pastimes

Sumo continued to draw large crowds. Wrestling stables flourished, passing down training methods that combined Edo tradition with some new influences like diet changes. Tea ceremony clubs, flower arranging circles, and poetry gatherings also thrived, often among older or more conservative groups. This lively mix of old and new activities made Tokyo feel like a city brimming with cultural possibilities.

12.11 Educational Paths for Aspiring Leaders

The early Meiji government prioritized training a new generation of officials and experts. Tokyo, as the capital, hosted most of these endeavors.

Government Scholarships

Promising students from various backgrounds received scholarships to study at the capital's new schools. Some eventually traveled abroad to learn advanced engineering, law, or medicine. Upon returning, they took government posts, where they shaped policies on infrastructure, finance, and legal reforms. This cycle of studying abroad and bringing knowledge back accelerated Tokyo's modernization.

Women's Higher Education

While limited, the government founded a few institutions for girls beyond basic schooling. These taught practical subjects like sewing, hygiene, and moral studies, but also introduced math, science, and literature at a modest level. Graduates from such schools sometimes became teachers themselves, quietly expanding opportunities for women. Still, the path to high-level leadership positions for women remained blocked, reflecting deeper social barriers.

Practical vs. Classical Studies

A debate emerged between those who valued Western scientific disciplines—like chemistry or mechanical engineering—and those who insisted on retaining Chinese classics and Confucian ethics as the core of education. Many schools combined both approaches, mixing modern science with moral lessons about loyalty and family duty. This compromise aimed to produce graduates who could handle modern technology without abandoning traditional virtue.

12.12 The Blossoming of Meiji Literature

A new form of Meiji literature arose, influenced by translations of Western novels and the changing social landscape.

Social Realism

Some writers began crafting stories about everyday life in Tokyo—families adjusting to job losses, young people dreaming of study abroad, or older samurai grappling with irrelevance. This realism resonated with readers more than the old tales of heroic battles. Serialized novels in newspapers tackled themes like poverty, the clash between old and new, and even romantic love, which was rarely the focus in traditional Japanese literature.

Translations and Adaptations

Dostoevsky, Shakespeare, and other Western authors were partially translated, stirring interest in broader human themes like individual rights, morality, and personal freedom. Local writers tried to adapt these ideas to the Japanese context, sometimes blending them with references to Edo's floating world or samurai lore. This fusion produced a unique literary style that reflected Tokyo's transitional spirit.

Censorship and Limits

The government, wary of radical thoughts, censored writings deemed too critical of the emperor or state. Even so, a modest amount of debate persisted, especially in reading clubs or small magazines. These seeds of free expression would later grow, but for now, authors walked a careful line between innovation and caution.

12.13 Ceremonies and the Role of the Imperial Court

The imperial family played a key role in fostering cultural unity, organizing ceremonies that combined old imperial traditions with modern trappings.

Public Rituals

Court rituals once confined to Kyoto became more visible in Tokyo. Festivals celebrating the emperor's birthday or national milestones involved parades and official speeches. Public squares filled with onlookers, some wearing Western-style hats, others in traditional attire. Fireworks and lantern displays delighted crowds. These events were intended to build national pride and support for the Meiji regime.

Honors and Awards

The government introduced medals and decorations modeled after European honors. Citizens who contributed to modernization—be it in education, industry, or public service—could receive these awards at an imperial ceremony. This recognized new forms of merit, rather than inheritance or samurai status, reflecting the government's emphasis on achievement.

Imperial Patronage of the Arts

Artists who impressed the court might get official backing or invitations to decorate new government buildings. A few Western-style paintings graced palace halls, while some members of the imperial family learned to play Western instruments. These gestures set the tone for a capital city open to blending foreign techniques with Japanese aesthetics, at least among the elite.

12.14 Shifting Gender Norms

While full equality was distant, subtle shifts in gender roles occurred in early Meiji Tokyo.

Government Outlook

Policy documents stressed that women should be "good wives and wise mothers," supporting modernization from the home. Officially, men led in public affairs. Yet a few forward-thinking bureaucrats acknowledged that educating women boosted the nation's overall strength, especially in raising literate children.

Women Writers

A small circle of educated women began writing articles or short stories for magazines. Their works often discussed family life, moral dilemmas, or gentle critiques of social norms. Some used pen names to avoid backlash. Even this limited outlet marked progress, as Edo-era constraints rarely allowed women's voices in public print.

Challenging Customs

Occasionally, a bold woman cut her hair short in the Western style, sparking gossip. Others tried partial Western dress. These actions were not widespread, but they symbolized the curiosity some women had about new freedoms. In middle- and upper-class circles, such changes led to quiet debates about a future in which women might have a larger role beyond the household.

12.15 Popular Songs and Street Entertainment

Walking through Tokyo's streets in the early Meiji years, one could hear echoes of modern influences mixing with older sounds.

Street Performers

Street musicians who once sang about legendary heroes now included ditties about rickshaws or railroads. Some adapted foreign melodies, turning them into short, catchy tunes with Japanese lyrics. Vendors hawked snacks, performing jingles to attract passersby. Children learned these tunes, humming them on the way to school.

Music Halls

A few music halls or small theaters tried featuring Western instruments like pianos or brass bands. Audiences, split between excitement and bewilderment, might politely applaud, then request traditional shamisen pieces. This blend exemplified the city's cultural swirl—new forms landed, but old favorites still reigned in many hearts.

Evolving Folk Songs

In neighborhoods with strong community bonds, local folk songs carried on, preserving stories from Edo times. Over sake or during festivals, people sang about legendary warriors, local legends, or comedic gossip. Sometimes new verses were added, referencing telegraph wires or Western hats, folding the modern era into age-old melodies.

12.16 Architecture and Urban Style

Early Meiji Tokyo saw architecture diverge along two paths: modern government buildings and traditional homes.

Government and Commercial Structures

Ministry offices, banks, and some upscale shops used brick or stone in Western designs. They featured symmetrical facades, larger windows, and sometimes small domes or spires. Foreign architects or Japanese who studied abroad led these projects. For many Tokyoites, these buildings were dazzling proof that the city was catching up with Europe or America.

Residential Streets

Ordinary people still lived in wooden row houses, with paper doors and tatami floors, just as in Edo. Fire remained a concern, but many could not afford to switch to brick or stone. Some owners painted walls with a protective coating to reduce fire risk, a small nod to modernization. Over time, wealthier citizens experimented with "Western-style homes" combining tatami rooms and furniture like chairs or tables. This hybrid style was both practical and symbolic of Tokyo's transition.

Bridges and Public Works

The city replaced some old wooden bridges with iron or stone structures. Colorful Western-style lampposts appeared, though gas lighting was still limited to certain districts. Stray dogs and open drains on the roads reminded everyone that Tokyo was not yet a fully modern metropolis, but steps were being taken to present a new face to the world.

12.17 Festivals of Innovation

Besides traditional festivals, early Meiji Tokyo hosted public exhibitions to show off inventions and modern products.

Industrial Expositions
Periodically, the government organized small expositions where local manufacturers displayed steam-powered devices, textiles, or agricultural tools. Visitors, many from rural areas, marveled at spinning machines or glass-blowing demonstrations. Officials hoped this would spark nationwide enthusiasm for modern industry. Inspired by international fairs, these expositions blended spectacle with education, hinting at a future where Tokyo would be a hub for science and technology.

Cultural Showcases
Some expositions also featured cultural displays, like ikebana (flower arranging) or calligraphy, to emphasize Japan's artistic heritage. This allowed foreign visitors to appreciate older arts side by side with modern machinery. Japanese attendees enjoyed seeing how their traditions might stand proudly next to Western innovations, reinforcing the idea that modernization did not require discarding cultural roots.

Public Reception
Ordinary families found these fairs both thrilling and puzzling. Fathers might be excited by a new mechanical rice mill, while mothers worried about losing home-based tasks they had refined for generations. Children loved the bright banners, occasional music, and the chance to eat festival foods. The events were a microcosm of Tokyo's broader changes—filled with promise, yet leaving some unsure about what modernization would truly bring.

12.18 Conflicts of Identity

Throughout these cultural developments, Tokyo residents faced real questions about identity.

Embracing the West vs. Preserving Tradition

Some believed wholeheartedly in adopting Western science, fashion, and even social norms, arguing Japan must "catch up" to avoid colonization. Others saw foreign influence as a threat, urging a cautious approach or a return to purely Japanese aesthetics. In homes and workplaces, these debates shaped choices as small as the type of teapot to buy or the style of clothing to wear.

Regional Influences

Tokyo attracted people from all over Japan, each bringing local dialects, festivals, and crafts. This mixing meant new cultural fusions, but it also created friction. Longtime Edo residents sometimes looked down on "country folk," while newcomers saw city dwellers as snobbish. The Meiji government tried to forge unity under a national identity, but local pride and old rivalries lingered.

Samurai Memories

For families of former samurai, these cultural changes could feel like a betrayal of their heritage. Yet some found new purpose in teaching martial arts as a cultural treasure, instructing police officers or young students. This helped preserve elements of bushido in peacetime. At the same time, foreign guests occasionally took fencing or jujutsu lessons, impressed by Japan's warrior traditions. Such cross-pollination offered a silver lining to those who mourned the end of the feudal era.

12.19 Everyday Moments and Lasting Impressions

In sum, the cultural and social changes of early Meiji Tokyo were both dramatic and uneven. For every new building or modern institution, there were still countless alleys echoing with the old Edo spirit.

Morning Routines

A typical day might start with the crowing of roosters or the distant whistle of a steam factory. People woke in wooden houses, slid open paper screens, and prepared rice for breakfast. Children hurried to school, some wearing partial Western clothing, others in kimonos. Meanwhile, men in suits and bowler hats dashed to government offices, while rickshaw pullers readied their carts.

Markets and Shops

Merchants displayed both Japanese fabrics and imported cloth. Tea sellers offered traditional blends beside small samples of coffee beans. In a single market, one might see a shop advertising Western medicines while next door an herbalist recommended age-old remedies. Bargaining took place with the same lively banter that had filled Edo's streets, but now references to new products and foreign coin occasionally slipped into conversations.

Evening Scenes

At night, paper lanterns and a few gas lamps lit the roads. Families relaxed over simple meals. Some read from new magazines about foreign travel or looked at picture prints of modern Tokyo. Others listened to old tales passed down through generations. In wealthier districts, social gatherings merged sake with Western wines, geisha songs with piano tunes. In quieter neighborhoods, one might still hear a shamisen echo softly from a wooden house.

12.20 Conclusion: The Soul of a City in Flux

Cultural and social change in early Meiji Tokyo was not a straight path from old to new. Instead, it was a tapestry woven from the threads of Edo's heritage and the bright, sometimes harsh fibers of foreign influence. Traditions like kabuki, sumo, and tea ceremony lived alongside rickshaws, gas lamps, and Western-style buildings. Literature and theater bridged samurai tales and Western plots, while festivals celebrated both ancient gods and modern achievements.

In many ways, this era laid the foundation for Tokyo's character as a place where innovation mingles with deep respect for the past. Residents navigated each day with a blend of curiosity, pride, fear, and hope. While the transformation was far from complete—diseases persisted, economic gaps widened, and political freedoms were limited—these cultural shifts pointed to a future in which Tokyo would continue evolving, shaping Japan's identity in an ever-connecting world.

CHAPTER 13

Education, Arts, and Traditions

13.1 Introduction: The Ties That Bind

By the early Meiji era, Tokyo stood at a crossroads, blending fresh ideas from abroad with centuries of Japanese heritage. Education became an urgent priority for the new government, as leaders wanted a population prepared for modern challenges. At the same time, the city's creative spirit—rooted in traditional arts—did not simply vanish. Skilled painters, poets, and performers adapted to changing tastes, weaving old and new styles into their works.

In this chapter, we will explore how educational structures shifted, how arts both transformed and preserved legacies, and how everyday traditions remained a crucial part of city life. While samurai families navigated a world without stipends or feudal duties, artisans responded to new opportunities and competition. Through schooling, artistic expression, and time-honored customs, the people of Tokyo balanced a desire for modern progress with a deep respect for the past.

13.2 The Growth of Public Education

Shortly after the Meiji Restoration, the government issued policies aimed at creating a literate society. Officials saw Western nations' successes and believed that universal schooling would strengthen Japan. In Tokyo, these goals took shape through a network of primary schools. Some were built from the ground up, while others adapted old temples or samurai estates.

- **Curriculum:** Basic reading, writing, and arithmetic formed the core. Early textbooks also included moral lessons about loyalty to the emperor and respect for elders. Over time, more subjects—like geography and science—were added.

- **Structure:** The government separated schools by age group, with elementary education intended for both boys and girls, though not always equally enforced. Secondary education for boys expanded faster than for girls, reflecting old biases about gender roles.

- **Challenges:** Many families could not afford to lose a child's labor, especially in lower-income neighborhoods. Some parents feared that Western-style teaching might erode traditional values. School fees, supplies, and uniforms added to the burden, limiting who could attend regularly.

Yet Tokyo's public schools kept growing. Over the 1870s, modest successes encouraged more families to give schooling a try. By blending moral instruction with practical skills, these schools helped raise basic literacy rates, a key step in modernizing the city.

13.3 The Rise of Private Academies

Alongside public schools, private academies—often called *juku*—played a vital role in Tokyo's education scene. Many were founded by former samurai or scholars who believed in specialized teaching approaches.

- **Confucian Tradition:** Some academies continued to focus on Confucian texts and Chinese classics. Samurai families who missed the old ways found comfort in these lessons, which emphasized loyalty, filial piety, and ethical conduct.
- **Western Influence:** Other *juku* introduced foreign languages like English, French, or German. They employed instructors who had traveled abroad or learned from foreign experts in Japan. These academies drew ambitious students eager for government posts or diplomatic careers.
- **Innovative Methods:** Private academies often experimented with teaching styles, combining rote memorization with discussion groups or debates—a novelty at the time. Some even used foreign textbooks, translating or adapting them for Japanese readers.

These academies gave Tokyo's education system a dual character: on one side, the state-driven push for universal schooling, and on the other, smaller institutions with specialized or traditional curriculums. Students with means could pick and choose, shaping their education to fit personal or family aspirations.

13.4 Traditional Learning vs. Western Learning

Tensions arose as people debated whether Japan should embrace Western-style subjects entirely or preserve older methods of instruction.

- **Pro-Western Advocates:** Government reformers argued that subjects like modern science, mathematics, and world geography were essential if Japan hoped to stand equal with European powers. They pointed out that feudal learning had not prepared the country for advanced military technology or international diplomacy.
- **Traditionalists:** Scholars rooted in Confucian or Buddhist teachings insisted that moral education was vital to maintain social harmony. They warned that a purely Western approach might weaken cultural identity and lead to selfish individualism.
- **Compromise in Practice:** Many schools attempted a blend. Students might read Confucian texts in the morning, then study a foreign language or modern science in the afternoon. This balancing act was not always smooth, but it allowed Tokyo's population to expand its knowledge without abruptly discarding its heritage.

In daily life, a child might memorize classic Chinese poetry at home, then learn about steam engines at school. This coexistence of old and new study materials shaped a generation that could adapt to modern needs while still valuing traditional roots.

3.5 The Emergence of Women's Education1

Although women's roles remained constrained, the early Meiji era saw the first organized efforts to offer formal education for girls.

- **Official Policies:** The government recognized that educated mothers could raise children with modern skills. New guidelines encouraged families to send daughters to elementary schools, though attendance rates trailed behind boys.

- **Private Girls' Schools:** A few pioneers founded schools specifically for girls, teaching basic academics along with "good wife, wise mother" values. Sewing, etiquette, and household management were common additions, reflecting ongoing expectations about women's domestic duties.
- **Barriers:** Parents worried about costs, as well as exposing daughters to unfamiliar ideas. Some believed advanced learning might make girls "unmarriageable." Still, the trend toward opening schools for females gained momentum, especially in Tokyo's more progressive families.

These small steps toward women's education did not instantly grant equal standing, but they laid groundwork for greater female participation in the public sphere. Over time, more girls gained literacy, eventually contributing to new voices in literature, teaching, and social activism.

13.6 Art in Transition: A Living Heritage

Tokyo's visual arts scene mirrored the city's broader shifts. With the collapse of feudal patronage, many artists had to find new markets or adapt their styles.

- **Decline of Samurai Commissions:** In Edo times, samurai lords funded certain art forms—like folding screens, ink paintings, or fine calligraphy. Once stipends ended, these commissions dwindled. Some artists struggled to make a living.
- **Rising Merchants and Foreign Buyers:** Wealthy merchants or foreign collectors became new patrons. Ukiyo-e prints featuring modern cityscapes or Western visitors drew the interest of travelers and diplomats. Artists who catered to foreign tastes found fresh revenue streams.
- **Government Support:** The Meiji government occasionally sponsored exhibitions or offered recognition to talented artists, hoping to preserve "national essence" while showcasing Japan's

cultural sophistication to the West. This led to official "Art Schools" teaching both Japanese and Western painting methods.

Amid uncertainty, Tokyo's art community remained active. Skilled painters experimented with brighter pigments, new perspectives, or even borrowed techniques like oil painting. While some critics accused them of losing authenticity, others praised their versatility, seeing it as proof of Japan's ability to evolve.

13.7 Traditional Painting and Crafts

Not all artists pivoted to modern themes. Many continued producing classic works grounded in Edo-era aesthetics.

- **Nihonga (Japanese-Style Painting):** This term emerged to distinguish native painting techniques from *Yoga* (Western-style art). Nihonga artists used mineral pigments, ink, and soft lines to depict landscapes, flowers, or historical scenes. Even if influenced by Western ideas, they strove to maintain a "Japanese essence."
- **Craftsmanship in Lacquer and Ceramics:** Artisans skilled in lacquerware or ceramics faced pressure from cheap foreign goods, but they also found new export markets. Ornate, hand-painted pieces appealed to Western buyers seeking exotic designs. Government expositions promoted these crafts as symbols of national excellence.
- **Family Workshops:** Traditional craft families in Tokyo passed down secrets to younger generations. While the scale of feudal patronage shrank, some workshops thrived by selling items in local markets or to foreigners. This continuity helped keep Edo craftsmanship alive, even as the city's economy modernized.

Such crafts and paintings remained a source of pride, reminding Tokyo residents that progress did not have to erase the subtle beauty cherished for centuries.

13.8 Western Influences on Visual Arts

Foreign instructors and returning Japanese students who had studied abroad introduced new artistic concepts, sparking creative fusions.

- **Oil Painting:** Western oil painting techniques, with their use of shadow, perspective, and bright colors, fascinated some local artists. Studios teaching these methods popped up in Tokyo, attracting curious novices. Some critics initially mocked the "realism" as too blunt or lacking the refined simplicity of Japanese art.
- **Landscape and Portraiture:** While traditional painting often focused on nature in stylized forms, Western-style artists attempted lifelike portraits of real people. Government figures sat for formal oil portraits, wearing modern uniforms. Landscapes also included telegraph poles or train tracks, reflecting Tokyo's changing skyline.
- **Art Societies and Exhibitions:** Groups like the Meiji Fine Arts Society organized small shows, inviting artists of both Western and Japanese traditions to display work side by side. These exhibitions were educational for visitors, prompting conversations about style, technique, and Japan's place in global art trends.

Gradually, a hybrid style emerged, blending Western realism with Japanese composition. Paintings might feature the perspective and shading of Western art, yet incorporate the calm, spacious feeling of classic East Asian landscapes.

13.9 Theatrical Arts and New Performance Styles

Theater served as a key source of both entertainment and cultural reflection.

- **Kabuki's Ongoing Popularity:** Despite modernization, kabuki theaters remained packed. Famous actors, once financed by wealthy daimyo, now relied on ticket-paying audiences and occasional government support. New kabuki plays might address current events—like the arrival of Western ships—or incorporate comedic bits about rickshaws and telegraphs.

- **Shinpa (New School Theater):** A small movement, Shinpa drama attempted more realistic plots, often focusing on family strife or moral dilemmas in modern times. Instead of kabuki's exaggerated costumes and acting, Shinpa aimed for subtle emotions, simpler staging, and some Western theatrical techniques. It attracted younger urbanites who wanted stories reflecting their own changing lives.
- **Noh and Bunraku:** Traditional forms like Noh drama or Bunraku puppet theater continued but faced a decline in patrons. The government recognized them as cultural treasures, so occasional subsidies helped maintain training schools. Some enthusiasts worried these slow-paced art forms might fade amid the excitement for Western innovations.

The coexistence of kabuki, Noh, and new drama mirrored Tokyo's broader cultural landscape—revering old forms yet experimenting with fresh narratives.

13.10 Poetry and Literature: Embracing Modern Voices

Even as woodblock prints and kabuki changed, written literature also underwent a transformation.

- **Haiku and Tanka:** Japan's classic short poems retained popularity. Newspaper columns featured haiku competitions, inviting readers to capture fleeting moments of city life. Writers blended images of telegraph poles or foreign hats with traditional seasonal references, creating fresh twists on old forms.
- **Western-Style Novels:** Translations of works by authors like Jules Verne or Victor Hugo excited young readers. Japanese writers imitated these adventure or romance themes, crafting longer fictional narratives than typical Edo-period stories. Readers found new emotional depths in novels about individual struggles, love, or personal ambition—subjects not always central in older Japanese tales.
- **New Literary Clubs:** Students and aspiring authors formed clubs where they read Western novels, shared original works, and discussed writing techniques. Literary magazines emerged,

publishing serialized stories that reflected the restless energy of a city in flux. While censorship could curb overt criticism of the government, many writers tackled social issues through fictional plots, fueling debates about modernization's costs.

Literature became a window into the soul of Meiji Tokyo: eager to learn from the world while grappling with identity and tradition.

13.11 Traditional Ceremonies and Rituals

Though modernization advanced, many families continued to observe centuries-old practices.

- **Weddings and Funerals:** Shinto or Buddhist ceremonies still guided major life events. Brides wore layered kimonos, sometimes complemented by Western elements like a veil or gloves if the family was more progressive. Funerals followed established rites—offering incense, chanting sutras—reinforcing the community's shared heritage.
- **Seasonal Observances:** Events like Setsubun (warding off evil spirits), Tanabata (star festival), or Obon (honoring ancestors) remained popular. Even newly educated youth tended to join in, scattering beans to chase away demons or lighting lanterns for returning ancestors. Such customs tied the present generation to past beliefs, providing a sense of continuity amidst change.
- **Shrine and Temple Visits:** On special occasions, families visited local shrines or temples, praying for good fortune in exams, business, or health. Government guidelines had separated Shinto from Buddhism in official records, yet at street level, the overlap persisted. People continued lighting incense at Buddhist altars before going to a Shinto shrine, illustrating how layered religious practices remained in everyday life.

These traditions gave comfort and unity to Tokyo's diverse population. Regardless of new schooling or Western fashions, the city's spiritual core endured.

13.12 Folk Traditions in a Changing City

In the outskirts of Tokyo, many folk customs survived or adapted to the urban environment.

- **Music and Dance:** Regional folk songs—originally sung in rural villages—came to the city with migrant workers. Over time, these tunes blended with Edo street rhythms. Improvised dances sometimes occurred during festivals, merging local styles with urban flair.
- **Storytelling and Fairground Events:** Traditional storytellers, known as *kodan* or *rakugo* performers, continued to amuse crowds with tales of heroic deeds or comedic skits. Fairs featured traveling entertainers who showed off illusions, acrobatics, or fortune-telling. Although Western circuses and foreign amusements appeared, the local traveling showman remained a beloved figure in many neighborhoods.
- **Craft Fairs and Seasonal Markets:** Farmers from surrounding areas brought handmade items—woven baskets, straw sandals, or carved toys—into Tokyo's markets. City folks appreciated these familiar products, even as machine-made goods became more widespread. Seasonal fairs, with their colorful booths and lively chatter, gave neighborhoods a taste of old Edo's communal spirit.

In this way, the "village heart" remained alive, reminding Tokyo residents that not all traditions had to fade in the face of modernization.

13.13 The Role of Festivals in Education and Arts

Festivals played a vital role in teaching younger generations about their heritage while also showcasing the city's evolving culture.

- **Student Participation:** Some schools encouraged pupils to join local festival preparations, carrying floats or performing dances. This hands-on approach let children connect with community traditions, balancing their classroom lessons with practical experiences.

- **Art Displays:** During large festivals, temporary art exhibitions or craft stalls allowed artisans and students to display work. School clubs showed painted fans or calligraphy, merging old techniques with modern themes. Spectators admired how the younger generation merged textbooks knowledge with Edo-style creativity.
- **Government Involvement:** Occasionally, officials used festivals to promote national unity. They incorporated small speeches on civic duty or posted notices about health measures. While some frowned on mixing official announcements with revelry, others found it an effective way to reach the public in an enjoyable setting.

Through festivals, Tokyo sustained links between education, the arts, and the collective memory that shaped the city's character.

13.14 Samurai Traditions and the Concept of Bushido

Though samurai as a class no longer held formal power, their values and martial practices still influenced Tokyo's identity.

- **Martial Arts Schools:** Many dojos shifted from training professional warriors to instructing civilians, including police recruits or interested townspeople. Jujutsu, kenjutsu, and later judo or kendo taught discipline and respect for hierarchy. This preserved elements of bushido—courage, loyalty, self-control—even in a non-feudal context.
- **Philosophical Debates:** Writers and educators discussed how bushido could guide modern citizens. Some believed it fostered national pride and moral strength; others warned it might encourage blind obedience or aggression. Nonetheless, bushido remained a common reference point in Meiji literature, speeches, and educational texts.
- **Samurai Aesthetics:** Swordsmiths, though less in demand, kept alive the art of forging blades, selling them as decorative or ceremonial items. Tea ceremony teachers emphasized samurai-era etiquette, maintaining the spirit of quiet focus and discipline. In

these ways, the city did not forget the values once held by Japan's warrior class.

Thus, bushido lived on as a cultural ideal, evolving to fit new societal frameworks where the actual carrying of swords was no longer permitted.

13.15 Traditional Music and Dance

Alongside the new Western tunes creeping into concert halls, traditional music thrived in smaller venues.

- **Shamisen and Koto Ensembles:** Geisha houses and private gatherings still enjoyed the gentle plucked sounds of the shamisen or koto. Some skilled musicians also traveled to small theaters, delighting audiences with classical repertoires that had been refined in Edo's pleasure quarters.
- **Folk Dances:** Neighborhood associations organized group dances during festivals or communal events. Drums and flutes accompanied dancers wearing yukata (light cotton kimonos). Children learned steps from elders, continuing a lineage of movement passed down for generations.
- **Court Music (Gagaku):** In the newly named Imperial Palace, the court preserved gagaku—ancient ceremonial music played for imperial events. Although fewer people experienced gagaku firsthand, its existence showcased Japan's long artistic lineage at the heart of national governance.

Such music and dance traditions reminded Tokyoites that, despite the surge of new cultural imports, the sweet and steady rhythms of old Japan endured.

13.16 Popular Culture and Street Performances

Daily entertainment in Tokyo was not limited to theaters or official ceremonies—street culture played a huge part.

- **Variety Shows:** Small performance troupes staged comedic skits or magic tricks in open squares. These shows combined slapstick humor with occasional references to modern novelties like rickshaws, telegraphs, or foreign officials. Audiences of all ages gathered, paying a few coins or simply watching from the side.

- **Puppetry and Shadow Plays:** Inspired by bunraku traditions, traveling puppet shows adapted classical tales or even told new stories reflecting modern struggles, like a samurai father losing his stipend. Shadow plays, using candlelight and paper silhouettes, offered low-cost thrills, especially at night.

- **Print Culture Tie-Ins:** Illustrated pamphlets or cheaply printed "story sheets" were sold at these performances, retelling the drama in cartoon-like sequences. People who wanted to remember the show or share it with family bought these ephemeral publications, linking street art to the broader world of mass printing.

This vibrant popular culture kept Tokyo's commoners connected to both longstanding forms of entertainment and inventive twists on contemporary happenings.

13.17 Changes in Language and Writing

Language, the foundation of all arts and education, underwent shifts in early Meiji Tokyo.

- **Rise of Modern Japanese:** Official documents and newspapers began using a style closer to spoken Japanese, breaking from the older, formal syntax heavily influenced by classical Chinese. This shift aimed to reach broader audiences and reduce confusion, though it happened gradually.

- **Furigana and Kana Usage:** To make texts more accessible, publishers added small kana script over difficult Chinese characters (*kanji*). This helped new readers, including children and those from lower-literacy backgrounds, to pronounce words correctly.

- **Borrowed Words and Neologisms:** As foreign technology and ideas arrived, Japanese speakers created new terms or borrowed foreign words. Items like "telephone" (denwa) and "train" (kisha) became common, expanding the vocabulary of city dwellers. Some older folks disliked these modern borrowings, yet younger people found them practical.

By adapting language to be clearer and more inclusive, Tokyo's literate circles grew, linking art, education, and daily communication.

13.18 Preservation Societies and Cultural Awareness

Amid the rush to modernize, some citizens worried traditional arts would be lost forever. A few organized preservation groups.

- **Purpose:** These societies aimed to document local festivals, record old songs, or sponsor exhibitions of classic crafts. Members included former samurai nostalgic for Edo, scholars studying folklore, and officials anxious to keep a sense of national identity.
- **Activities:** They collected old manuscripts, interviewed senior artisans, and organized small competitions to reward masters of older techniques. Periodically, they published booklets describing vanishing customs, hoping younger generations would carry the torch.
- **Impact:** While these societies were small, they had a lasting effect, influencing later national policies that recognized intangible cultural assets. By valuing tradition as a living part of Japan, they balanced out the fervor for Westernization that sometimes threatened to overshadow everything else.

In this way, even as Tokyo changed, a self-conscious effort took shape to guard the cultural heart of the city.

13.19 Everyday Arts: Home Crafts and Customs

Not all arts required formal training; many thrived in ordinary households.

- **Embroidery and Textile Arts:** Mothers taught daughters how to embroider family crests or decorative patterns on clothing. Some included small Western motifs, like roses or alphabet letters, in the design, showcasing a playful fusion of influences.

- **Paper Arts:** Origami and paper-cutting remained popular among children and adults alike. New patterns emerged, depicting steam locomotives or foreign carriages in folded form. Families displayed these creations during local fairs, celebrating both creativity and tradition.
- **Seasonal Decorations:** Whether for the New Year, Doll Festival (Hina Matsuri), or Boy's Day, households arranged special ornaments that reflected both older beliefs and modern tastes. A samurai helmet display might stand next to a small Western-style portrait, symbolizing the household's blend of identities.

These small-scale arts and customs anchored families in familiar rhythms, offering reassurance that, despite the city's whirlwind transformations, the warmth of home-based traditions endured.

CHAPTER 14

Changes in City Planning and Infrastructure

14.1 Introduction: Building a Modern Capital

While education and the arts reshaped Tokyo's cultural life, another vital shift happened beneath everyone's feet: the transformation of city planning and infrastructure. During the Edo period, the city grew organically around the shogun's castle, with moats, narrow roads, and waterways. Now, under Meiji rule, leaders aimed to construct a capital that would impress foreign dignitaries and support modern industry.

In this chapter, we will examine how roads, bridges, public transportation, and new buildings changed Tokyo's landscape. We will see how old districts adapted or disappeared, how Western engineering influenced city layouts, and how everyday life improved—or struggled—due to these large-scale projects. Even as the government made bold plans, it faced financial limits, fires, and earthquakes, testing its resolve to forge a city that symbolized Japan's entry into the modern world.

14.2 From Castle Town to Government Hub

When the Tokugawa shogunate ended, Edo Castle became the Imperial Palace, and surrounding areas turned into government quarters. This brought a shift in priorities:

- **Administrative Buildings:** Ministries sprang up in former samurai districts, often using Western architectural designs with brick walls and large windows. The new Meiji bureaucrats felt these modern structures projected power and sophistication.
- **Clear Streets around the Palace:** Unlike the feudal era, when castle moats were key for defense, the Meiji government wanted easier access. Some moats were filled in or reduced, replaced by roads for carriages and the occasional horse-drawn tram.

- **Space for Embassies:** Foreign legations needed secure locations near the political center. Grand residences with European-inspired gardens emerged, prompting local builders to learn new construction methods.

Though these developments mainly affected areas close to the palace, they set a tone of modernization that rippled outward. The once-winding roads designed to slow attackers were widened and straightened, making room for parades, official processions, and more efficient travel.

14.3 Road Improvements and Paving

During Edo times, roads were mostly dirt or gravel. Rain turned them into mud, and in dry spells, dust clouds filled the air. The Meiji government realized decent roads were essential for trade and public health.

- **Paving Efforts:** In the 1870s, officials selected a few key streets to pave with cobblestones or crushed stone. This provided a smoother ride for horse-drawn carriages and reduced flooding. However, paving was expensive, so it advanced slowly and mainly in central districts.
- **Street Widening:** Some narrow alleys were merged or demolished to create broader thoroughfares, allowing two-way traffic. Residents often resisted, fearing the loss of homes or shops. Compensation disputes arose, leading to delays in construction.
- **Lighting:** Oil or gas lamps appeared along major roads, improving nighttime visibility. At first, these lamps were few in number, concentrated near government offices or foreign embassies. Locals marveled at how the flickering light extended evening activities, though maintaining them posed challenges.

These early road projects laid foundations for further expansion, yet the city remained a patchwork—modern streets in some areas, rustic lanes in others.

14.4 Bridges and Canals: Linking Neighborhoods

Historically, Edo's canals and bridges were crucial for shipping goods and controlling water flow. In Meiji Tokyo, they gained new roles.

- **Reinforcing Old Bridges:** Wooden bridges were prone to fire and rot. The government began replacing them with iron or stone structures, more durable under heavy traffic. Designs often mimicked Western engineering techniques, with arches or metal trusses.
- **Canal Maintenance:** Some older canals were dredged or expanded for steam-powered barges. Officials hoped to boost trade by allowing larger boats to deliver raw materials and finished products. However, many canals were still too shallow or winding for modern vessels.
- **New Thoroughfares vs. Traditional Water Routes:** As roads improved, reliance on boat transport gradually decreased in some districts. Fishermen and traders, though, still found waterways a cheap option. Balancing road traffic with canal use was an ongoing puzzle, especially with limited government budgets.

Despite these efforts, flooding remained an issue in low-lying parts of the city. Dikes and embankments needed constant repair, reminding everyone that Tokyo was still at the mercy of nature.

14.5 Early Public Transportation: Rickshaws and Horse-Drawn Trams

Tokyo's first forays into organized public transport changed how people moved around.

- **Rickshaws (Jinrikisha):** Introduced in the 1870s, rickshaws quickly became a common sight. They were faster and less expensive than palanquins. Rickshaw pullers often hailed from rural backgrounds, drawn to city life. While convenient, some critics saw the labor as too strenuous, sparking debates about worker conditions.
- **Horse-Drawn Trams:** Responding to the need for mass transport, the government licensed companies to build tracks on major roads.

A single horse could pull a small tramcar with a dozen passengers. Fares were affordable to middle-class residents, though day laborers often stuck to walking.

- **Impact on City Layout:** Tram lines encouraged the development of new commercial strips along their routes. Shops, eateries, and small inns sprang up near stations, turning once-quiet stretches into bustling avenues.

Though slow by modern standards, these systems cut travel times significantly, drawing more people into central Tokyo for work or leisure.

14.6 Attempts at Modern Water Supply

Clean water had long been a concern in Edo, which relied on wells, rivers, and simple aqueducts. As Tokyo grew, new solutions were needed.

- **Western-Style Pipes:** Engineers, some foreign-trained, designed water pipes to distribute cleaner river or spring water. Early attempts were limited to neighborhoods near government offices. Installing pipes required digging up roads, leading to complaints from shopkeepers.
- **Filtering and Storage:** Small filtration facilities emerged, though technology was basic and capacity limited. Some sections of the city continued drawing water from older canals. During hot summers, contamination caused outbreaks of cholera or dysentery, reminding officials that more upgrades were essential.
- **Resident Response:** Wealthier households sometimes built private water tanks, collecting rainwater or paying for piped connections. Poorer districts depended on communal pumps or rivers, lacking funds for better options. The uneven access highlighted class divisions, a challenge the government struggled to address.

Despite the difficulties, these water projects hinted at a future where Tokyo might have a comprehensive infrastructure comparable to Western capitals.

14.7 Sewers and Waste Management

Keeping the growing capital sanitary was no easy task. Traditional waste disposal methods were stretched thin.

- **Night Soil Collectors:** In Edo times, human waste was a valuable fertilizer. Collectors gathered it at night for sale to farmers. As Tokyo's population soared, these operations became more complex. Narrow alleys and overcrowded housing increased health risks.
- **Early Sewer Construction:** Inspired by Western cities, some Tokyo officials planned underground sewers. Funding constraints meant slow progress. A few main streets got basic brick-lined drains, while side streets kept shallow ditches. Heavy rains often overflowed these ditches, spreading filth.
- **Public Awareness:** Newspaper articles criticized the filth in certain wards, demanding better drainage. Local groups urged government action, but with limited resources, progress remained uneven. In wealthier quarters, some landowners financed private drainage projects, but poorer areas lagged behind.

This haphazard approach to sanitation underscored how Tokyo's modernization was partial and uneven—modern roads and trams on one side, stagnant ditches on the other.

14.8 Firefighting and Disaster Preparedness

Fires had always been Edo's greatest threat, and modernization introduced new types of hazards.

- **Traditional Fire Brigades:** Edo's *hikeshi* (firefighters) wore protective padded coats and specialized in tearing down buildings to create firebreaks. They remained active, but now the government also encouraged Western-style water pumps and organized municipal brigades.
- **Fireproof Buildings:** Brick or stone structures were more fire-resistant, appealing to government ministries and banks. However, these materials were costly. Most residents still lived in

wooden houses with paper walls. A single spark could wipe out entire blocks.

- **Earthquake Worries:** Tokyo, like much of Japan, faced seismic risks. Early Meiji engineers lacked modern quake-proof design, so buildings were vulnerable. Big quakes caused fires from tipped lanterns or broken stoves, compounding the damage. Officials tried to raise awareness, though actual protective measures were minimal.

In times of crisis, local communities rallied to contain flames, proving that some Edo-era communal spirit still thrived amidst modernization.

14.9 Western Architectural Styles and Land Reclamation

Ambitious urban planners dreamt of broad boulevards and neat grid patterns. While funds were limited, a few showcase projects took shape.

- **Brick and Stone Landmarks:** Government halls, embassies, and large commercial buildings showcased columns, arches, and decorative facades reminiscent of European cities. These structures stood out among wooden shops, symbolizing Meiji ambitions.
- **Reclaiming Coastal Lands:** Some planners proposed land reclamation along Tokyo Bay to create new districts for industry and trade ports. Though expensive, small-scale reclamation allowed for wharves where larger ships could dock. This opened global routes for importing machinery and exporting goods.
- **Disputes and Delays:** Such grand schemes often clashed with local realities. Landowners resisted expropriation, and labor costs soared. Frequent fires or financial crises interrupted progress. As a result, major transformation moved slowly, leaving Tokyo as a city of striking contrasts—modern enclaves near medieval pockets.

Nonetheless, each finished project gave the government confidence that Tokyo could indeed become a world-class metropolis.

14.10 The Influence of Foreign Engineers and Planners

Many of Tokyo's infrastructure projects relied on foreign experts brought in by the Meiji government.

- **Advisors from the West:** British, French, and German engineers helped design bridges, water pipes, or gas lighting systems. They negotiated contracts, trained Japanese apprentices, and often clashed with local officials over budgets or methods.
- **Language Barriers and Cultural Differences:** Translators became indispensable. Misunderstandings sometimes caused errors in measurements or materials. But over time, local engineers picked up foreign techniques and adapted them to Japan's climate and resources.
- **Innovation vs. Tradition:** Western engineers pushed for iron frames or reinforced concrete—new concepts in Japan. Local builders, skilled in wooden architecture, had to learn different safety standards. This merging of knowledge gradually birthed a distinct Japanese approach to modern construction.

Tokyo's reliance on foreign expertise showed how urgently the government desired rapid development, even if it meant navigating cultural and technical hurdles.

14.11 Electric Innovations and Communication

While the telegraph and telephone were still in their infancy, they had a noticeable impact on Tokyo's layout and daily life.

- **Telegraph Lines:** Poles carrying telegraph wires lined key roads, linking Tokyo to Yokohama and beyond. Government offices used them for fast communication, especially regarding diplomatic or military matters. Private businesses slowly adopted telegraph services, though costs remained high.
- **Early Telephone Trials:** In the late 1870s, experimental telephone sets arrived. Only government ministries and a handful of wealthy individuals could afford them. Lines were few, and the technology

was unstable. Nevertheless, the possibility of voice communication across distances excited the public.

- **Street Clutter:** Wires and poles added to the city's visual chaos. Along with gas lamps, signboards, and horse tram lines, they created a new type of urban clutter that confused some residents used to simpler Edo landscapes.

Though limited, these electric innovations hinted that Tokyo would not remain a patchwork forever—it was inching toward a more connected future.

14.12 Commercial Districts and Marketplaces

Rising commerce reshaped certain pockets of Tokyo, as new shops and businesses clustered in strategic spots.

- **Ginza and Other Modern Districts:** The Ginza area, rebuilt after a major fire in 1872, became a showcase for Western-style shops and brick buildings. Visitors found clothing stores selling both kimonos and Western suits, plus cafes offering imported coffee. Wide sidewalks encouraged strolling, a novelty in the city.
- **Traditional Markets Endure:** Neighborhood markets—selling fish, vegetables, and household goods—remained lively centers of daily life. Street vendors called out prices, children ran errands, and local gossip flowed freely. Even as large department stores appeared later, these smaller markets did not vanish, serving customers who preferred familiar faces and modest prices.
- **Credit and Banking:** Modern banks, some financed by the government, emerged to handle transactions and loans for merchants. This formalized the economy, though many smaller tradespeople still relied on private moneylenders. Over time, banks stimulated bigger projects, fueling further development in Tokyo's commercial zones.

Economic growth through these bustling districts illustrated how infrastructure upgrades—like better roads and trams—boosted trade and consumer culture.

14.13 Housing Developments and Real Estate

Population growth brought pressure on housing, forcing Tokyo residents to adapt.

- **Rental Rooms and Tenements:** In older neighborhoods, traditional row houses (nagaya) subdivided into smaller units. Landlords squeezed more families in, raising rents. Overcrowding led to sanitation issues and frequent disputes over noise or shared facilities.
- **Western-Style Homes for Elites:** Wealthy merchants or high-ranking officials built houses using brick foundations, glass windows, and sometimes furniture like chairs or tables. Gardens mixed imported flowers with Japanese landscaping. Such homes symbolized status and openness to modern lifestyles.
- **Speculative Building:** Some entrepreneurs bought cheap land on the outskirts, anticipating new tram lines or roads. They erected modest houses to rent out, hoping to profit when expansion reached those areas. This speculative real estate trend occasionally led to haphazard development, as the city lacked strict zoning laws.

While a few neighbors enjoyed airy Western villas, many more struggled in cramped backstreets. Tokyo's housing scene displayed both aspiration and hardship.

14.14 Public Spaces, Parks, and Recreation

Alongside roads and buildings, city planners recognized the need for green areas and leisure spots.

- **Birth of Public Parks:** Ueno Park, once part of temple grounds, became Tokyo's first major public park under Meiji rule. Open to everyone, it hosted picnics, strolling paths, and occasionally small fairs or exhibitions. Other parks, like Shiba or Asakusa, followed suit, though their size and facilities varied.
- **Playgrounds and Sport Fields:** Encouraged by Western ideas of physical education, some schools and military grounds opened space for sports. Early baseball games or gymnastics events took

place on vacant lots. Over time, these gatherings turned into semi-public events, drawing curious crowds.

- **Lake and Riverfront Improvements:** The city attempted to beautify riverbanks, planting trees or installing benches. Though budgets were tight, officials believed scenic water views would elevate Tokyo's image and give residents a healthy pastime.

These recreational areas, though still sparse, hinted at a more balanced urban environment—one with room for both commerce and relaxation.

14.15 Street Regulations and Policing

As the city grew busier, controlling traffic and enforcing rules became vital to public safety.

- **Traffic Directions:** Horse trams, rickshaws, and carts needed some coordination to prevent collisions. Police stations posted signs directing traffic flow on major roads. While few rules existed about staying on the left or right side, informal conventions arose, enforced by police whistles and gestures.
- **Vendor Regulation:** Street hawkers and small shops often spilled into the roads, creating bottlenecks. Authorities tried licensing vendors, designating certain areas off-limits. Merchants complained about fees and lost foot traffic, while pedestrians appreciated clearer walkways.
- **Nighttime Curfews:** Though not as strict as in Edo times, some areas enforced early closing hours to curb crime. Police patrolled commercial centers, ensuring shops closed on time. This prevented rowdiness but frustrated owners who wanted longer operating hours in a modernizing city.

These measures revealed the government's push for orderly streets, even if old habits of spontaneous stalls and irregular traffic died slowly.

14.16 Earthquake and Fire Reconstruction Efforts

Natural disasters frequently tested Tokyo's growing infrastructure.

- **Frequent Earthquakes:** Minor quakes rattled houses and occasionally destroyed vulnerable buildings. After each event, officials and local builders would debate stricter construction standards. However, cost constraints meant truly earthquake-resistant designs were rare.
- **Fire Outbreaks:** Large fires sometimes swept entire wards, fueled by wooden homes packed closely together. Rebuilding provided a chance to widen roads or mandate brick walls, but owners often rebuilt quickly with cheaper wood. The cycle of destruction and partial modernization repeated, slowing the city's push for uniform safety standards.
- **Community Aid:** Neighborhood groups organized relief for fire or quake victims, distributing food and temporary shelter. This spirit of mutual help reflected Edo-era traditions. However, the government also took more active roles, deploying newly trained fire brigades or sending in military engineers to clear rubble.

Over time, repeated disasters shaped Tokyo's character: a city that learned, step by step, to adopt modern building methods, but never fully escaped natural threats.

14.17 The Role of the Imperial Household in Urban Development

The emperor's move to Tokyo influenced many planning decisions.

- **Roads for Imperial Processions:** Major avenues near the palace were designed to accommodate imperial carriages. Decorative arches, lights, and carefully tended trees lined these routes. They served as a stage for national pageantry, showing off Tokyo's growth to both locals and foreign guests.
- **Imperial Projects:** The court sometimes funded projects like improved drainage near palace grounds or landscaped gardens around important shrines. These investments highlighted the monarchy's support for modernization, though critics noted that many poor districts received less attention.

- **Symbolic Landmarks:** Monuments or gates honoring the emperor's rule popped up in strategic locations. Planners wanted Tokyo to reflect loyalty and progress, weaving imperial symbolism into the city's physical design.

In these ways, the Meiji government fused tradition—embodied by the emperor—with the forward-looking drive for infrastructure, leaving a distinct stamp on Tokyo's evolving map.

14.18 Challenges for City Officials

Building a modern capital was not straightforward. Officials grappled with multiple constraints:

- **Financial Limitations:** Collecting taxes in a still-developing economy meant limited revenue. The cost of hiring foreign experts, importing materials, and compensating landowners often exceeded budgets. Debt and inflation loomed, complicating large-scale projects.
- **Resistance and Protests:** Residents resented demolitions, expropriations, or new regulations. Street vendors, rickshaw pullers, and local associations sometimes staged protests against fees or forced relocations. Police had to balance maintaining order with allowing people to earn a living.
- **Competing Visions:** Different factions in the government had diverging ideas. Some argued for a rapid Western-style grid system, while others wanted to preserve certain Edo-era charms. The resulting compromises produced a city with a mixed personality, neither fully modern nor purely traditional.

These struggles highlighted that city planning was more than technical engineering; it was also about social negotiation and cultural adaptation.

14.19 Everyday Life Amid Construction

For ordinary people, living in a city under constant renovation had daily impacts.

- **Noise and Dust:** Construction sites, with workers hammering stone or forging metal, disturbed once-quiet lanes. Dust from roadwork irritated shopkeepers who had to clean merchandise repeatedly. Neighborhoods near major projects endured months of disruption.
- **Opportunities and Jobs:** Public works created new employment for laborers, carpenters, and masons. Rickshaw pullers or tram operators found stable incomes. Even roadside stalls selling food to workers saw brisk business. Modernization offered a path out of poverty for some.
- **Ongoing Inconveniences:** Not all improvements were beneficial. Partial sewer systems and half-finished roads created patchwork neighborhoods. A traveler might enjoy a paved boulevard in one ward, then trudge through muddy alleys in the next. These uneven conditions shaped daily routines and tested patience.

Still, many Tokyoites believed that inconvenience now meant a better future. The vision of a grand, functional city fueled a sense of possibility, even as frustrations mounted.

14.20 Conclusion: Laying the Foundations for Tomorrow

By the close of the early Meiji period, Tokyo's infrastructure had advanced beyond Edo's constraints, yet it was far from a sleek modern metropolis. Some districts featured stone buildings, trams, and gas lighting, while others clung to narrow wooden rows with limited access to clean water. Disasters like fires and earthquakes repeatedly tested the city's resolve.

And yet, the seeds of transformation were firmly planted. Public roads allowed greater mobility, enabling commerce and cultural exchange. Government ministries, foreign embassies, and local businesses shaped new hubs of activity, reflecting Tokyo's growing role on the world stage. Engineering feats—like iron bridges and experimental sewer lines—suggested a future where the city could overcome its natural vulnerabilities.

For the people living amid this transition, each day offered glimpses of progress—from paved thoroughfares to horse-drawn trams—and reminders of old challenges, like cramped housing and patchy sanitation. In all these contrasts, Tokyo evolved from a feudal stronghold into a capital city blending Western innovations with deeply rooted traditions. As we move forward in our history, we will see how these initial infrastructure efforts set the stage for even more dramatic changes, ultimately shaping the Tokyo we know today—resilient, ever-growing, and proud of its layered identity.

CHAPTER 15

Everyday Life in Tokyo During Transformation

15.1 Shifting Patterns of Work and Family

After decades of rapid changes since the Meiji Restoration, daily life in Tokyo combined old habits rooted in Edo times with new pressures brought by modernization. In many homes, mornings began with the familiar sound of wooden shutters opening. Men and women dressed for their day, but whereas a father might still don a traditional kimono, his grown son—now employed in a government office or commercial company—might wear trousers and a jacket. Children navigated narrow alleys to reach schools that taught both classic Confucian morals and the basics of Western science.

Households remained structured around the extended family, with grandparents, parents, and children often sharing tight quarters. The father typically held formal authority, but mothers managed household finances and child-rearing. Family gatherings continued to follow rhythms passed down through generations, such as bowing in respect before meals or lighting incense at a small Buddhist altar. Despite this cultural continuity, new job opportunities altered traditional roles. Sons no longer had to inherit their father's trade; they might enter the expanding bureaucracy or find work in small factories. Daughters, while still guided toward marriage, could attend girls' schools or learn to sew Western-style clothing, which sold well in certain districts.

The city's growth placed stress on families of modest means. Landlords subdivided old row houses into smaller units, pushing more people into cramped spaces. Even though public works progressed, sanitation lagged behind the population surge. Housewives spent time hauling water, disposing of waste, and trying to keep tatami mats free of dust. Fathers faced new anxieties over rising prices and uncertain wages. The comfort of Edo-era job security—where one might apprentice for years under a family friend—was being replaced by the unpredictability of a cash economy. Yet families adapted in creative ways, using side jobs or small shops to supplement incomes. Some mothers sold homemade sweets or crafts to local vendors, while children might help deliver parcels or run errands for neighbors.

While small, these changes rippled through everyday routines. The family table might include staple foods like rice and pickled vegetables, but adventurous cooks could incorporate Western seasonings, new vegetables, or even the once-taboo beef. At times, older relatives grumbled that modern dishes lacked the harmony of traditional meals. Younger members, however, found the novelty exciting, especially when local papers praised the nutritional value of meat or touted Western recipes. In this dynamic mix, family life became a microcosm of Tokyo's transformation, tugged between the comfort of the past and the possibilities of the future.

15.2 Neighborhood Rhythms and Community Spirit

Despite modernization, neighborhood bonds—carried over from Edo days—remained the glue that held communities together. People often spent their entire lives in the same ward, surrounded by families who had known each other for generations. Children played in the same cramped side streets where their parents once ran about, forging early memories that blended old Edo festivals with new amusements like street performers referencing Western ships or railroads.

Neighborly ties were especially visible during crises. Fires broke out regularly, and the local watch groups sprang into action. Residents kept ropes, buckets, and damp straw mats ready to protect homes from sparks. Despite new firefighting measures championed by the government, it was still these tight-knit groups that responded first, tearing down fences or smaller structures to stop flames from spreading. Afterwards, when the ash settled, survivors pooled whatever resources they had to rebuild. Similar solidarity appeared when sickness struck. If a household lost income due to illness, neighbors often pitched in with food or small donations. Mutual-aid societies continued the Edo-era custom of rotating funds, helping people afford emergency expenses or ceremonies like weddings and funerals.

Yet subtle changes affected neighborhood life. Some old alleyways were widened, displacing a few homes. Larger roads carved paths through once-intimate wards, encouraging new shops to open, including those selling Western clothes, imported fabric, or foreign sweets. Younger residents took advantage of the better roads by commuting outside their immediate neighborhood for work, something far less common in Edo times. Electric telegraphs and horse-drawn trams connected distant parts of Tokyo, diminishing the insular feel of local communities. Though daily greetings and neighborly respect persisted, the rapid influx of newcomers—workers, students, and merchants from other provinces—created a sense of flux that was both stimulating and unsettling.

In this evolving environment, small local festivals became a means to reinforce identity. The same shrines that once gathered local samurai or artisans now welcomed government clerks, factory workers, and even a few foreigners curious about Japanese customs. Even as official Shinto and state ceremonies gained prominence, wards hosted vibrant summer festivals, with portable shrines carried through streets to the beat of taiko drums. Laughter and music filled the air, forging a kind of unity that reminded everyone that Tokyo, no matter how modern it became, was still built on age-old communal foundations.

15.3 The Evolving Role of Women

Modernization opened a few doors for women, though most lived under traditional constraints that prioritized marriage, family care, and obedience to male relatives. Still, change was underway, especially in Tokyo where new ideas took root faster than in rural areas. Girls attending schools gained basic literacy, allowing them to read novels, newspapers, and the occasional foreign magazine. Government policy promoted the concept of "good wife, wise mother," implying that women needed education to raise children fit for a modern nation. While the message still centered on domesticity, the very act of sending daughters to school marked a significant shift from Edo practices that limited formal learning for most girls.

In wealthier families, some women pursued more advanced studies. A handful learned English or French and were hired as translators or governesses. Others found work in new textile factories, using mechanical looms. Factory life, though harsh, represented a path to earning wages independently. For lower-income households, service jobs remained the main option: maids in Western-style hotels, shop assistants in modern department stores, or servers in tea houses. These roles exposed them to foreign customers and business practices, gradually eroding the assumption that women could not handle public-facing tasks.

Yet the majority of women continued to fulfill traditional roles. They woke at dawn to prepare meals, launder clothes, and manage household finances. Wives of former samurai coped with reduced incomes by opening small businesses—perhaps sewing Western-style garments or teaching calligraphy. Merchant families often needed the mother's help in the store, balancing child care with serving customers. As they navigated these demands, women displayed remarkable resilience and ingenuity, even as their achievements rarely appeared in official records.

Social gatherings among women became more common in districts influenced by Western customs. Mothers of schoolchildren might share ideas about modern hygiene or home economics. Some took lessons in Western cooking or piano, adapting them to Japanese spaces. Others joined small charity groups aiding orphanages or running literacy programs. Step by step, women in Tokyo began laying the groundwork for broader participation in public life, though it would take many more years before their voices were heard in government or professional arenas.

15.4 Emerging Pastimes and Leisure

Amid new work routines and social shifts, Tokyo residents still found moments for enjoyment. Traditional pursuits like kabuki theater and sumo matches thrived, drawing large crowds who craved a break from the rigors of modern living. Younger viewers thrilled at fresh kabuki storylines referencing telegraphs or the marvels of a Western ship, while older fans scoffed at gimmicks, preferring classic tales of samurai valor. In this coexistence of old and new, performers deftly balanced loyalty to tradition with an eagerness to reflect current fascinations.

Public parks, such as Ueno or Shiba, gave families a space for strolling. Men might practice Western calisthenics or baseball with colleagues, while women gathered on benches to chat and watch children play. The blossoming of cherry trees in spring drew crowds from across the city, echoing Edo-era flower-viewing picnics yet featuring occasional foreign visitors or Japanese dressed in Western coats. Even though roads were sometimes muddy or incomplete, these parks offered a vision of a city that aspired toward modern urban planning.

New amusements arose. Imported board games like chess or card games gained a foothold among curious youth, alongside well-established favorites such as go or shogi. Book lending shops circulated translations of Western novels, and a few cafés experimented with coffee, ice cream, or Western pastries. Some well-to-do residents formed music clubs where they performed Western compositions on violin or piano. Meanwhile, commoners still enjoyed street performers, rakugo storytellers, and puppet shows that explored the comedic side of modernization. This layered entertainment scene meant that on any given evening, a passerby might encounter the clash of shamisen strings from a teahouse and, just around the corner, a group of men engrossed in a new card game taught by a foreign acquaintance.

The city's nightlife also expanded. Horse-drawn trams and gaslit streets allowed shops to remain open later, and wealthier patrons visited establishments serving Western spirits like beer or whiskey. Genteel social gatherings at European-style ballrooms coexisted with boisterous gatherings at traditional inns. The diversity of recreational venues underscored Tokyo's status as a hub of cultural fusion, where one could feast on Western pastries after a kabuki play or ride a rickshaw to a modern coffee shop.

15.5 Money Matters and the Cash Economy

While barter and rice-based transactions once defined much of Edo society, money became increasingly central in Meiji Tokyo. Currency reforms under the new government aimed to unify Japan's chaotic monetary system, encouraging the use of yen coins and banknotes. Everyday people, especially shopkeepers and artisans, learned to handle modern bookkeeping, often leaving behind Edo-era ledgers that recorded debts in koku of rice or local scrip.

This growing cash economy transformed daily transactions. City dwellers paid tram fares, bought bread or newspapers, and saved coins in small wooden boxes at home. Merchants who had relied on personal trust and local networks now navigated more formal banking relationships. Moneylenders still existed, but banks expanded, offering small loans for budding businesses. The shift was not always smooth. Some older merchants distrusted new financial instruments, such as promissory notes or shares in joint-stock companies, fearing they might lead to debt traps.

Prices fluctuated as imported goods, like kerosene for lamps or foreign textiles, entered the market. Families felt these pressures acutely when salaries in newly formed offices or factories failed to keep pace with rising rent and food costs. Inflation, fueled by government spending on modernization, forced mothers to stretch household budgets further. Meanwhile, those with capital to invest reaped benefits. Resourceful Tokyoites who owned land near new tram lines saw property values soar.

Others opened shops selling Western-style shoes or hats, catering to officials who wore them as part of a modern uniform. In the midst of these opportunities, many still struggled, living day to day in cramped quarters. The cash economy thus created winners and losers, reshaping social hierarchies that were once dictated by samurai status or merchant lineage.

15.6 The Everyday Sounds and Sights

Stepping onto Tokyo's streets offered a sensory collage. From morning to dusk, rickshaw pullers shouted for fares, vendors hawked steaming sweet potatoes or tofu, and public announcers read out government notices in lively voices. Horse-drawn carriages clattered over uneven roads, while carpenters' hammers rang out from buildings under repair. In more modern districts, the clang of construction for new brick structures contrasted with the hush of older neighborhoods still dominated by wooden walls and paper doors.

People of all backgrounds wove through these streets. A samurai-turned-official might stride by in a Western frock coat, followed by a shopkeeper's daughter in a colorful kimono. Students wearing a mix of Japanese and Western attire hurried to school, balancing books and lunchboxes. Merchants carried tall paper lanterns advertising their shops, while foreigners from embassies occasionally passed in carriages, prompting curious stares from local children. Market stalls displayed both local produce and imported goods like foreign biscuits or new chemicals for dyeing cloth. The city's fabric stalls now featured cotton prints decorated with patterns of steam locomotives, signifying how daily objects had started reflecting modern imagery.

Nighttime brought a different set of impressions. Lanterns glowed in narrow alleys where small inns catered to tired travelers, and watchers patrolled to guard against thieves or late-night fires. Gaslights brightened major roads near government offices, revealing brick buildings that stood as symbols of Tokyo's desire to rival Western capitals. Beneath that modern glow, people still gathered at communal bathhouses to soak away the day's fatigue, exchanging gossip as steam rose into the night. Even in the quiet hours, the city never truly slept. Distant temple bells mixed with the occasional rumble of a late-night horse tram, underscoring a tension between Edo's lingering spirit and Meiji's forward thrust.

15.7 Health, Hygiene, and Coping with Disease

Though the government promoted sanitation reforms, daily hygiene was often a personal battle. People relied on well water or public pumps. Boiling water became more common in homes that could afford fuel, an effort to stave off diseases like cholera, which flared whenever contaminated water reached crowded wards. Street cleaners tried to maintain cleanliness, but with horse droppings and open gutters, it was an ongoing challenge. Children in poorer districts might run barefoot through puddles, risking infection, while wealthier families purchased imported soap or disinfectants.

When epidemics struck, schools closed and neighborhoods quarantined themselves. Families burned incense or hung protective charms, blending medical advice with folk remedies. Some turned to Western-trained doctors who had set up private clinics, where they might receive vaccinations or treatments like quinine for fevers. Traditional healers also persisted, offering herbal concoctions, acupuncture, or moxibustion. The cohabitation of these different medical practices mirrored Tokyo's overall blending of old and new.

Mortality rates remained high compared to Western cities. Government statistics, rudimentary as they were, revealed that young children suffered the most. Even so, life continued. Neighbors supported each other in times of sickness, delivering simple foods or making runs to local shrines for blessings. Over time, efforts to improve water supplies, build sewers, and expand medical facilities did help, but the transition to a healthier city was slow and uneven, especially in districts far from the central heart of government initiatives.

15.8 Schoolchildren and Youth Culture

Despite the hardships, children often experienced the Meiji shift as a grand adventure. Many attended new schools, where they recited Confucian morals one hour and learned arithmetic in a Western style the next. During recess, they might play old Edo games like spinning tops or battledores, side by side with attempts at Western sports—like tossing a rubber ball or even practicing basic forms of baseball taught by a foreign instructor.

Homework occasionally included reading short newspaper articles, introducing them to headlines about government decrees or foreign affairs. This exposure to wider issues shaped a generation more outward-looking than their parents, who in Edo times rarely worried about events beyond their neighborhood or domain. Young people also influenced home life by teaching older relatives a few words of English or describing the scientific concepts they learned—such as simple experiments showing how steam power worked.

Outside school, peer groups formed around modern amusements, like visiting traveling exhibits or collecting small items with Western motifs. Daughters of modestly progressive families might gather to practice needlework that combined Japanese embroidery with glimpses of European patterns they saw in books. Even the routine act of wearing a school uniform, especially if it had Western-style features like pleated skirts or collared shirts, set youth apart from older siblings who never had such attire. Slowly, an emerging youth culture took shape, bridging the gap between tradition and modernity in playful, day-to-day ways.

15.9 Rites of Passage and Changing Celebrations

Personal milestones adjusted to the new social fabric. Ceremonies for coming of age, marriage, and funerals kept elements of Edo tradition but adapted to practical realities. For instance, a merchant's wedding might now integrate a Western-style photo session, complete with formal attire, after the Shinto ceremony. Families cherished these photographs, which became status symbols of modern living. Yet the main ceremony still involved sake-sharing rituals, shrine visits, and family crests marking the union of two lineages.

Funeral customs similarly combined old rites with subtle modern influences. People wore traditional mourning clothes, bowed before an incense brazier, and recited Buddhist prayers. But the funeral notices might also mention the deceased's occupation in a modern firm or government office, and a few lines of Western-style eulogy might be read out if the family had foreign ties. Graveyards began to display occasional Western-style stone markers, standing incongruously among wooden tablets inscribed with posthumous Buddhist names.

New ceremonies arose too. With the introduction of official school graduations, families celebrated children's achievements in events that had no Edo-era equivalent. Diplomas were handed out, sometimes with printed covers featuring both Chinese characters and English words like "Certificate." Proud parents looked on, often unsure what the foreign script meant, but satisfied their child was stepping into a future that promised stability and respect. Thus, across births, weddings, and death, the city's expanding set of customs enriched the tapestry of daily life, even as it stirred nostalgic yearnings for a simpler time.

15.10 Conclusion: The Quiet Pulse of Transformation

Despite all the headlines about infrastructure projects or political reforms, Tokyo's transformation truly lived in the quiet pulse of everyday life. Families wrestled with new jobs, new foods, and new ways of learning. Neighborhoods adapted to changing demographics, holding onto communal bonds while absorbing an influx of strangers seeking opportunity. Women found small openings to participate beyond domestic spheres, and children bridged the gap between traditional morality and Western knowledge. The city's amusements, social customs, and financial systems reflected modern influences, yet old Edo rhythms lingered in every festival drumbeat or neighborly act of kindness.

Even as telegraph wires and horse-drawn trams signaled progress, many facets of life remained remarkably consistent with the past. Lantern-lit alleyways, the smell of grilled fish at twilight, the warm chatter at a local bathhouse—these reminders of continuity coexisted with a growing sense that Tokyo's pace would never slow again. In the next chapter, we will explore how commerce and industry further accelerated this transformation, shaping both the skyline and the fortunes of citizens who rode the unpredictable waves of Meiji modernization.

CHAPTER 16

Growth of Commerce and Industry

16.1 Introduction: A Thirst for Prosperity

By the 1880s, Tokyo's ambitions stretched far beyond being simply a
political center for the Meiji state. Government leaders and entrepreneurs
alike saw the city as a crucible for economic development, eager to prove
Japan could stand on equal footing with Western nations. Factories
cropped up along rivers, modern banks financed new ventures, and
department stores introduced urbanites to an array of local and imported
goods. As commerce and industry expanded, they reshaped the capital's
social fabric and physical landscape. Family businesses reinvented
themselves, samurai turned into company managers, and rural migrants
arrived to find factory jobs. In this chapter, we will examine how Tokyo's
economic awakening came with both promises of wealth and challenges
that tested the city's resolve.

16.2 Merchants Rising in Influence

Under the Tokugawa system, merchants had been ranked below samurai
and peasants in official status. However, the Meiji era reversed this social
order in practice, if not always in name. Financial success allowed some
merchants to wield more power than former samurai who struggled
without feudal stipends. In Tokyo, established merchant houses thrived by
pivoting to modern banking and foreign trade. For instance, shops that
once sold rice or sake expanded into real estate or foreign imports, learning
from European business models.

Smaller vendors also found opportunity in the growing city. As roads
improved, they shipped goods faster, meeting the demand of new
neighborhoods. Street markets teemed with fresh produce from the
countryside, as well as novel items like bread or Western canned foods.
Educated sons of merchant families often managed the transition, applying
arithmetic or basic foreign language skills to forge partnerships with

overseas agents. This shift toward a cash economy and broader trade networks elevated the merchant class from a tolerated necessity under feudalism to a critical driver of modernization.

Commerce also became more visible. Brick-faced shops along Ginza displayed both Japanese crafts and imported clocks, perfumes, and textiles. Shoppers, including government officials' families, strolled wide sidewalks that echoed Western boulevards. Advertisements popped up in newspapers or on signboards, showcasing everything from foreign soaps to local teas rebranded for export. This energy signaled Tokyo's readiness to compete internationally, even as many merchants remained humble in public gestures, mindful that conspicuous wealth could stir envy or criticism.

16.3 Emergence of Modern Banking

Crucial to this commercial surge was the establishment of modern banks. The Meiji government recognized that if Japan intended to finance railways, factories, and large-scale trade, it needed stable institutions for savings, loans, and currency exchange. In Tokyo, the first national banks issued paper money backed by the government, phasing out the chaotic array of domain-specific currencies from the Edo period. Wealthier families and businesses deposited funds, earning interest—an unfamiliar concept for many used to the old practice of storing gold or silver at home.

Banks offered loans that allowed small entrepreneurs to expand. A textile merchant, for instance, could borrow to purchase mechanical looms or open a second shop. As these ventures succeeded, the merchant repaid the bank with interest. In some cases, banks helped form joint-stock companies, which let multiple investors pool capital. This structure introduced the idea of stock ownership, a leap from Edo traditions where businesses typically stayed in one family for generations.

Yet the banking system was not without controversy. Periodic financial panics rattled confidence, as over-ambitious loans or speculative investments went sour. Some newly minted bankers had limited training, and enforcement of regulations was inconsistent. Debtors who defaulted could ruin a bank's reputation. Newspapers reported dramatic tales of bankruptcies or fraud, feeding skepticism among everyday Tokyoites who worried that depositing their life's savings might lead to ruin. Despite these fears, banks gradually gained trust by demonstrating that secure deposits and careful lending fueled genuine growth, reinforcing the city's broader economic momentum.

16.4 Factories and Industrial Districts

The most visible sign of Tokyo's commercial revolution was the appearance of factories. Early ventures focused on textiles, especially silk reeling, taking advantage of Japan's existing sericulture. In older wards, low, smoky buildings housed whirring machines imported from Europe, powered by coal and managed by foremen taught in basic mechanical engineering. Over time, these factories clustered in certain districts near rivers or canals, which provided water for steam engines and a means of shipping raw materials in and finished products out.

Working conditions varied. While some owners tried to maintain clean environments and limit work hours, many factories subjected laborers to long shifts, poor ventilation, and minimal safety measures. Young women from rural provinces formed much of the workforce, drawn by promises of steady wages. Once they arrived, they found themselves living in cramped dormitories with strict supervisors. Their pay, though better than peasant farming in some cases, still barely covered living costs in the city. Health problems like respiratory illnesses were common, as dust or fumes accumulated in closed workrooms.

Nevertheless, the factories offered a foothold for families seeking upward mobility. Some laborers managed to save or send money back home, supporting aging parents or paying off debts. Entrepreneurs reinvested profits into machinery upgrades, aiming to boost efficiency and quality. Government officials lauded these industrial districts as proof of Japan's modernization, hosting foreign dignitaries to show how the once-feudal society had embraced mechanized production. But the sweat and hardship behind these success stories also prompted discussions about factory reform, foreshadowing future labor movements.

16.5 Trade and Global Connections

As Tokyo became the Meiji capital, foreign diplomats and merchants flocked to negotiate treaties, supply machinery, or establish joint enterprises. Steamships crossed the seas carrying raw silk, tea, or artifacts from Japan, returning with iron rails, engineering tools, and Western goods. Tokyo's port facilities, though still developing, reflected this global exchange. Warehouses stored crates of foreign textiles or advanced equipment waiting to be distributed across Japan.

Among local businessmen, a fascination with foreign markets grew. Silk reeling and tea exports already formed a robust trade pipeline, but new possibilities emerged for processed foods, ceramics, or even modern manufactured goods. Eager entrepreneurs hosted Western-style tea parties to court potential investors or sign distribution contracts. A handful of bilingual brokers specialized in bridging language gaps, earning healthy commissions. Publications like The Japan Mail or Kaigai Bukkyō promoted cross-border business, offering translations of foreign economic news and shipping schedules.

This outward-facing commerce affected everyday consumers, too. Shops stocked European flours, wines, and household gadgets that middle-class Tokyoites purchased as novelties. Wealthy patrons tried foreign furniture or cutlery, integrating them into homes otherwise furnished in traditional Japanese style. Even if the average family could not afford such imports, the city's commercial district displayed them as symbols of a cosmopolitan future. At the same time, exported Japanese crafts—lacquerware, porcelain, ukiyo-e prints—found eager buyers overseas, fueling pride that Tokyo's arts were admired in prestigious European salons. This interplay of export success and import fascination drove much of Tokyo's commercial dynamism, weaving the city more tightly into global currents.

16.6 Department Stores and Shoppers' Revolution

One striking innovation in Tokyo's retail landscape was the rise of early department stores. Borrowing concepts from Europe and America, local entrepreneurs opened large, multi-story shops where customers could browse a range of products in a single, stylish environment. Ginza, with its modern brick architecture and broader sidewalks, became an ideal location for these emporiums. Windows displayed Western dresses and hats, but also sold kimono fabrics and traditional items, creating a bridge between foreign-inspired consumer habits and Japanese tastes.

The department store experience differed from Edo-era shops in several ways. Prices were marked openly, discouraging the haggling that was once standard. The stores had fixed operating hours, posted on modern signboards. Electric lighting, introduced in the more advanced outlets, extended shopping into the evening, lending an aura of sophistication. Some even had tearooms serving both green tea and Western confections, encouraging browsers to linger. Female customers found the environment somewhat liberating: they could shop without the pressure to negotiate with male shopkeepers or worry about social hierarchies. Although these establishments mostly catered to the wealthier classes, they captured the public imagination, with newspapers calling them windows onto the modern world.

Yet not all embraced this revolution. Traditional merchants felt threatened, fearing the decline of small neighborhood shops. Critics lamented the impersonal nature of big stores, where a customer's face no longer mattered as much as their wallet. Additionally, the earliest department stores faced logistical hurdles, from managing complex inventories to training staff in modern sales techniques. Over time, however, their popularity soared, symbolizing Tokyo's shift toward a consumption-driven urban culture and introducing concepts like seasonal sales or Western-style gift-giving during holidays.

16.7 The Role of Government in Economic Growth

While private enterprise expanded, the Meiji government played a key role in guiding Tokyo's commercial and industrial development. Officials promoted certain industries—textiles, shipbuilding, and armaments—by funding pilot factories and dispatching students overseas to learn cutting-edge technologies. Tokyo, as the seat of power, benefited from this strategy. Government ministries oversaw the awarding of contracts, the formation of state monopolies on goods like tobacco or salt, and the regulation of currency.

Tax incentives and low-interest loans favored well-connected entrepreneurs who founded large corporations. Many were either ex-samurai or wealthy merchant families aligned with influential bureaucrats. Critics complained that these cozy relationships created cartels, stifling smaller players. Nonetheless, defenders argued that forging strong, state-backed businesses was necessary for Japan to compete internationally.

In addition, the government orchestrated grand expositions in Tokyo, showcasing machine tools, electric devices, and modern crafts. These events aimed to educate the public about industry's potential and impress visiting foreigners. Newspapers covered these expositions in detail, writing effusive praise about Japan's modernization efforts. By the turn of the century, the partnership between government and big industry, known as the "zaibatsu" system, became a defining feature of Japan's economy, setting the stage for even more dramatic growth in the following decades.

16.8 Laborers, Artisans, and the Seeds of Discontent

Behind the headlines of booming trade and industrial triumph lay a workforce grappling with low wages, long hours, and limited protections. While some skilled artisans, especially those producing fine crafts for export, maintained stable livelihoods, many faced competition from mass-produced goods. In factories, employees often endured harsh discipline. Supervisors enforced strict timetables, docking pay for tardiness or minor mistakes. Workers had few legal avenues to demand better conditions, as labor laws were rudimentary and unions barely existed.

Life was somewhat better in small family-run workshops, where artisans balanced tradition with modern methods. They took pride in their craft, passing down knowledge through apprenticeship. But these workshops struggled to scale up to meet foreign demand unless they compromised on quality or found outside capital, which could dilute family control. In newly developed industrial zones, the clamor of steam engines overshadowed the patient artistry of Edo-era manufacturing. Over time, some artisans learned to adapt, merging their craftsmanship with mechanical tools to boost output.

Yet pockets of discontent emerged. Occasional work stoppages—small strikes or walkouts—signaled mounting frustration. During these protests, laborers complained about unsafe conditions, delayed wages, or abusive foremen. Authorities often responded by sending police to quell disturbances, reflecting a broader fear that labor activism might spread. Though these early protests rarely led to lasting reforms, they planted seeds for the labor movements that would gain traction in later years, challenging the myth that modernization automatically benefited all of Tokyo's citizens.

16.9 Transportation of Goods: Railways and Steamships

A revolution in how goods moved to and from Tokyo underpinned its industrial ascent. The first railway lines, connecting the city to Yokohama, allowed faster transport of raw materials and manufactured items. Entrepreneurs invested in additional rail spurs extending to inland regions, enabling Tokyo's factories to reach new markets. Steam locomotives symbolized modernity, their whistles echoing across farmland once traversed by packhorses. The improved speed and capacity slashed shipping costs, energizing commerce in ways unthinkable under Edo's slower road networks.

In Tokyo's harbors, steam-powered ships replaced or supplemented traditional sailing vessels. Loading cranes and modern dock facilities cut turnaround times. Foreign lines established offices near the waterfront, forging direct routes to Asia, Europe, and America. Merchants tracking silk prices in London or tea auctions in New York could react quickly, shipping goods out on short notice. This fluid connectivity knitted Tokyo into a global web of commerce.

The benefits, though, accrued unevenly. Harbor neighborhoods saw land values soar, while some interior wards stagnated. Lower-skilled laborers who once carried loads on foot now competed with rail freight or mechanized cranes. Environmental side effects also appeared. Coal smoke from ships and trains blanketed nearby districts in soot. Yet for investors and city planners, railways and steamships were the arteries of modernization, promising to keep Tokyo's economic pulse strong.

16.10 Technological Curiosity and Industrial Exhibitions

Tokyo's thirst for innovation expressed itself in public events dedicated to technological marvels. Government-sponsored expositions showcased everything from modern looms to telegraph equipment. Crowds walked through large exhibition halls, gazing at mechanical models that performed tasks at astonishing speeds. Foreign companies sometimes set up displays to pitch engines or steam turbines, hoping to secure Japanese buyers. The events offered a carnival atmosphere. Children munched on sweet buns while wide-eyed visitors marveled at miniature railroads or mechanical puppet shows.

These exhibitions served educational purposes. School groups toured them to learn about the science behind electricity, steam power, or chemical processes. Manuals and pamphlets explained how factories in Britain or Germany structured their production lines. Samurai-turned-bureaucrats took notes on potential new industries to champion. Newspapers published enthusiastic reports, and rumor had it that the emperor himself occasionally visited incognito to witness Japan's progress.

For average Tokyoites, the exhibitions sparked debate. Some were enthralled, seeing proof that the city was on par with Western capitals. Others felt uneasy about machines replacing handcrafted artistry or worried that technology might disrupt social harmony. Yet with each successive expo, the momentum behind industry grew, reinforcing the notion that progress demanded mechanical efficiency, large-scale production, and the willingness to adapt to global standards.

16.11 Rural Migration and Urban Pressures

As factories multiplied, so did the demand for workers. Rural villagers seeking better lives trickled into Tokyo, often carrying little more than a small bundle of clothing and local produce as gifts for new neighbors. Many found lodging in cheap inns or overcrowded tenements near factory districts. They stood in lines each morning, hoping a foreman would pick them for day labor. If fortunate, they might land a steady position. Others survived on temporary gigs, sweeping factory floors or loading freight at the railway station.

This influx fueled tensions. Longtime residents complained about rising crime, as the newcomer population soared. City officials worried about the spread of disease in poorly built dormitories, where multiple families shared latrines and cooking facilities. Traditional neighborhood associations struggled to integrate strangers unfamiliar with local customs. Nonetheless, these migrants contributed vitality to Tokyo's economy, accepting low wages that kept factories competitive and small businesses staffed. Some saved enough to eventually move family members to the city, forging new communities that combined provincial dialects and traditions with the fast-paced routines of urban life.

Gradually, a pattern emerged. Migration to Tokyo was no longer an occasional phenomenon for samurai or wealthy merchants. It became a steady stream of common folk, responding to the lure of factory wages or service jobs in booming commercial districts. While poverty and hardships shadowed many, the possibility of climbing the economic ladder—perhaps by opening a street stall or learning a trade—gave hope to those seeking a better future. In this way, commerce and industry reshaped not just the city's skyline, but the very composition of its people.

16.12 Changing Consumer Habits and Advertising

With rising incomes for some segments of society came new consumer behaviors. The Meiji government encouraged citizens to buy domestic products rather than imported ones, to bolster local manufacturers. Slogans like "Enrich the Country, Strengthen the Army" extended to everyday shopping. Patriotic newspapers urged readers to purchase Japan-made textiles or use domestic coal, framing it as an act of national duty.

Nevertheless, foreign goods retained allure. Branded soaps, perfumes, and even tinned biscuits were sold as status items. Western-style furniture or porcelain sets were prized in upper-class homes. Advertising strategies evolved. Posters and handbills employed bright colors, bold lettering, and occasional foreign words to capture attention. Department stores placed small ads in daily papers, listing upcoming sales. Some even sponsored parades with floats displaying their latest merchandise.

Artisans in older wards adapted by marketing their products with modern flair. Silk weavers added small tags describing how their fabric matched

European fashion trends. Potters introduced novel glazes or patterns that appealed to buyers abroad. The city's consumer landscape thus became a theater of innovation, where old and new marketing techniques coexisted, and every enterprise, large or small, sought to carve a niche in the expanding marketplace.

16.13 Small Business Resilience

Amid the growth of factories and big commerce, countless small shops and family-run businesses continued to anchor city life. Corner teahouses offered warm rice porridge or miso soup to laborers before dawn. Candle makers, fishmongers, and book lenders plied their trades as they had for generations, albeit with minor adjustments to new economic realities. These enterprises served as a reminder that modernization did not obliterate the everyday needs once fulfilled by Edo's vibrant network of craftspeople and merchants.

Some thrived by embracing modern touches without losing their identity. A traditional sweets shop might introduce new varieties that incorporated Western jam or cream, appealing to younger customers. A small bookstore could stock translations of foreign novels while still featuring the popular woodblock-printed story sheets. In the dynamic swirl of Tokyo's economy, these small-scale entrepreneurs displayed agility and creative spirit, forging personal relationships with customers that big department stores or mass manufacturers could not match.

Yet survival was not guaranteed. Big money projects—like large breweries, cotton mills, or hardware companies—could undercut smaller operators with bulk pricing. Small business owners sometimes fell into debt, forced to seek help from banks that prioritized larger clients. As a result, some old family shops shuttered. Others consolidated, forming local cooperatives to purchase supplies in bulk or share resources. The resilience of these small players underscored Tokyo's dual nature: while industrial capitalism roared ahead, the city's pulse still beat in the modest trades and personal connections that had flourished for centuries.

16.14 Women in the Workforce

Industrial growth created job openings for women outside domestic service or farm labor. Textile mills, in particular, hired large numbers of young women for spinning and weaving. While wages were often low and hours long, these positions offered a taste of independence. Factory women sometimes formed informal networks, supporting each other in disputes with management or pooling savings. At the same time, parents worried about moral dangers in the city, pushing supervisors to maintain strict dormitory rules.

In shops and offices, a few women gained roles as clerks or typists, especially once typewriters became available in limited forms. Educated women from middle-class families found such positions more respectable than factory work. Magazines published accounts of "modern girls" balancing modest clothing with the responsibilities of office tasks. These stories, while not widespread, hinted at shifting attitudes toward what women could achieve.

However, most female employment remained tied to low-paying, labor-intensive jobs. Efforts to unionize or campaign for better treatment were minimal, as social norms discouraged women from public protest. Still, the presence of so many working women in Tokyo's commercial districts underscored how modernization changed gender roles piece by piece, not through sweeping legal reforms but through daily economic necessity.

16.15 Foreign Entrepreneurs and Cultural Exchange

Economic expansion also lured foreign entrepreneurs to Tokyo. Some set up small factories producing goods for local consumption, such as chemical dyes or processed foods. Others ran trading firms, connecting Japanese artisans with overseas clients. Their offices became hubs of cultural exchange. Japanese employees learned foreign business customs, while expatriates discovered Japanese negotiation tactics. Business lunches at Western-style cafés might end with a shared pot of green tea, bridging culinary traditions.

These cross-border partnerships inspired hybrid products. Japanese breweries, for example, launched beer brands that combined German techniques with local tastes. Craft studios produced porcelain shaped in European forms but decorated with classic Japanese motifs. Buyers in

Europe and America often prized such items for their novelty, fueling a continuous loop of design fusion.

The city's foreign entrepreneurs faced challenges, including language barriers, unfamiliar legal systems, and occasional anti-foreign sentiment. Some overcame these obstacles by hiring bilingual clerks or forging ties with influential Japanese patrons. Diplomatic events at Western embassies provided networking opportunities, where deals were struck amid formal dances or dinners. Over time, the presence of foreign businesses in Tokyo normalized, blending into the city's diverse commercial tapestry.

16.16 The Imperial Factor: Military Procurement and National Projects

The Meiji leadership championed the phrase "Enrich the Country, Strengthen the Army." Tokyo's factories often included military contracts, producing uniforms, ammunition, and even warships in newly developed shipyards near the bay. This melding of commerce and nationalism shaped the city's industries, as large sums of government money flowed to strategic enterprises. Skilled labor in shipbuilding or arms manufacturing commanded decent wages, sparking competition for trained workers. Some technology transfers from abroad centered on building up the arsenal, which the government deemed essential for international respect.

Civilians saw the results in official parades. Troops marched in newly made uniforms, while artillery, cast in modern foundries, clattered along cobblestone streets. Newspaper articles praised the advanced rifles and well-forged cannons. Meanwhile, critics warned that too much spending on military hardware diverted funds from infrastructure or social welfare. Still, in a climate where Western powers threatened Asia, many citizens accepted the military buildup as a necessary investment.

This state-driven militarization also boosted ancillary industries—steel mills, railway expansion to transport troops, and chemical plants producing gunpowder. The synergy between government procurement and private enterprise strengthened the city's industrial base, yet it also meant Tokyo's economy would remain, in part, at the mercy of the national agenda. Even everyday items—like boots or canned provisions—found new markets in the military, further entrenching the city's reliance on large-scale production.

16.17 The Birth of Corporate Culture

As businesses expanded, a new corporate ethos emerged. Instead of a master-apprentice model, many factories and trading houses adopted hierarchical management structures with defined ranks, job titles, and standardized wages. Employees used clock cards to track attendance, reflecting Western notions of punctuality. Work behavior shifted from personal loyalty to a family master, to formal loyalty to the firm. Social events—like company picnics or sports matches—built morale, forging an identity around corporate success rather than clan or lineage.

Executives studied foreign texts on management, budgeting, and industrial psychology. They introduced concepts like employee uniforms, which symbolized unity and discipline. Some companies published internal newsletters, spreading information about sales figures and praising diligent workers. A sense of corporate pride grew, with employees referring to their workplace as if it were a clan of its own. This transition was starkest for ex-samurai who had joined commercial firms. They replaced swords with ledgers, recasting their sense of honor to revolve around product quality or sales targets.

Workers at lower levels were not always comfortable with these changes. They missed the personal ties of smaller shops or the paternal guidance of a master craftsman. In large factories, they felt anonymous. Still, as wages slowly rose and the promise of promotion dangled before them, many embraced this corporate system as a pathway to steady, if sometimes impersonal, success.

16.18 Everyday Scenes of Industry and Commerce

Walking through Tokyo's business districts, one might see a swirl of modernization. Clerks in Western suits rushed between bank offices, carrying documents in leather satchels. Storekeepers swept brick sidewalks before opening, carefully arranging new displays of imported goods and local crafts. Delivery boys, sometimes on bicycles, wove past horse-drawn carts loaded with barrels or bolts of cloth.

In the industrial zones near the river, factory whistles signaled shift changes. Streams of laborers hurried to cramped eateries serving cheap rice bowls. The air echoed with the hum of spinning machines and the hissing of steam pumps. Coal smoke tinted the sky, a constant reminder of progress's environmental toll. Along the canals, barges moved raw materials—bales of cotton or logs for lumber mills—while finished products returned in crates headed for ports or rail depots.

Meanwhile, neighborhoods near major department stores or modern markets bustled with middle-class shoppers. Women in refined kimonos, sometimes accompanied by children in school uniforms, admired window displays. Men discussed new business ideas over tea in second-floor cafés, scanning newspapers for the latest commodity prices. The infusion of commercial life into everyday routines reinforced Tokyo's evolving identity as a capital not just of government, but of enterprise and ambition.

16.19 Challenges and Aspirations

Tokyo's booming commerce and industry were not without friction. Strikes and small riots occasionally broke out when factory owners cut wages or extended hours. The city also faced environmental degradation: rivers that once sparkled with fish turned murky from industrial runoff. Traffic jams near major thoroughfares slowed deliveries. Land prices soared, pushing laborers to live on the outskirts, far from their workplaces.

Yet these troubles did not dampen the city's aspirations. Newspapers championed the notion that Tokyo was the engine propelling Japan into the modern age. Business associations formed, pressing for better rail connections, advanced port facilities, and protectionist tariffs to nurture local industries. Intellectual circles debated how to balance Western capitalism with Confucian ethics. Was unbridled profit-seeking undermining social harmony? Or did national strength depend on the energy of a free market? In response to these questions, the city pressed on, adopting partial regulations, forging alliances between government and corporations, and seeking to refine a uniquely Japanese brand of capitalism.

16.20 Conclusion: Forging a Commercial Metropolis

By the close of the 19th century, Tokyo had become a showcase of Meiji ambition. Its factories churned out textiles and consumer goods. Modern banks and department stores redefined commerce, while international trade channeled the city's products into distant markets. The swirl of entrepreneurial energy delivered prosperity to some, whereas others struggled with meager wages and cramped housing. Traditional artisans adapted or vanished in the face of machine-driven mass production. Yet, in the midst of smoky factories and bustling shops, Tokyo's resilience glowed. Small businesses found niches, local festivals continued, and the rhythms of daily life still bore traces of old Edo.

In many ways, the city's growth laid the groundwork for Japan's emergence as an industrial power in the 20th century. Even so, the seeds of social tension and environmental stress were sown alongside the factories and railroads. Modernization in Tokyo was neither flawless nor universal, but it was unstoppable, propelled by the dreams of a nation determined to stand among the world's great powers. The next chapters will further trace how these economic shifts tied into evolving social classes, Western ideas, and Japan's expanding role on the global stage—shaping a capital city poised at the threshold of a new century.

CHAPTER 17

Social Class Changes and Shifts

17.1 The Unraveling of Old Hierarchies

In the early Meiji era, Tokyo's people were learning to live without the rigid class system of the Edo period. Under the Tokugawa shogunate, society was divided into four main groups—samurai, peasants, artisans, and merchants—with samurai standing at the top. But with the collapse of feudal rule and the rise of new economic opportunities, these lines blurred. By the late 19th century, many samurai families had lost their stipends, peasants had migrated to the city for factory work, and merchants often held far more wealth than former lords.

This shift brought both excitement and uncertainty. For some, it felt like liberation: no longer were people bound to a single occupation by birth. A peasant's child might study in a government school, then find a job in a modern office. A samurai's son could leave behind swordsmanship and become a merchant or banker if he learned enough about business. But the transition also created chaos. Samurai who once wielded swords of authority found themselves overshadowed by ambitious merchants who had built strong connections in finance and trade. Older folks lamented the loss of the strict social rules that once kept everyone in a clear place, while younger generations embraced the idea that skill or knowledge could lead to upward mobility.

Public discussions sprang up about what really defined a person's worth—was it loyalty, lineage, education, or money? Confucian ideals, which once legitimized samurai dominance, still mattered to many. Yet Western ideas about individual merit also caught on, persuading some that personal achievement, not birth, should guide a person's fate. Navigating these mixed messages became a daily challenge for city dwellers. The changes in social class were not just lofty abstractions for philosophers, but practical realities affecting wages, marriages, and community standing.

17.2 Samurai Losing Privilege

Nowhere was the shake-up more visible than among the samurai class. Under the shogunate, samurai wore two swords as a sign of status, received rice stipends, and served in military or administrative roles for their domains. Once the Meiji government formed, the domains were dissolved, stipends were reduced or ended, and a law eventually banned carrying swords in public. Thus, the proud warrior class saw its main symbols stripped away.

Some samurai adapted successfully. Those with literacy and math skills found posts in the new government. They became teachers, policemen, or low-level officials in the Ministry of Finance or Agriculture. A few ambitious ones studied abroad, returning with advanced knowledge of law, engineering, or medicine. These men then rose to leadership roles and influenced how Tokyo shaped its modernization.

Many more, however, struggled mightily. A large portion of samurai had never needed to master a trade or run a business. They lacked the capital or know-how to open shops in a competitive market. Some sold family heirlooms or swords just to pay rent in the fast-changing city. Others borrowed from merchants at high interest rates, leading to mounting debts. Bitterness set in, as they watched commoners surpass them financially. In certain neighborhoods, ex-samurai formed tight-knit communities, supporting each other while reminiscing about the old days.

This sense of displacement led a few hotheaded samurai to join revolts against the Meiji government, hoping to restore the old ways or at least reclaim some privileges. But these uprisings typically failed. Over time, most samurai families accepted that they were just ordinary citizens now, learning to navigate a Tokyo where wealth, education, and connections often mattered more than lineage. Despite their frustration, many ex-samurai contributed to society in new forms, carrying forward ideas of discipline and loyalty but applying them in schools, businesses, or local administration.

17.3 Merchants on the Rise

While samurai mourned lost power, merchants experienced a surge in status. During Edo times, they were technically at the bottom of the social ladder, though some grew wealthy through clever trade. The Meiji era, with its emphasis on commerce and industry, brought them a new legitimacy. Merchants who had once hidden their fortune to avoid samurai disdain began openly investing in banks, railways, and shipping lines. Government officials courted these successful entrepreneurs, seeking loans for modernization projects.

Ginza's modern storefronts showcased this shift clearly. Shrewd merchants, armed with capital, leased or bought prime real estate, opened shops selling imported goods, and transformed the district into a showpiece of Western-influenced consumer culture. Customers from all walks of life flocked to these stores, eager to purchase the latest fashions or try unusual foods. Meanwhile, older corners of Tokyo saw smaller merchant houses expand into producing or trading new items like kerosene lamps or telegraph components.

Some members of the merchant class faced backlash. Commoners felt local shops were being overshadowed by big businesses that used modern marketing and possibly unfair advantages, like cozy relationships with government officials. Samurais who had turned into bureaucrats might still harbor a hidden bias against "money-minded" merchants, even though they needed them for Japan's economic plans. Yet the unstoppable tide of commerce made these disagreements secondary. By the end of the 19th century, many Tokyo residents recognized that wealthy merchants—and the corporations they founded—had become major pillars of the city's future, shaping job markets and influencing city policies.

17.4 Farmers, Artisans, and the New Urban Workforce

Peasants were once seen as vital food producers tied to the land. But in Meiji Tokyo, farmland lay beyond the city edges, and the line between "peasant" and "urban worker" blurred. Many rural families sent sons or daughters to the capital for factory or service jobs, hoping remittances would improve life back home. Consequently, Tokyo's population grew with an influx of people who no longer identified strictly as peasants. They were now city laborers—an emerging class not neatly defined by old feudal categories.

Artisans faced similar changes. Skilled in Edo-era crafts, they battled the rise of machine-made goods, which threatened to render hand production quaint or expensive. Some artisans found a niche catering to wealthier clients, preserving traditional quality in items like pottery, lacquerware, or textiles. Others learned to run modern machinery, merging craftsmanship with mass production. Apprenticeship traditions changed too. Young people still learned from masters, but they might train in a workshop that used steam-driven looms or metal presses, mixing old methods with new technology.

A new type of laborer emerged: the factory worker. This person was neither peasant nor artisan in the Edo sense. Some had minimal skills and endured tough conditions. Others specialized in operating imported machinery, earning slightly better pay. Urban laborers rarely owned land and had limited job security. But they also had a freedom unknown to peasants—if wages in one factory were too low, they could try their luck in another, or even switch to a different industry altogether. Over time, these factory employees, shop clerks, and city laborers developed a sense of shared experiences, hinting at the birth of a broader urban working class.

17.5 The Government's Role in Class Restructuring

Although many changes in social class sprang from economic forces, the Meiji government shaped them, too. Officials enacted reforms that eliminated old feudal ranks—daimyo, samurai, peasants—and replaced them with new categories like kazoku (nobility), shizoku (former samurai), and heimin (commoners). Initially, the government continued to pay stipends to ex-samurai, but gradually converted these payments into government bonds or one-time lump sums, forcing many samurai to manage their finances wisely or risk losing everything.

The government also introduced universal conscription and compulsory education, policies that broke down class barriers. Samurai families, once the only warriors, found that any physically fit young man could be drafted

for military service. Meanwhile, samurai children who once studied
Confucian texts in private academies now shared classrooms with the
children of peasants or merchants. Though personal bias lingered, official
rules demanded that all be treated equally in matters of education and
national service. Some resented these changes, but for others, it fueled the
dream that diligence and skill, rather than birth, would open doors to a
government career or leadership role.

These reforms generated a mixed legacy. On one hand, they fostered a
sense of national unity, forging a society where "Japanese" identity
overrode local domain loyalties. On the other hand, not all classes
benefited equally. Wealthy commoners who pivoted to big business soared
higher. Poor peasants or struggling ex-samurai sometimes sank into deeper
poverty without feudal protections. Nonetheless, the government's
dismantling of the old caste system set a foundation for social mobility,
however uneven, marking a stark contrast with Edo times.

17.6 New Elites and the Rise of a Middle Class

As Japan's economy boomed, a new elite emerged—a fusion of ex-samurai
officials, wealthy merchants, and business-minded nobles. These people
lived in Western-style mansions or upscale Japanese homes with modern
amenities. Their children attended advanced schools, sometimes even
traveling abroad. They dined on Western courses at formal dinners, wore
suits or dresses for official gatherings, and employed servants from
lower-income backgrounds. This new elite, often called the "Meiji
oligarchs" or simply "the privileged," wielded considerable influence over
policymaking and corporate affairs.

Below them, a modest but growing middle class took shape in Tokyo. Civil
servants, teachers, bank clerks, engineers, and mid-level managers at
factories or trading firms formed its backbone. Many had enough education
to read newspapers regularly, discuss public matters, and invest a bit in
small luxuries—like a modern stove or a piece of Western-style furniture.
Their daily routines included commuting by horse tram to offices, sending
children to primary schools, and shopping for both traditional items and
occasional Western treats. Over time, these families developed shared

aspirations: stability, modest upward mobility, and respectability. They might not have been as wealthy or powerful as the top elite, but they were far from the precarious life of day laborers.

This middle class also contributed to the cultural life of Tokyo. They bought books, supported local theater, and donated to charitable groups, shaping public opinion. Their blend of traditional values—like respect for family ties—and new habits—like reading Western novels or using foreign products—became a model many others tried to follow. In short, the middle class served as a bridge between the old Edo world and the modern Tokyo, proving that moderate success was attainable outside the strict boundaries of samurai or merchant identities.

17.7 Education's Impact on Social Mobility

Compulsory education, though unevenly applied, was a powerful lever for change. Boys and girls from common backgrounds learned to read, write, and do math. They were exposed to the idea that diligence and academic performance could lead to better job prospects. Government scholarships allowed bright students with limited means to continue their studies, sometimes advancing to specialized schools in teaching, engineering, or foreign languages. These young graduates formed a new professional layer—teachers, technicians, translators—filling gaps in Tokyo's rapidly evolving industries.

Some ex-samurai families embraced education wholeheartedly, seeing it as the path to restoring lost prestige. They encouraged children to excel in modern subjects like Western medicine or law, hoping this expertise would secure them high-ranking roles in government. Meanwhile, merchant families used schooling to hone business skills for international trade. Even a bright peasant child might catch the eye of a patron, bridging class lines that once seemed insurmountable. This cross-class integration in schoolyards, albeit limited by financial realities, slowly carved cracks in the notion that one's birth fixed their destiny.

Not everyone applauded the results. Traditionalists argued that too much Western learning undermined Confucian ethics and filial piety. Some feared that a scholar who succeeded in Tokyo might abandon his rural home, leaving old parents behind. Moreover, wealthy families had access to private tutors or advanced academies, reinforcing their advantage. But as decades passed, the transformative power of education became clear. Tokyo's new generation, less bound by birth status, found fresh ways to climb socially, forging ties and forming networks that spanned old class barriers.

17.8 Women and Changing Roles in Society

Shifts in class structure also affected women, who historically were restricted in public life. The Meiji government's "good wife, wise mother" slogan formalized a role that included education—but mainly to foster well-rounded children. Nonetheless, some women ventured beyond these confines. Daughters of middle- or upper-class families, especially if their fathers believed in modern ideals, enrolled in girls' academies. There, they studied moral lessons alongside basic science or Western language. A few gained enough credentials to work as teachers, clerks, or telephone operators.

Such roles did not necessarily erase old class distinctions, but they allowed women from non-samurai backgrounds a chance to move up. For instance, a merchant's daughter who excelled in English might land a position in a foreign trade office, earning respect usually reserved for men. Factory women, on the other hand, toiled under tough conditions, yet the mere fact of earning wages offered a form of independence. With money in hand, they could send funds home or buy items once off-limits to those of peasant origin.

Socially, these changes sparked debate. Some men felt threatened by educated women, worrying they might question patriarchy. Conservative voices warned that unrestrained female involvement in commerce would harm family harmony. But as Tokyo's growth demanded more labor in offices, shops, and factories, practical needs overrode conservative fears. Slowly, a wedge formed in the old class system, where being a capable woman with modern skills held weight, regardless of one's birth. Though progress was slow and partial, the idea that women from various backgrounds could contribute to national development opened new doors, fueling further shifts in social norms.

17.9 The Tug of War Between Old and New Ideals

For many Tokyoites, navigating the changing class landscape felt like standing between two worlds. Respect for elders and Confucian family hierarchy remained deeply ingrained. Bowing to superiors, showing reverence for ancestry, and valuing group harmony did not vanish overnight. Yet daily encounters with Western ideas—through schools, newspapers, or foreign visitors—introduced concepts of individual rights, personal ambition, and merit-based advancement. City dwellers wrestled with questions like: Should a son always obey his father's choice of career, or follow his own calling? Did a merchant surpass a samurai if he managed bigger profits?

This tension surfaced in literature and theater. Kabuki scripts occasionally featured stories about an ex-samurai marrying a merchant's daughter, or a young clerk defying his father to join a modern company. Authors wrote serialized novels about characters torn between loyalty to family tradition and the excitement of forging a personal path. Public debates and magazine articles tackled the moral dilemmas. Some warned of social chaos if old virtues disappeared, while others argued that stiff traditions blocked the nation's progress.

Despite the strain, the city's pulse thrived on these discussions. Families improvised solutions—perhaps encouraging a child to respect Confucian ethics at home while developing modern skills for the workplace. Many discovered they could cherish old customs like tea ceremony or festivals, even if they also participated in capitalist ventures or studied foreign languages. This blending of values became a hallmark of Meiji Tokyo: not a clean break from the past, but a careful layering of new practices onto traditional foundations.

17.10 Neighborhood Identity and Class Mixing

As class lines reshuffled, Tokyo neighborhoods became more mixed than before. In Edo times, samurai resided near the castle, merchants lived in designated quarters, and artisans clustered by their specific trades. Under Meiji reforms, ex-samurai sold or leased their large homes, sometimes sharing streets with merchants who had grown wealthy enough to move into samurai districts. Factories sprouted near waterways, attracting laborers who built shanties in once-respectable wards.

While this mingling could spark friction, it also created opportunities for everyday friendships across old boundaries. A retired samurai might buy groceries from a commoner's shop. A skilled artisan who employed a few laborers might rent a spare room to a lower-ranking samurai's widow in need of income. Public schools further blended children from different backgrounds, normalizing cross-class interactions that once were taboo.

Over time, wards developed new identities less tied to class and more to shared activities or industries. A district might become famous for its textile factories, with owners and workers living side by side. Another ward might be known for modern banks, drawing government clerks and middle-class families. Though some pockets of elitism persisted, especially among old noble families, the city's daily life turned more fluid, forging a social environment in which personal connections and professional success gradually overshadowed feudal rank.

17.11 The Kazoku: Japan's New Nobility

Despite promoting broader equality, the government did not fully abandon aristocracy. It created a new peerage system called kazoku, blending ex-daimyo and high-ranking ex-court nobles into a Western-style nobility. These individuals were granted titles—prince, marquis, count, viscount, or baron—based on family prestige and government favor. In Tokyo, kazoku families lived in grand homes or estates, sometimes adopting European decor. Their members participated in the upper house of the legislature, influenced political decisions, and often married among themselves to preserve status.

For many commoners, the kazoku system felt like an awkward remnant of feudal times. They questioned why Japan needed a hereditary nobility if the old caste distinctions were supposedly gone. But the Meiji oligarchs believed that preserving some aristocratic structure would unify the nation, offering a sense of continuity from imperial history. In practical terms, the kazoku families served as cultural intermediaries, hosting Western diplomats in lavish events, wearing tuxedos or dresses, and showcasing Japan's ability to blend tradition with modern courtly elegance.

Over the decades, some kazoku families invested heavily in commerce, founding companies or banks. Others stuck to more ceremonial roles, preferring the quiet prestige of noble life. While they did not dominate everyday Tokyo life the way daimyo once dominated their domains, kazoku stood as an example that, amid social upheaval, certain elite privileges continued. Their presence underscored how Meiji Japan carefully fused the new with the old, retooling feudal forms into modern frameworks.

17.12 Rising Entrepreneurs and "Nouveau Riche"

Just as the kazoku represented old aristocracy refashioned for modern times, a new wave of "nouveau riche" entrepreneurs emerged from humble origins. Some started as small merchants, made risky investments in industries like silk reeling or railway construction, and struck gold. Suddenly wealthy, they built fancy homes, wore Western suits, and sent children to expensive schools. These families often clashed with old elites who viewed them as lacking refinement or lineage.

The nouveau riche tried to carve out social acceptance by sponsoring charities, donating to public works, or forging alliances with top officials. They might fund local improvements—like a bridge or a school building—while hoping to receive public praise. Banquets in lavish Western-style mansions became symbolic occasions, where these new capitalists mingled with politicians, foreign businessmen, and sometimes even kazoku members. Such interactions helped them shape policies beneficial to their ventures and cement their standing among Tokyo's influential circles.

Among ordinary people, opinions varied. Some admired these entrepreneurs as proof that class mobility was possible in Meiji Japan. Others grumbled about the ostentation, mocking their sometimes-gaudy taste or lack of old-world manners. Satirical newspapers occasionally published cartoons depicting nouveau riche families fumbling with Western tableware or speaking awkward English. Despite the teasing, many recognized that these self-made figures drove economic expansion, employing thousands and fueling the city's modernization. Thus, the nouveau riche stood as both a catalyst for change and a point of contention in Tokyo's ongoing social transformations.

17.13 Cultural Clubs and Cross-Class Mixing

One surprising outlet for cross-class interaction was the rise of cultural clubs. Groups devoted to poetry, theater, music, or foreign languages welcomed members from varying backgrounds, provided they could pay minimal dues or show genuine interest. Middle-class teachers, ex-samurai intellectuals, wealthy merchants, and even a few laborers who loved art or books found these clubs a place to share enthusiasms.

Some clubs focused on preserving older arts, like Noh chant or tea ceremony, believing that Japan's heritage anchored national identity. Others specialized in Western pursuits, such as piano recitals, Western painting, or reading translated novels. Members might gather weekly in a borrowed hall or someone's parlor, discussing new trends, performing short recitals, or debating cultural news from overseas. In these gatherings, formal social rank mattered less than talent or curiosity. A merchant's skill in calligraphy could earn admiration from an ex-samurai who once thought merchants were beneath him.

These clubs quietly accelerated social blending. Friendships formed across lines of old status. A tea ceremony master from a samurai background might discover a loyal disciple in the daughter of a former peasant. Participants realized that shared passions—for music, drama, or scholarship—bridged differences that once seemed insurmountable. While not everyone in Tokyo joined such clubs, their influence rippled through newspapers and word of mouth, demonstrating that social class was no longer the ultimate divider if individuals shared common cultural interests.

17.14 Tensions Among Rural-Urban Relations

The city's changing class dynamics also affected relations between Tokyo and rural areas. Former peasants who found success in the capital might return to their villages wearing modern clothes, speaking about factory wages or business opportunities. This sparked both envy and hope among those left behind. Some villagers saved money or borrowed from relatives to send more family members to Tokyo, chasing the same dream of upward mobility.

However, not everyone thrived once they arrived. Failed attempts to secure decent work or unscrupulous labor brokers left some migrants destitute. When such people returned home, they carried stories of hardship in the city—crowded living, exploitation by employers, or the cold indifference of big-town society. Rural elders who clung to Edo-era rhythms found these tales disturbing, strengthening their suspicion that Tokyo's modernization was eroding Japan's moral fabric.

Moreover, the new tax system placed heavier monetary burdens on villages, sometimes fueling resentment toward Tokyo-based officials who demanded payments for national projects. A farmer might lose land if harvests failed and taxes went unpaid. This tension revealed that the class changes in Tokyo—where ex-peasants could become workers or entrepreneurs—did not simply free everyone from old hardships. Instead, it created a more complicated web of winners and losers, linking city fortunes to country struggles. Over time, the government tried to balance Tokyo's needs with rural welfare, but regional disparities remained a sore point that occasionally boiled over into protests.

17.15 The Spread of Western Social Customs

Western influence did not only alter the economy; it also shaped manners, dress, and daily etiquette in ways that affected class interactions. Government officials encouraged men to cut their topknots, adopt short hairstyles, and even wear Western suits for official gatherings. The upper classes and emerging middle class followed suit, eager to appear modern. Over time, Western-style dining halls and ballrooms opened for special occasions, hosting soirees where men wore tuxedos and women wore gowns. The presence of foreign diplomats in Tokyo made these events more frequent.

Still, not everyone could afford fine Western clothes or felt comfortable wearing them. Lower-income families stuck to traditional kimonos or adapted partial Western items, like a jacket over a kimono. Some ex-samurai insisted on retaining at least a hint of their old style, perhaps wearing a short sword ceremonially at home or opting for a fusion outfit—traditional hakama pants with a Western coat. This sartorial diversity mirrored the shifting class lines: no single style dominated, and appearances became a statement of both personal choice and social ambition.

Public behavior also changed. Bowing remained essential, but in certain offices, a handshake replaced the standard bow among colleagues, showing a Western form of courtesy. Younger city dwellers tried to speak a few foreign phrases, especially if they worked in trade or government offices. This partial adoption of Western manners sometimes confused older folks or caused comedic misunderstandings. Even so, the spread of these new customs exemplified how modern class identities were formed not just by money or rank, but by daily expressions of refinement and knowledge, further mixing old hierarchies into new patterns.

17.16 Religious Institutions and Evolving Class Influences

Throughout these transitions, religious institutions in Tokyo also experienced change. Shinto shrines and Buddhist temples had once received patronage from samurai or wealthy families, reinforcing class structures. Now, with many samurai impoverished and merchants ascendant, donations might come from successful business owners who wished to gain social prestige through philanthropy. Temples, in turn, offered blessings or memorial services for donors' ancestors, subtly reshaping how religious support aligned with class.

Shrine festivals that once glorified local feudal lords now served broader communities of mixed class origins. At the same time, some shrines welcomed foreign visitors or introduced bilingual signs to accommodate curious foreigners. Buddhist monks occasionally ran small charity schools or orphanages, drawing funds from new elites or from volunteer groups that included ex-peasants and ex-samurai. In such settings, class lines blurred, since spiritual merit overshadowed older rank-based privileges. The shift was gradual, but it reinforced the idea that financial support and moral commitment carried more weight in the new Tokyo than inherited status alone.

Christianity also made inroads. Missionaries built churches and schools, attracting some city dwellers who found Christian ethics appealing or saw an advantage in learning English. Converts ranged from low-income laborers seeking a sense of community to upper-class students wanting modern education. Though Christianity never became dominant, its presence added another layer to Tokyo's evolving social tapestry, suggesting that faith and moral values, too, were subject to the city's transformation beyond rigid class boundaries.

17.17 Policing, Crime, and Class Perceptions

As the city expanded and class structures loosened, Tokyo authorities faced rising crime rates, partly spurred by economic desperation and partly by the transient population. Policing methods modernized. Samurai sword-bearing patrols were replaced by officers in Western-style uniforms, sometimes carrying firearms. This police force had to manage not just petty theft or brawls, but also new forms of fraud tied to evolving business practices. Swindlers took advantage of uneducated migrants, forging documents or tricking them into fake job offers.

Class perceptions influenced law enforcement. There were complaints that wealthy businessmen or ex-samurai officials received lighter treatment for white-collar crimes, while poor laborers faced harsher punishments for small offenses. Newspapers occasionally criticized corruption in local precincts, suggesting bribes or influence determined outcomes. These criticisms reflected the incomplete nature of class reform. Though the state tried to say "all are equal before the law," actual practice sometimes favored those with connections and money.

Nevertheless, public order improved in some respects. Widespread violence or feudal vendettas were a thing of the past. Samurai no longer carried swords, and territorial disputes between domains vanished. The newer forms of crime, while troubling, tended to revolve around property or money rather than lethal clan rivalries. In that sense, Tokyo's transition to a modern society brought a redefinition of what conflict looked like—less about inherited feuds, more about socioeconomic tensions. Policing itself became a career path for ex-samurai seeking stable income, meaning that once-lethal swordsmen now enforced laws designed to protect a broad, mixed-class public.

17.18 Entertainment and the Class Melting Pot

As the capital modernized, leisure became a space where class distinctions softened. Theaters like kabuki or new Western-style halls drew spectators from various backgrounds. Ex-samurai, wealthy merchants, and middle-class clerks might find themselves in the same audience, united by curiosity about the latest play. People with little money could stand in the cheaper sections, still enjoying a glimpse of high society entertainment.

Similarly, sumo matches remained an event for all. Though sumo had ties to old Edo traditions and samurai patronage, the sport's popularity grew among city folk of every rank. Crowds roared together as favorite wrestlers clashed, forgetting for the moment any differences in wealth or ancestry. Betting on sumo outcomes formed a small underground pastime, bridging class lines in a shared thrill. Street food stalls around arenas sold inexpensive snacks, letting even poor laborers partake in the festival atmosphere.

Coffeehouses and small music venues also popped up. Some catered to middle-class tastes—quiet places to read newspapers or discuss politics—while others offered boisterous evenings of Western instruments, attracting foreigners and locals alike. A new brand of entertainer emerged: the showman who could blend Japanese puppet acts with comedic commentary on modern city life. These performances poked fun at class pretensions, ex-samurai still clinging to old ways, or nouveau riche families showing off gaudy wealth. In poking fun, they reminded everyone that Tokyo's social transformations, however serious, could also be faced with humor and acceptance.

17.19 The Changing Face of Marriage and Family Ties

Family arrangements adapted to the new times. In Edo, marriages often served to maintain or advance a family's social rank, with samurai marrying samurai, merchants marrying merchants, and so on. Now, cross-class unions, while still rare, became less shocking. A bright ex-samurai with a stable job in a government office might wed a merchant's daughter, forging beneficial ties. A factory foreman's son could find a wife whose family had rural farmland. Such alliances balanced old prestige with new wealth or job security. Families might still rely on matchmakers, but the range of matches was broader.

Inside households, younger members occasionally challenged parental authority regarding career paths or spending. Fathers discovered they could not always force a child to become a tradesman or scholar, especially if that child found another calling in the city's diverse economy. Mothers often served as mediators, blending maternal guidance with an understanding that modern children needed some autonomy.

Elders, for their part, felt the erosion of the feudal structure that once gave them absolute authority. Confucian respect for parents endured, but the father's word was no longer law if it directly clashed with new social realities—like the demand for specialized education or the allure of factory jobs. Some older parents adapted by becoming proud grandparents, watching as the family's younger generation excelled in roles unimaginable just a few decades before. This gradual shift in family power dynamics reflected the broad changes stirring Tokyo's social classes from within.

17.20 Conclusion: A City Recast by Fluid Identity

By the late 19th century, Tokyo had become a stage for unprecedented social fluidity. The strict hierarchy of samurai, peasants, artisans, and merchants gave way to a more complex mix of ex-samurai officials, thriving merchants, industrial workers, middle-class clerks, and a rising professional class shaped by modern education. Even the newly minted kazoku nobility found themselves sharing influence with self-made magnates and government-connected oligarchs. Women, once confined to domestic tasks, ventured into factories, offices, and schools, challenging gender norms as they contributed to family incomes or pursued knowledge.

Everyday life in Tokyo showed that while old titles and rituals lingered, birth status no longer guaranteed or prevented success. Personal effort, education, and capital trumped lineage in many spheres, leading to a city both invigorated and anxious. Times were uncertain: a samurai heritage might grant prestige but no money, whereas a humble background could transform into wealth if one seized the right opportunity. Tokyo's people wrestled with moral quandaries, balancing Confucian ideals with Western individualism, forging a distinctive cultural blend.

In the next chapter, we will explore how Western ideas—spanning technology, philosophy, art, and more—further influenced the city's mindset. We will see how Tokyo's classes, newly reconfigured, responded to foreign concepts and wove them into the city's evolving identity. Through it all, the capital's social fabric continued to shift, ensuring that no one remained locked in an old mold, but neither did they find a simple, uniform path to belonging in Japan's restless metropolis.

CHAPTER 18

Influence of Western Ideas

18.1 A Curious City Looking Outward

By the late 19th century, Tokyo was not only reconstructing its class system but also absorbing a steady stream of Western influences. Ship routes and telegraphs connected the city to Europe and America. Foreign diplomats, teachers, engineers, and merchants roamed the streets in bowler hats or tall boots, chatting in languages that locals found both intriguing and baffling. Western-style buildings rose beside traditional wooden homes. In schools, students recited lessons about global geography and science. Magazines printed translations of foreign essays on law, government, or personal freedom.

This outward gaze resulted from Japan's drive to modernize quickly, to catch up with nations that once threatened its sovereignty. Meiji leaders believed adopting Western knowledge—especially in technology, medicine, and warfare—would strengthen the country. For everyday Tokyo residents, however, Western influence also touched daily life in unexpected ways. Some found it thrilling to sample new foods, wear partial Western outfits, or learn bits of English. Others worried that an uncritical embrace of foreign ways might undermine the essence of Japanese culture. As each year passed, new concepts and products arrived, fueling debates, experiments, and collaborations that shaped Tokyo's character.

18.2 Learning from Abroad: The Students' Journey

One of the most direct paths for Western ideas to enter Tokyo was through Japanese students who studied overseas. The Meiji government funded bright scholars, sending them to universities in America, Britain, France, or Germany. There, they absorbed modern disciplines: mechanical engineering, chemistry, Western law, political theory, and more. They returned with suitcases of foreign textbooks, heads full of theories, and the drive to apply these insights back home.

Some of these returnees became key advisors in government ministries, drafting laws or policies that mirrored European systems. Others set up private academies in Tokyo, teaching specialized subjects never before included in standard Japanese curriculums. They introduced the notion of critical thinking, where students analyzed texts rather than memorizing them. This approach clashed with the old Confucian emphasis on rote learning, causing friction among conservative teachers. Yet over time, the new methods caught on, especially for scientific and technical fields where hands-on demonstration proved more effective than classic memorization.

Not every returning student found acceptance. Some were ridiculed for imitating Western habits too closely—eating bread at every meal, or insisting on shaking hands rather than bowing. Yet the overall impact was huge. Through these educated pioneers, Tokyo gained direct knowledge of how Western cities functioned, how their parliaments were run, and how their factories achieved efficiency. In turn, these ideas filtered into textbooks, government agencies, or private firms. The city's top leaders, themselves ex-samurai or nobles, recognized that if Japan hoped to avoid colonization and command respect abroad, it had to harness what these students learned. As a result, their experiences became stepping stones to major reforms in law, infrastructure, and social policy.

18.3 The Role of Foreign Experts

While Japanese students traveled west, foreign experts came east. The Meiji government signed contracts with doctors, engineers, military officers, and teachers from Europe or America, inviting them to help modernize Japan. Known as "oyatoi gaikokujin," or "hired foreigners," they worked in ministries, schools, and industrial plants across Tokyo. A British railway engineer might oversee track construction; a French military instructor could teach modern tactics; an American teacher might guide the curriculum at a newly established school.

For many locals, these foreigners represented a living glimpse of the outside world. They wore unfamiliar clothes, ate bread and meat regularly, and brought families with them who set up Western homes in designated neighborhoods. Their daily presence, whether instructing a class or advising city planners, fueled curiosity. Some foreigners learned basic

Japanese to communicate, forging friendships with local colleagues. Others stuck to enclaves, socializing mainly with fellow expatriates.

Their influence was broad. City hospitals adopted Western medical procedures after foreign physicians demonstrated surgery or introduced vaccines. Civil engineers from Britain guided the construction of Tokyo's first iron bridges. French architects influenced the design of government buildings, adding arches and columns. Some foreigners taught Tokyo's budding entrepreneurs about modern accounting, shipping, or communications. Critics worried about relying too much on outsiders—would Japan lose cultural sovereignty? But on the whole, the city benefited from their knowledge. As local engineers and officials gained skills, they gradually took over projects, ensuring the learning remained in Japanese hands.

18.4 Western Medicine and Public Health

Before the Meiji era, Japanese healthcare mixed herbal remedies, acupuncture, and folk practices with some imported ideas from China or the Netherlands. With Western doctors arriving, Tokyo opened new avenues of science-based treatment. Hospitals adopted antiseptic methods, sterilizing instruments and using disinfectants. Surgeons performed operations once considered too risky, employing anesthesia that eased patient suffering.

Public health campaigns emerged. Foreign-trained doctors warned that contaminated water and poor sewage caused cholera, dysentery, and other epidemics. Government officials, influenced by these lessons, printed leaflets advising residents to boil drinking water and build better latrines. Over time, vaccination programs against smallpox and other diseases saved countless lives. Western medicine also brought updated concepts of anatomy, often demonstrated via dissections in medical schools.

Such changes sparked debates. Traditional healers felt threatened, insisting their methods were time-tested and more holistic. Some patients distrusted hospital surgery or new chemical drugs. Yet as success stories mounted—like surgeons saving limbs from infection or doctors halting smallpox outbreaks—acceptance grew. By the late 19th century, Tokyo's leading hospitals blended foreign techniques with local wisdom. Wealthy individuals sought Western checkups, while poorer folks sometimes combined old remedies with the new when they could afford them. In this gradual melding, the city's overall life expectancy began to inch upward, a testament to the practical value of foreign ideas adapted for local needs.

18.5 Architecture and Urban Design

Western architectural styles added a fresh look to Tokyo's skyline. Along major avenues, new government halls featured brick or stone facades, tall windows, and decorative pillars. Banks and trading companies commissioned similar buildings, each trying to outshine the other in grandeur. Although earthquakes posed a challenge, foreign engineers introduced stronger foundations and iron frameworks, which local builders studied and refined for Japan's seismic reality.

Private residences also showed Western influence, especially among the elite. A nobleman might erect a manor with a Victorian-style garden, complete with rose bushes and wrought-iron fences. Inside, he might display plush chairs, chandeliers, and large dining tables, while still maintaining a separate tatami room for tea ceremony or receiving guests in traditional fashion. Middle-class families, meanwhile, usually could not afford fully Western homes. Instead, they incorporated minor elements: glass windows, partial flooring, or small chairs in one corner. This fusion was often called "wafū yōsai," or "Japanese-Western style," reflecting the city's dual identity.

On the streets, Western urban planning showed up in attempts to create broad boulevards or symmetrical layouts. Ginza's rebuild after a major fire in 1872 was the first large-scale test of such planning. While older wards kept their winding alleys, newer districts boasted straighter roads, brick sidewalks, and lined trees that evoked European capitals. Critics complained that Tokyo was losing its cozy Edo charm. Advocates insisted modernization demanded more orderly street grids and building codes. In practice, money and land disputes slowed sweeping changes, so Tokyo ended up with a patchwork cityscape: half modern grid, half ancient warren of lanes. This unique blend shaped the city's character, one where Western design coexisted beside quiet temples and wooden row houses.

18.6 Western Cuisine and Dining Culture

Food habits, too, were not immune to Western influence. Restaurants serving beef or bread—both once taboo or unusual—became common in certain neighborhoods. Some were modeled after European cafés, with chairs, tables, and menus listing dishes like beef stew, potato croquettes, or French-style pastries. Middle-class diners who could afford these spots enjoyed tasting the "new flavors," sometimes to show off their modern sensibilities. Families who stuck to traditional meals at home occasionally splurged on a Western feast to celebrate special occasions, thus bridging old and new culinary worlds.

At formal state banquets, foreign dignitaries and Japanese elites sat at long tables lined with cutlery instead of chopsticks, sipping on wines instead of sake. This shift, though only affecting a small portion of society, generated headlines in local papers whenever a notable politician or prince introduced Western dining manners. Meanwhile, cheaper Western-inspired foods—like curry rice—spread among the masses. Curry, originally from India but adapted by the British, was introduced to Japan through foreign navy contacts. Soon, small eateries sold mild Japanese-style curry ladled over rice, offering an exotic flair that gradually became a local staple.

Yet the adoption of Western cuisine did not erase classic Japanese dishes. Neighborhood stalls still served grilled fish or soba noodles, teahouses dispensed green tea, and families gathered around low tables for communal meals. Instead, Tokyo's food culture broadened. Even humble workers might sample Western bread or canned goods when available. In this ongoing mix, foreign flavors complemented, rather than replaced, traditional staples—symbolic of the city's approach to Western ideas overall: selective, adaptive, and woven into existing habits.

18.7 Language and the Spread of English

One of the most significant Western influences was linguistic. English emerged as the main foreign language taught in many schools, though French and German had strong followings too. Government agencies encouraged officials to learn enough English to read treaties or communicate with foreign envoys. Educated city dwellers recognized that speaking English might secure them better jobs, especially in foreign trade, diplomacy, or advanced studies abroad.

Print culture reflected this shift. Bilingual dictionaries and English grammar books filled bookstore shelves. Newspapers included small sections summarizing foreign news in English for advanced readers. Some private academies specialized in English conversation, using teachers from America or Britain to guide pronunciation. The government eventually standardized romanized spellings of Japanese place names, making it easier for foreigners to navigate the city. Street signs in key areas also adopted roman letters, helping foreign visitors and signaling Tokyo's openness to global traffic.

At home, families who placed high value on modern aspirations might hire English tutors for their children, even if they themselves barely grasped the language. Middle-class students, proud of new phrases, occasionally inserted English words into everyday talk, though older relatives found this habit pretentious or puzzling. Over time, the presence of English textbooks, signs, and casual speech among the youth planted the idea that Tokyo was not just a city for Japanese speakers, but a budding cosmopolitan hub with a language bridge to the outside world.

18.8 Western Literature and Thought

Translations of Western literature flowed into Tokyo's growing library system and bookstores. Works by Shakespeare, Goethe, Hugo, and more introduced themes of individual desire, romantic love, moral struggle, and social justice that differed from many traditional Japanese tales. These novels broadened readers' horizons, spurring local authors to experiment with new narrative techniques. Some wrote about personal conflicts in a direct, emotional way that was uncommon in older Japanese storytelling.

Philosophical texts also emerged, translating Enlightenment ideas about reason, liberty, and human rights. Intellectual circles in Tokyo debated these works fervently. Were individual rights and democratic principles compatible with Confucian-based respect for hierarchy? Could Japan adopt a parliamentary system like Britain's, or would that undermine the emperor's authority? Magazines serialized discussions on social contract theory, the role of the state, and the balance between personal freedom and communal duty. Although not every commoner read these texts, the ideas trickled down through newspapers and conversation, shaping a new generation's vision for society.

Conservative voices warned that Western literature glorified personal pleasure and independence at the expense of filial piety or social harmony. They urged caution, claiming such ideas might spark unruliness or moral decay. Yet as Tokyo's modernization advanced, more people found these global perspectives invigorating. Local writers penned their own novels exploring personal growth, challenging arranged marriage, or questioning blind obedience to elders. Over time, Western literary and philosophical currents became part of Tokyo's cultural bloodstream, woven alongside older Japanese forms in a tapestry of creative expression.

18.9 Christian Missions and Religious Exchange

Christian missionaries played a notable role in bringing Western views to Tokyo. They established schools, hospitals, and churches, attracting locals interested in foreign languages or modern medicine. Some Japanese students attended mission schools simply because they offered quality education and language practice, not necessarily seeking conversion. Others, however, were drawn to Christian teachings about universal love, human dignity, or moral equality—ideas that resonated with new thoughts on individual rights.

While the number of actual Christian converts remained small, the presence of churches offered a space for public gatherings and lectures. Missionaries taught music, particularly hymns, thus introducing Western choral traditions. They also organized charity efforts, such as soup kitchens or orphan care, that sometimes reached beyond class lines. These activities demonstrated Western-style philanthropy, encouraging local citizens to form volunteer groups or social service clubs. Over time, a few Christian converts from merchant or samurai backgrounds used their foreign connections to travel, study theology, or engage in interfaith dialogues, furthering cultural exchange.

Not everyone welcomed missionary influence. Traditional Buddhist and Shinto authorities feared losing followers or moral authority. Some critics labeled Christianity as a foreign intrusion that disrespected national beliefs. Occasionally, local hostility flared into protests, and for a time in the 1870s, the government had laws banning direct evangelism. But as foreign pressure for religious freedom grew, Tokyo adopted a more tolerant stance. In a city grappling with many transformations, Christianity became one more thread in the tapestry—never dominant, but visible enough to spark questions about faith, morality, and how religion fit into the modern age.

18.10 Military Reforms and Western Strategies

Western influence also restructured Japan's military. The Meiji government recognized that the samurai-only model was obsolete in the face of Western armies, which relied on conscription, advanced firearms, and disciplined drills. Foreign advisors, especially French and German officers, instructed Tokyo's soldiers in modern tactics. They introduced new rifles, artillery methods, and the concept of a general staff that planned comprehensive warfare strategies.

Samurai pride resisted at first. Former warriors balked at wearing Western uniforms or marching in tight formations without the elegance of swordsmanship. But Japan's leaders insisted modernization was crucial. They built modern barracks in Tokyo and established the Imperial Japanese Army. Conscripts from varied backgrounds trained together, forging a national identity that transcended local loyalties. By the 1880s, large military parades in Tokyo showcased columns of uniformed men with rifles, overshadowing the old image of individual sword-bearing samurai.

Naval reforms paralleled these changes. British advisors helped design ships and train crews, enabling a modern Japanese navy. Shipyards in

Yokosuka and other harbors near Tokyo employed Western tools and blueprint methods. The success of these reforms in subsequent regional conflicts bolstered support for Western military ideas. It also heightened national pride and shaped public attitudes about the city's role as the seat of power for a newly formidable Japan.

18.11 Debates on Democracy and Rights

One of the most striking Western imports was political ideology. Japanese intellectuals devoured texts on constitutional government, individual rights, and representative assemblies. Tokyo turned into a hotbed of debate, with rallies and lectures sometimes filling rented halls or open squares. Political clubs, though monitored by police, spread the call for a national assembly where commoners and nobles alike could voice opinions. Newspapers like the Yokohama Mainichi or Tokyo's own local papers printed editorials championing or criticizing these movements.

Leaders of the "Freedom and People's Rights Movement" argued that if Japan truly wished to be on par with Western nations, it needed a constitution guaranteeing freedoms such as speech, press, and assembly. Government moderates worried about upheaval, preferring a more cautious approach. When the emperor declared in 1881 that Japan would adopt a constitution, euphoria swept Tokyo's political circles. Intellectuals and reformers saw it as a victory, though the final constitution, enacted in 1889, still granted significant power to the emperor and the oligarchic elite.

For common people, these abstract ideals sometimes felt remote. Survival, rent, and wages took precedence over high-minded politics. But the notion that Japan might build a parliamentary system akin to Britain or Germany stirred hope among some workers, artisans, and small merchants who saw democracy as another step toward social leveling. Tokyo's streets buzzed with talk of potential elections and party platforms, though real power changes were slow. Even so, this infusion of Western political thought confirmed that Tokyo's modernization extended beyond material gains, touching the very soul of governance and civic life.

18.12 Western Influence on Arts and Entertainment

Theater and art responded dynamically to Western influences. Some kabuki plays introduced characters with Western attire, comedic bits about telegraphs, or storylines involving foreign visitors. Meanwhile, new drama forms, known as shimpa or "new school," emerged, mixing kabuki's emotional style with Western realism. Playwrights wrote scripts exploring personal conflicts, love marriages, and social injustice—reflecting European novelistic themes.

Visual arts likewise experienced a fusion. Students learned oil painting techniques from foreign teachers in government-sponsored art schools. Their canvases depicted Japanese landscapes with Western shading and perspective, creating the so-called "yōga" style. Critics worried about losing the refined subtlety of ink-based nihonga. But many artists argued that adopting Western realism expanded creative horizons. Exhibitions displayed both yōga and nihonga works, inviting comparisons and conversations about national identity. Some painters even traveled to Europe, returning with new brush techniques that they applied to Japanese subjects—like Mt. Fuji or local festivals—seen through a Western lens.

Music, too, underwent change. Military bands performed Western marches at public events. Schools taught choral singing, sometimes with Western-style scales. Middle-class families bought pianos or organs, practicing simple tunes in living rooms that once only heard shamisen strings. Gradually, a new generation grew up comfortable with chords and harmonies alien to Japanese traditional music. Still, the older forms—kabuki chanting, Noh flutes, or folk drumming—remained beloved, weaving a dual soundtrack for Tokyo's everyday life.

18.13 The Growth of Print Media and Foreign Journalism

Western ideas also entered Tokyo through journalism. Foreign newspapers published in Yokohama or Shanghai circulated, carrying stories about global politics, science breakthroughs, and cultural trends. Some well-educated Japanese read them eagerly, feeling connected to events like the Franco-Prussian War or American industrial expansion. Soon, local newspapers in Tokyo adopted Western reporting styles: shorter paragraphs, bold headlines, coverage of social issues, and serialized fiction.

Editorialists championed free speech as a pillar of modern society. They criticized government censorship, calling it a relic of feudal times. Though the government tried to maintain tight control, many articles slipped through with subtle critiques. Readers devoured news on foreign technology, praising or lamenting how slowly Japan kept pace. Interviews with foreigners living in Tokyo sometimes appeared, revealing outsider views of the city's progress. This exchange gave impetus to local reformers pushing for more transparency, accountability, and public debate.

Western magazines—on topics like science, fashion, or religion—found niche audiences. Translators summarized interesting articles, fueling imaginative leaps in business, design, or everyday living. A tailor might adopt European cutting techniques after reading a piece on modern suiting. An engineer might glean new approaches to steam turbine design from a British publication. Over time, Tokyo's knowledge base widened, reinforcing the sense that the city was plugged into a global conversation, not just passively receiving foreign teachers but actively shaping and sharing ideas.

18.14 Criticisms and the Backlash Against "Too Much West"

Despite enthusiasm, a sizable portion of Tokyo's population felt uneasy about Western influence. Conservatives feared that copying foreign customs—eating beef, wearing suits, letting women read foreign novels—eroded Japan's moral core. They worried the emperor's divine status might be overshadowed by democratic talk or that communal loyalty would fracture under individualism. Some intellectuals wrote essays condemning "bunmei kaika" (civilization and enlightenment) as blind Western worship, calling instead for a measured approach that protected Japanese essence.

In more tangible forms, small protests erupted. Traditional shrine associations or guilds of old artisans demanded the government scale back Western-style city planning or building codes that threatened time-honored architecture. Rural visitors to Tokyo sometimes felt alienated by the city's Western trappings. They viewed gaslit streets or baroque bank facades as proof that city folks were abandoning national roots. Popular plays occasionally mocked flamboyant Western dressers, portraying them as buffoons who could barely handle chopsticks.

The Meiji leadership tried to calm these fears. Officials insisted that modernization was selective: adopting what was strong in the West while preserving the imperial institution, Shinto rites, and core values of loyalty and harmony. Over time, policy and social practice found a middle path. Tokyo continued to borrow foreign science and law while reaffirming the emperor's centrality and Japanese cultural forms. The city's identity thus remained dual-faced, an interplay of tradition and modernity rather than a complete Western makeover.

18.15 Hybrid Practices and Selective Borrowing

One of Tokyo's greatest strengths in this era was its ability to borrow Western ideas without discarding local traditions entirely. Schools used foreign textbooks for science or math, yet continued teaching Japanese history and classical literature. Factories installed imported machinery, but local engineers customized designs to suit domestic resources. Western suits appeared for formal events, while casual daily wear might still be a kimono. Families served bread and coffee for breakfast yet ate miso soup and rice at dinnertime.

This pattern was not random. It was guided by a national strategy: keep the emperor's prestige intact, maintain social order, and adopt foreign elements that clearly enhanced security or economic growth. Spiritual beliefs, language, festivals, and centuries-old aesthetics were too precious to cast aside. City planners, intellectuals, and craftsmen found that merging foreign knowledge with local ways produced innovative results. The new drama style, for instance, became distinctly Japanese in flavor, even if it owed something to Western realism.

Foreign visitors marveled at these hybrids. They reported on how Tokyo's shops sold telegraph parts next to wooden sandals, how sumo tournaments might feature a British brass band playing anthems before bouts. Some labeled it an odd mismatch, others praised Japan for forging a path unique among Asian nations. Tokyo's residents themselves felt moments of confusion or pride. On one hand, they juggled contrasting practices daily. On the other, they recognized this flexible blending gave them a sense of control over modernization, shaping a future that was distinctly theirs, not a carbon copy of Europe or America.

18.16 Influence on Manners and Etiquette

Western ideas also touched social behavior. Bowing remained standard, but in certain government offices or social clubs, a handshake replaced it. Dining etiquette saw more forks, knives, and multiple courses in upper-class households. The concept of "ladies and gentlemen" as a polite form of address took hold among the educated, mixing with traditional honorifics in Japanese. Even the notion of private space changed: some wealthier Tokyo homes featured a living room with chairs and tables for receiving visitors, adopting the idea that formal guests did not always need to sit on the floor.

Timekeeping also became more precise. Western-style clocks replaced hour-based clocks used in Edo, where day and night hours varied by season. Railroad timetables demanded punctuality, pushing city dwellers to track minutes carefully. Government offices posted fixed hours, expecting employees to arrive at the stroke of a clock. This shift in temporal discipline affected daily routines. Traditional craftspeople who worked at a slower pace found themselves adjusting to schedules if they wanted to sell to big companies or keep up with new demands.

More subtly, Western concepts of privacy, personal space, or individual property rights seeped into legal codes. Even family relations changed slightly as new laws permitted separate property ownership for married couples or made divorce more accessible in certain situations. Although these were incremental steps, they showed how Western jurisprudence forced a rethinking of how individuals related to each other and to social institutions—again reflecting the city's overall process of blending foreign lessons with homegrown values.

18.17 Western Science and Technological Curiosity

Science fairs and public lectures introduced topics like electricity, magnetism, or Darwin's theory of evolution to Tokyo audiences. University faculties and research institutes sprang up, employing returning Japanese scholars and foreign professors. Observatories used Western astronomical instruments to refine calendars. Zoological or botanical collections displayed creatures and plants from overseas, expanding local knowledge of the natural world.

Ordinary people often viewed these scientific wonders with a mix of awe and skepticism. Electricity, especially, seemed magical—few understood how wires carried power to light bulbs. Some worried about the health effects or whether lightning would strike the new poles in storms. Others applauded the convenience of electric lighting in certain factories or public buildings, which extended working hours and nighttime activities. Over time, demonstrations of telephones or electric motors became public spectacles, drawing curious onlookers who paid a small fee to watch wires transmit voices or power small machinery.

This fascination with science paralleled the city's industrial surge. As factories needed better production methods, scientists and engineers introduced Western chemistry for dyes or improved steelmaking processes. At the same time, local tinkerers attempted to replicate foreign inventions, sometimes unveiling home-spun electric fans, mechanized looms, or early cameras. The result was a blossoming culture of invention, with Tokyo serving as the hub for workshops, entrepreneurial labs, and cross-disciplinary gatherings. Even if not everyone grasped the deeper theories, the city's willingness to adopt Western science accelerated modernization in nearly every sector.

18.18 Critiques of Western Materialism

While technology and commerce thrived, some Tokyo intellectuals challenged what they saw as excessive materialism in Western teachings. They criticized the pursuit of profit over communal well-being, warning that unbridled capitalism could lead to social ills like exploitation, class conflict, or moral decay. Writers pointed to slums forming around factory districts, asking if Western-style industrialization was a double-edged sword.

Others worried that Western emphasis on individual achievement undermined group harmony and respect for elders. They called for a "Japanese spirit" guiding modern practices, echoing the phrase "wakon yōsai"—"Japanese spirit, Western technology." According to this view, technology was valuable, but society should keep hold of virtues like humility, loyalty to family, and self-restraint. If everyone only chased personal success in a Western manner, critics believed the social bonds that held communities together might fray.

Teachers who followed this line taught students moral lessons from Confucian tradition even as they introduced algebra or foreign language. They reminded the young that knowledge should serve society, not just individual ambition. Government policy often echoed this stance, promoting loyalty to the emperor and national unity as moral cornerstones. Thus, Tokyo's adoption of Western ways remained a carefully moderated affair, with influential voices urging a balanced approach that did not let foreign materialism overshadow Japan's ethical roots.

18.19 Grassroots Incorporation of Western Tidbits

Far from the policy debates, everyday folks found small, inventive ways to integrate Western influences. Street food vendors experimented with new spices, combining them with local dishes. Rickshaw pullers occasionally learned bits of English to attract foreign tourists, painting signs that read "Quick and Safe Ride!" on their carts. Artisans carved cheap metal spoons or forks styled after foreign cutlery but adorned with Japanese motifs, satisfying local curiosity about Western eating utensils.

Local associations hosted small shows where European music might be performed on a local stage. Amateur actors tried comedic sketches about a country bumpkin's first encounter with a "gentleman" in Western attire, generating laughter at stereotypes. Children used chalk to mimic English letters on walls, even if they had no idea what they spelled. Temple fairs sometimes featured a "Western corner," displaying mechanical novelties or letting people try out bizarre items like a bicycle, which seemed a marvel of balance and technology.

These grassroots touches made Western ideas more approachable, less alien. They allowed people who did not read fancy books or attend government banquets to taste modernity on their own terms. By weaving foreign elements into mundane routines, the city ensured that Western influence permeated not just official institutions but the colorful fabric of local life. This bottom-up adoption also revealed Tokyo's spirit of ingenuity: it took imported ideas, reshaped them, and made them part of daily fun or utility.

18.20 Conclusion: An Ongoing Fusion

By the end of the 19th century, Western influence had profoundly shaped Tokyo's government, industry, education, arts, and social customs. The city had embraced foreign technology—railways, factories, telegraphs—alongside Western architectural styles and academic disciplines. People tried new foods, wore new fashions, listened to new music, and read new books. Yet Tokyo did not become "Western." It remained a Japanese capital, preserving festivals, shrines, language, and deep cultural values that gave the city its own identity.

Indeed, the mixture of Western thought with local tradition spurred a creative bloom. Samurai discipline blended with foreign military tactics to form a modern army. Confucian morality interfaced with Western liberal ideas, shaping an emerging constitutional framework. Merchants retooled foreign commerce methods in synergy with Japanese guild-like networks. Even the intangible realm of manners, family norms, and aesthetics found fresh expressions, yielding a dual city that was neither fully Edo nor purely European.

In the chapters ahead, we will see how these influences continued to evolve, setting the stage for Tokyo's late 19th-century transformations and beyond. For now, it is enough to note that Western ideas served as catalysts—sparks that ignited experiments in law, infrastructure, social roles, and personal lifestyles. Tokyo's people, for all their differences, largely proved open-minded, adopting or adapting foreign lessons with confidence that they could remain true to their roots. It was this spirit of selective adoption, tempered by national pride, that made the city's modernization a uniquely Japanese phenomenon, forging a metropolis that recognized no single boundary between East and West.

CHAPTER 19

Late 19th Century Reforms

19.1 The Push for a Constitution

By the mid-1880s, Japan's modernization had advanced quickly in many areas—industry, infrastructure, education—yet the country still lacked a formal constitution. Influential voices in Tokyo, from intellectuals to businessmen, argued that if Japan wished to be seen as a modern power on the same level as Western nations, it needed a constitutional framework. The emperor and his top advisors had already hinted at this path, but drafting a constitution proved complex. What exact powers would the emperor hold? How much authority would rest with the people's representatives?

A group of high-ranking officials, many with experience studying abroad, gathered to craft a constitution that balanced Western models and Japanese traditions. They examined the constitutions of Prussia, Britain, and other European states, looking for ideas. Some advocated a British-style parliamentary system with stronger legislative power. Others favored a German-style model, granting more control to the executive branch under the emperor. While debate raged, the overall goal remained to protect imperial prestige while demonstrating Japan's commitment to modern legal structures.

In Tokyo's newspapers and coffeehouses, commoners and middle-class readers followed the constitutional debate with growing enthusiasm. Many hoped a constitution would secure rights such as freedom of speech or assembly. Some believed it might curb corruption or favoritism among government elites. Skeptics feared a merely symbolic constitution that reserved real control for a small circle around the emperor. Street rallies broke out, urging real popular representation. In quieter districts, conversations at small inns and teahouses wondered whether official promises would actually grant any new rights. Nevertheless, public anticipation built steadily toward what would become a landmark event in modern Japanese history.

19.2 The 1889 Constitution Takes Shape

In 1889, the Meiji Constitution was officially promulgated. The emperor stood at the center of this document, retaining the right to command the army, dismiss the Diet (parliament), and confirm laws. Meanwhile, the new Diet consisted of two houses: the House of Peers (mostly nobles and ex-samurai leaders) and the House of Representatives (elected by a fraction of the male population who met certain tax requirements). Citizens cheered the momentous announcement, which took place in Tokyo with a grand ceremony. Cannon salutes and festive decorations turned the capital into a scene of bright celebration.

Yet, the constitution's text revealed limits to popular power. Voting rights extended only to a small percentage of wealthy men, leaving most city laborers, farmers, and virtually all women unable to vote. The emperor could override decisions and controlled the military. Freedoms like speech or assembly were recognized but could be restricted by law when authorities deemed it necessary. Government bureaucrats, many from ex-samurai backgrounds or favored families, continued to manage the state with considerable authority.

Public response was mixed. Newspapers praised the emperor's benevolence and the symbolic leap toward Western-style governance. Reformist groups, though, noted that real democracy was still far off. Even so, the act of inaugurating a constitutional monarchy placed Japan in a different light internationally, helping renegotiate some unequal treaties with foreign powers. In Tokyo, intellectuals debated how to strengthen the Diet and broaden suffrage. Over time, these debates pushed further reforms, gradually expanding voter eligibility and clarifying rights. But in 1889, the constitution was a milestone—both a grand ceremony of modern progress and a guarded framework ensuring imperial leadership.

19.3 Parliament and the Birth of Political Parties

Once the constitution came into effect, elections for the House of Representatives occurred. Political parties emerged, offering candidates and publishing platforms. In Tokyo, party gatherings filled meeting halls, and posters plastered walls with slogans about taxation or social policies. Men who paid enough taxes to vote took these campaigns seriously, attending rallies where speakers promised new laws favoring commerce, education, or local autonomy.

Two main parties soon dominated the political scene. One faction, often backed by big business interests, supported close cooperation with government bureaucrats. Another grouping championed more robust parliamentary powers, seeking to curb the bureaucracy's influence. Elections sparked heated rivalries. In some wards, political clubs organized debates or distributed leaflets explaining party stances, an activity unheard of in Edo times.

For many commoners without voting rights, politics still felt distant. Factory workers, shopkeepers, and rural migrants were too busy earning wages to engage deeply. Yet a sense of political consciousness slowly filtered down. Newspapers reported on parliamentary sessions, describing fierce arguments over budget allocations, military spending, or tax rates. Restaurants near the parliament building welcomed visitors hoping for a glimpse of their representatives. This gradual exposure to party politics fostered a new image of Tokyo as a capital not just for bureaucratic edicts, but also for robust debate—even if severely limited by the narrow electorate.

19.4 Legal Reforms and Modern Courts

Law, too, underwent modernization. Before Meiji, Tokugawa-era legal processes were often informal, with local magistrates wielding broad discretion. Harsh punishments or public executions had been common. Now, the government aimed to craft civil and criminal codes reflecting European legal theory. Judges in Tokyo received training from French or German advisors, learning systematically codified procedures.

Courthouses arose, built with Western-style stone facades. Inside, trials followed set rules. Defendants had more formal rights to defense, though in practice many could not afford quality legal counsel. Officials hoped these reforms would demonstrate Japan's commitment to fairness and order, crucial for revising foreign treaties that placed foreigners under extraterritorial jurisdictions. The final goal was to prove Japan's legal system was on par with the West.

Common citizens found the new courts both puzzling and intriguing. Some recognized that codified laws offered clearer protections. Others missed the simpler, faster judgments of local Edo authorities who knew the community. Lawyers and notaries introduced fees many could barely pay, leading to grumbles that justice favored the wealthy. Nonetheless, as Tokyo courts handled cases involving property disputes, contracts, or criminal acts, residents gradually adapted to the idea of rule by written law. The shift was incomplete—old customs still guided many private matters—but with each passing year, the courthouse grew more central in resolving conflicts.

19.5 Expanding Education and Universities

Government schools had already spread basic literacy, but the late 19th century saw further growth in higher institutions. Tokyo University, initially formed by merging smaller colleges, expanded its faculties to include law, engineering, medicine, literature, and more. Graduates of these faculties often secured influential roles in ministries, banks, or large companies, symbolizing how higher education was becoming a gateway to the new elite.

Private universities also emerged. Christian mission schools, such as those founded by Western missionaries, added college-level courses. A handful of Japanese entrepreneurs or educators established academies focusing on specific fields—teaching advanced commercial skills or foreign languages. These institutions embraced Western teaching methods. Some invited foreign professors as guest lecturers, blending foreign textbooks with Japanese contexts. Students returning from overseas brought additional expertise.

For the average Tokyoite, higher education remained out of reach financially. But seeing bright young people earn degrees and move into well-paying positions demonstrated that knowledge was as crucial as birth status. Enthusiasm for education continued to rise. Families who could afford it scrimped and saved for tuition, hoping a diploma would open doors. Middle-class neighborhoods took pride in local students who matriculated into prestigious universities, while poor districts sometimes pooled funds to send at least one promising child upward. By the turn of the century, Tokyo had transformed from a city with pockets of high literacy under Edo to a bustling modern capital where formal schooling was increasingly seen as the path to personal and national success.

19.6 Women's Education and Social Change

Although men dominated most government and business roles, late 19th-century reforms made slow progress in women's opportunities. Girls' schools expanded beyond a handful of elite academies. Public elementary schools, legally open to both genders, improved attendance rates. Some forward-thinking leaders argued that Japan could not develop fully if half its population—women—remained uneducated in modern subjects.

Tokyo led the way. Families of modest means still focused on marrying daughters off, but more progressive parents recognized the value of schooling. Female normal schools produced certified teachers, who in turn spread literacy among younger girls. A few determined women began writing articles for magazines on family, childcare, or even broader social topics. Though rare, these voices challenged the idea that a woman's role was confined to cooking and child-rearing.

Yet major inequalities persisted. Women did not gain voting rights, and few advanced to university-level studies. Job opportunities outside factory labor or teaching were scarce. Social norms frowned on independent female activity, so forging a career required extraordinary support. Some women's groups, often backed by foreign missionaries or local reformers, organized small clubs to discuss issues like health, child rearing, or rights within marriage. While these meetings were small, they planted seeds for future women's movements, hinting at bigger changes in the next century. For now, the late 19th century reforms in Tokyo only cracked the door open, but that small opening hinted at a slow shift in how the city saw its daughters and mothers.

19.7 Policing, Public Order, and Modernity

As Tokyo restructured itself into a modern capital, maintaining order became an ongoing challenge. The government enlarged the city's police force, adopting Western-style uniforms, pistols, and hierarchical ranks. Police stations dotted busy districts, and officers patrolled on foot or horseback. The role of a policeman also shifted from Edo's night watch and fire control toward broader duties: controlling traffic, investigating crimes, and enforcing new regulations on street vendors, sanitation, and building codes.

This policing drive sometimes clashed with local traditions. Street peddlers, used to Edo-era freedoms, found themselves restricted by licenses and curfews. Police cracked down on gambling dens or unlicensed performances. Brothels and entertainment quarters faced tougher oversight as officials tried to present a civilized image to foreign visitors. Some quarters resented the intrusion. Newspaper columns occasionally criticized heavy-handed tactics, citing instances of police brutality or corruption.

Nevertheless, the police system developed into a hallmark of modernization. Communication improved, with officers using telegraph lines to coordinate responses. The city introduced official detective divisions trained in modern forensics—a major leap from Edo's reliance on confessions or community testimony. These new methods helped solve crimes more systematically, though they also fed concerns about government surveillance. Over time, Tokyo's police force served as both protector and enforcer of the city's changing values, balancing security demands against the era's expanding freedoms.

19.8 Economic Regulation and Worker Protections

While the Meiji government encouraged business growth, calls for worker protections emerged, especially in Tokyo's factories. Reformers pointed out dangerous conditions, child labor, and abusive foremen who overworked employees. Labor unrest bubbled up in sporadic strikes, leading officials to worry about social stability. Some officials, influenced by Western progressive ideas, argued that minimal labor regulations—such as limits on hours or safety standards—would reduce conflict and raise productivity in the long run.

Yet the government hesitated to pass comprehensive labor laws. Large industrialists, including ex-samurai oligarchs, feared any regulation would slow Japan's competitive edge. They insisted that Japan needed total dedication from its workforce to catch up with the West. Still, minor reforms appeared: guidelines recommended that children under a certain age not work at night, or that factory dormitories meet basic hygiene standards. Enforcement was spotty. Inspectors often lacked power or were easily swayed by company owners.

Despite these small steps, serious labor laws would not come until the 20th century. Meanwhile, philanthropic efforts occasionally stepped in. Some wealthy merchants or Christian missions funded medical clinics for workers or established mutual aid societies. At a few factories, forward-looking owners provided communal baths or simple meals, hoping to reduce absenteeism and boost morale. Though not official labor legislation, these measures hinted at a moral recognition that modernization brought heavy burdens for the working poor—and that ignoring their welfare risked unrest.

19.9 Infrastructure Upgrades and Social Services

Late 19th-century Tokyo witnessed fresh pushes to improve living conditions. Water and sewer projects grew, aiming to reduce cholera outbreaks that plagued the city. Although resources were limited, government-engineered pipelines gradually replaced shallow wells in some wards. Brick and concrete sewer lines improved drainage, if only in central districts. Lighting also advanced: gas lamps gave way to limited electric lighting in prime areas. Factories that generated their own electricity sold surplus to local grids, illuminating a handful of boulevards at night.

Hospitals with Western-trained staff expanded. Some specialized in infectious diseases, while others offered general care. City authorities also toyed with establishing specialized wards for mental health, an unfamiliar concept under Edo. Charitable hospitals run by religious groups or philanthropists served poorer neighborhoods. Meanwhile, the city's transportation progressed with horse-drawn trams evolving into early electric streetcars by the 1890s, providing faster service between commercial hubs.

Though these developments cheered residents, they highlighted social gaps. Outlying wards saw minimal upgrades. Lower-income families rarely had piped water in their homes. Streetcar fares, however cheap, were still beyond the reach of some laborers who walked miles to work. Social services beyond basic medical care were rare, and poor relief remained mostly a charitable affair. Nonetheless, the city's growing network of utilities and public services confirmed that Tokyo was on a path to becoming a fully modern metropolis, albeit one where prosperity and convenience were unevenly distributed.

19.10 Firefighting and Emergency Response

With denser housing and emerging factories, firefighting took on new urgency. The old Edo tradition of fire brigades—where volunteer teams wielded hooks and axes—gave way to more modern units equipped with hand-pumped or even steam-powered fire engines. As the century drew to a close, these specialized crews became more organized. The city established central fire stations and training programs, borrowing from Western methods that used pressurized hoses and protective gear.

Fires still struck periodically, tearing through wooden structures, but coordinated response times improved. Firefighters used telegraph lines to receive alerts and mobilize faster. Public awareness campaigns advised citizens to store fewer flammable items, build firebreaks, and adopt safer cooking methods. Though many poor districts remained vulnerable, Tokyo's shift toward better construction materials and professional brigades reduced the devastation. Over time, insurance systems also appeared, letting businesses or homeowners pay fees for fire protection coverage—another Western concept that fitted the city's modernization approach.

19.11 New Currency and Banking Initiatives

Economic reform underpinned many of these social changes. Tokyo's banks, encouraged by government policy, standardized the yen currency system, making trade smoother across the country. The Bank of Japan, established in 1882, acted as a central authority to issue banknotes and regulate money supply. This helped stabilize markets, especially after earlier periods of inflation or confusion due to multiple domain currencies.

Modern banking also spurred private loans, enabling entrepreneurs to open more factories or invest in shipyards. Urban development in Tokyo soared, with land speculation rising around potential tram routes or sites for foreign businesses. However, this environment bred some financial bubbles. Small investors lost savings when certain projects failed. Newspapers sometimes reported scandals involving bank directors who gambled with client deposits. Nonetheless, the central bank's oversight steadily increased trust in the currency. By the late 1890s, everyday Tokyo residents accepted yen notes with more confidence, a sign that the city's financial realm had left behind the patchwork system of Edo and embraced a unified modern economy.

19.12 Diplomatic Gains and Treaty Revisions

A hidden motive behind these reforms was Japan's desire to revise the unequal treaties forced upon it in earlier decades. Western nations had demanded extraterritorial rights for their citizens, limiting Japanese jurisdiction in legal matters. Tokyo's officials worked tirelessly to prove their legal and governmental systems were on par with those of Europe. The promulgation of the constitution, establishment of modern courts, and adoption of recognized legal codes all served this purpose.

By showcasing a stable government, advanced police force, and transparent justice, Japan gradually persuaded Western powers to renegotiate. Treaties were revised, restoring Japan's full sovereignty over foreign residents within its borders. This was a critical diplomatic victory, earning Tokyo global respect. It also unleashed new energies: foreign companies no longer confined themselves to treaty ports. More foreign businessmen opened offices or factories in Tokyo, intensifying the city's role as a commercial hub.

For citizens, the end of extraterritorial privileges bolstered national pride. The era of foreigners enjoying special legal status was over. Political leaders capitalized on this sentiment, reminding the public that modernization had yielded independence and equality. Newspapers trumpeted that Tokyo, once overshadowed by Western gunboats, now negotiated treaties on equal footing. This success further validated the reforms that had transformed the city and strengthened support for continuing the modernization path.

19.13 National Unity and Patriotism

With greater international standing, Tokyo became the heart of rising patriotism. The Meiji government urged schools and newspapers to emphasize loyalty to the emperor and nation. Classes included moral lessons on sacrifice for Japan's progress. The expansion of the military, partly led by ex-samurai but open to all conscripts, reinforced unity across social divisions. Public events like imperial birthday celebrations or military parades in the city drew crowds that cheered columns of uniformed soldiers. Patriotic songs and symbols, such as the rising sun flag, gained prominence.

Some critics worried that this nationalist fervor might overshadow individual freedoms just when the city was expanding rights. Occasionally, the police curtailed dissent by citing the need for national harmony. Still, the majority of Tokyo's population seemed proud that Japan had maintained independence, reorganized society, and proven its capabilities to the wider world. Patriotic festivals merged Western fireworks and orchestras with age-old traditions like shrine processions. Even children's games took on nationalist elements, with cardboard battleships or toy rifles reflecting the militaristic pride that accompanied modernization.

19.14 Innovations in Transport and Communication

Beyond the horse-drawn trams, late-century Tokyo introduced electric streetcars, partially financed by investors who believed swifter travel would boost commerce. The hum of streetcars soon replaced the clip-clop of horses on major lines. This new transport spurred suburban growth: families of modest means built homes along tracks, traveling to city jobs daily. High-end real estate developments also appeared, featuring tree-lined boulevards and Western-influenced architecture.

Telegraphs and telephone lines multiplied. While initial telephone use was limited to businesses or wealthy families, the novelty spread in government offices and banks, speeding up transactions. Telegrams allowed residents to send urgent news across the country or even abroad, forging a sense that Tokyo had bridged vast distances. Post offices offered combined mail and telegraph services, each branch outfitted with the latest equipment. Over time, these technologies subtly reshaped social habits: urgent messages could come at any hour, businesses stayed open longer, and schedules became more precise.

19.15 Modern Print Culture and Mass Readership

As education expanded, Tokyo's appetite for printed materials exploded. Publishers churned out textbooks, novels, magazines, and newspapers. Each major ward had at least one bookstore selling everything from Western science primers to local almanacs. Cheap reprints of foreign classics coexisted with serialized Japanese novels that captured everyday life in the city. Sensational newspapers covered crime stories, political gossip, and social trends, appealing to a broad audience.

This abundance of print boosted literacy rates further, since people wanted to read the latest stories or glean business tips from trade journals. Political parties used pamphlets to spread messages. Social reformers, Christian missionaries, and feminist writers also found platforms in small magazines or newsletters. Meanwhile, local libraries, still developing, provided a gathering space for curious minds. For the first time in Tokyo's history, even middle-class laborers might spend their free time reading, whether for entertainment or self-improvement.

Some conservatives bemoaned the flood of "trashy" literature—cheap romance tales or lurid crime fiction—accusing it of corrupting morals. Yet many recognized mass print as an essential feature of a modern society, one that allowed knowledge to circulate rapidly. Reading clubs formed, forging communities around shared interests in topics like engineering, foreign travel, or classical poetry. In effect, Tokyo's dynamic print culture extended the intellectual ferment that accompanied the city's legal and political reforms, making the late 19th century a true age of words.

19.16 Arts and Crafts Preservation

Amid the push for Western models, a movement to preserve Japan's cultural heritage gained ground. Officials and cultural figures worried that mass production would crush traditional crafts, that Western art forms might overshadow ukiyo-e prints or Noh drama. Scholars led efforts to document old techniques, photograph historic landmarks, and maintain classic styles of painting. The Imperial Household even sponsored certain artisans, commissioning them to create pieces that showcased Japan's aesthetic genius.

Museums opened in Tokyo, collecting artifacts from Edo and earlier periods. Exhibits displayed samurai armor, scroll paintings, ceramics, or kabuki costumes, framing them as national treasures worthy of admiration both at home and abroad. Universities added courses on Japan's literary and artistic classics, ensuring these were studied alongside Western subjects. Some kabuki troupes, while adopting new elements, staged special performances faithful to ancient scripts and stage conventions, drawing nostalgic crowds.

Artisans themselves adapted. Those who specialized in lacquerware, for example, might produce a line for export, featuring motifs that appealed to Western buyers, while reserving a separate line for domestic patrons who insisted on pure tradition. Woodblock artists tried new inks or printing techniques but retained the sense of composition and elegant lines that defined Edo aesthetics. The upshot was a city that, even while racing toward modernity, carved out deliberate spaces to celebrate and sustain old forms. This dual approach helped Tokyo remain a cultural center, fusing new and old in daily life as well as in formal policy.

19.17 Diplomatic Crises and Foreign Wars

Late 19th-century reforms also impacted Japan's foreign relations. A more modern military and stronger economy emboldened the Meiji leadership to stand firm in regional disputes. The Sino-Japanese War of 1894–1895, sparked by tensions over Korea, ended in a surprising victory for Japan, revealing the success of Western military reforms. Tokyo residents celebrated news of victories in newspapers and festive parades. War spoils and territorial gains reinforced national pride, though they also stirred condemnation from some who worried Japan was adopting the imperialist practices of Western nations.

These successes elevated Japan's global standing, encouraging further modernization to keep pace with other powers. In Tokyo, war commemoration ceremonies honored fallen soldiers, and the public erected monuments. Artists produced prints glorifying naval battles, while school textbooks emphasized patriotism and the duty to serve. Yet war also meant casualties, widows, and orphans, leading charitable groups to form in the capital to support them. As the century neared its end, Tokyo had become the nerve center for a nation that, after reforming its institutions, no longer hesitated to flex its strength on the international stage.

19.18 Changing Labor Patterns and Urban Challenges

Success in foreign wars did not erase the city's internal problems. As factories multiplied, labor conditions remained harsh, with minimal regulation. The population swelled, pushing more families into cramped housing. The government's incremental improvements in sewage or water systems lagged behind the city's expansion, creating pockets of filth prone to disease. Activists petitioned for public housing or better sanitation laws, but officials often prioritized showpiece projects—like modern boulevards—to impress foreign visitors.

Still, some incremental shifts took root. Building codes, though not strictly enforced, became more common for newer structures, using less flammable materials. Workshops that handled toxic chemicals faced inspections (albeit cursory) aimed at reducing health risks. Newspapers exposed particularly exploitative factory owners, prodding the government to intervene. Streetcar lines expanded gradually, easing congestion in commercial districts. Civic pride grew as Japanese-led construction firms, guided by partial Western training, completed new city landmarks.

Such developments offered glimpses of a better urban future, but they didn't solve all problems. Labor unrest and class disparities remained, with wealth concentrated among business and government elites. Still, the late 19th century reforms put Tokyo on a path where public authorities at least acknowledged duties to all citizens, not just the upper echelons—a mindset slowly laying ground for the welfare considerations that would follow in the next century.

19.19 The Dawn of a New Century

By the close of the 1890s, Tokyo stood as a vibrant capital marked by constitutional rule, partial democratic participation, and a bustling economy that melded Western and Japanese influences. Steamships at the harbor, electric lights in some neighborhoods, universities granting modern degrees—these were all signs that the city's transformation had gathered unstoppable momentum. Education levels soared, newspapers cultivated a more informed public, and daily life hummed with the rhythms of modern transport and commerce.

Yet Tokyo also wrestled with contradictions: archaic social rules coexisted with modern laws, and traditional festivals thrived near factories spewing smoke. Patriotism soared, but so did concerns over labor exploitation. Western suits and top hats marched beside kimono-clad neighbors, forming a social mosaic that defied simplistic descriptions of "East meets West." The city's leaders and citizens felt both pride in their achievements and unease about who might be left behind. Japan's rising global presence brought respect, but also suspicion from other powers in an era of colonial competition.

Nonetheless, the reforms of the late 19th century achieved their core goals: they solidified Tokyo as a legitimate capital, upheld the emperor's authority through a constitutional monarchy, and showcased Japan's readiness to stand equal among modern states. For better or worse, the city had broken from its Edo-era past. In the next and final chapter, we will reflect on how these centuries of development—from a small fishing village to a major seat of power—shaped the unique character of Tokyo before it entered the fully modern era of the 20th century.

CHAPTER 20

Reflections on Pre-Modern Tokyo

20.1 Tracing the Journey from Edo to Tokyo

Having traversed a broad sweep of time—from the land's earliest settlements through the Edo period to the late 19th century—it's clear that Tokyo's story is one of dynamic change. What began as a modest fishing village called Edo blossomed into the grand seat of the Tokugawa shogunate, marked by samurai governance, castle moats, and tightly regulated social classes. Then came the Meiji Restoration, unraveling feudal structures, inviting Western influences, and recasting the city as a modern capital in a few intense decades.

Reflecting on this transformation reveals both continuity and radical breaks. Edo's spirit of communal festivals, neighborly cooperation, and aesthetic traditions never truly vanished. Families continued to value group harmony and respect for lineage, even as new opportunities, schools, and Western ideas pulled them into modern careers. Samurai lost their stipends, peasants moved into factories, and merchants rose to economic prominence, melding old roles with new social mobility. By the end of the 19th century, Tokyo was a mix of the archaic and the contemporary—railways near temples, telegraphs beside shrines, foreign consultants advising ex-samurai bureaucrats.

Such rapid transition was neither smooth nor uniformly welcomed. Many faced hardship: factory laborers, ex-samurai drowning in debt, traditional artisans overshadowed by mechanized production. Others seized the moment: merchants building vast fortunes, students becoming the next generation of politicians, or reformers pushing for broader rights. Through it all, Tokyo's resilience stood out. It managed to absorb huge shifts—political, cultural, economic—without losing its core identity as a place of shared community life, strong family bonds, and a lasting reverence for history.

20.2 Key Themes: Adaptation and Selective Adoption

One overriding theme is adaptation. Whether it was shifting from feudal ranks to modern social classes or merging indigenous crafts with imported machinery, Tokyo excelled at taking outside concepts and fitting them into local frameworks. This was a deliberate process. Leaders weighed which Western models would bolster Japan's global standing—like railways, steamships, or a constitutional government—while trying to retain an imperial center, old festivals, and communal values.

The result was selective adoption, not blind imitation. Tokyo's city planners did not flatten every winding alley in favor of perfect grid streets. Instead, they modernized key routes, built showpiece districts like Ginza, and left much of the city's organic layout intact. Schools taught foreign languages but also maintained Confucian moral instruction. Even the constitution balanced Western forms with the emperor's supreme position. This approach gave Tokyo a distinctive hybrid identity, neither purely Edo nor fully Western, but a living blend that evolved with each wave of reform.

At times, these choices generated friction—conservatives resisted foreign dress, radicals demanded faster democratization, and artisans worried about losing heritage. But the city's overall strategy remained pragmatic:

keep what works, adopt what strengthens the nation, and adapt anything that threatens local culture. Hence, Japanese theaters performed Western plays while preserving kabuki. Factories used imported machines side by side with hand skills. The constant negotiation between external pressures and local tradition shaped a city that embraced change yet held onto older forms for spiritual grounding.

20.3 Remembering Edo's Legacy

Amid modernization, why does Edo's legacy matter? Because it laid the cultural bedrock that enabled Tokyo to adapt so robustly. Edo was known for disciplined administration under the Tokugawa shoguns, a strong emphasis on urban organization, and advanced artisan crafts. Those centuries of relative peace allowed literacy to rise among samurai and merchants, fostering wide appreciation for literature and theater. Neighborhoods formed tight communities, forging mutual aid in times of fire or disaster. This social cohesion and cultural richness did not vanish with the Meiji Restoration; rather, it provided a resilient base for transformation.

Edo also bequeathed Tokyo a sense of aesthetic sensitivity. Urban dwellers cherished cherry blossom viewings, meticulous art forms, and refined manners. Even as factories mushroomed and Western suits became fashionable, that love for beauty and tradition persisted in daily rituals—a short tea ceremony during a busy day, the custom of exchanging seasonal gifts, or the way festivals maintained color and music in otherwise modern settings. These practices anchored the city's soul.

Moreover, Edo's strong internal trade and merchant networks carried over into Meiji commerce. The same entrepreneurial spirit that once sold luxury fabrics to samurai houses now fueled the creation of department stores or banking ventures. People well-versed in Edo's market complexities quickly learned Western accounting methods, bridging old business savvy with new financial systems. Thus, Edo's foundation remained present in how Tokyo functioned economically, socially, and artistically, shaping the city's particular brand of modernization.

20.4 Social Bonds and Family Focus

One persistent thread in pre-modern Tokyo was the importance of family and community networks. Under Tokugawa rule, families were the fundamental unit, with clear roles for each member. While Meiji reforms loosened class barriers, they did not dissolve these household-centered principles. Even as young men and women found jobs in factories or offices, many returned to shared homes in the evenings, pooling earnings for communal support. Elders often remained advisors, guiding younger relatives through educational or marital decisions.

Neighborhood associations, once vital under Edo for firefighting or dispute mediation, continued in new forms. They helped manage street festivals, coordinate local improvements, or negotiate with authorities over building regulations. In an era of big administrative changes, these small associations retained a sense of continuity and belonging. Workers in factories, too, formed close-knit groups, sometimes carrying the same camaraderie that Edo artisans had known in guilds.

This family and community focus influenced how Tokyoans integrated Western concepts. For example, while some foreign advisers pushed for individual property rights and personal independence, local communities still valued group obligations. A father might quietly accept that his son studied Western medicine, yet expect that son to remain loyal to family traditions. Western manners and laws were woven into a collective ethos that prized empathy, respect for elders, and mutual aid. Even with all the modernization, Tokyo in the late 19th century was never just an anonymous urban sprawl; people cared about neighborly ties, though tested by migration and rapid growth.

20.5 The Role of Religion and Philosophy

Pre-modern Tokyo also inherited religious depth, blending Shinto and Buddhist beliefs with local folklore. In the Meiji era, Shinto gained prominence as a state-endorsed tradition, centered on emperor veneration. Buddhist temples adapted to less official support but remained vital in local rituals and funerals. Christianity found a foothold, but never dominated. Throughout these shifts, the city's spiritual life informed social values. Some families prayed for ancestors at Buddhist altars, then visited a Shinto shrine for protection. Edo's tolerance for multiple beliefs continued, with the state intervening only when it perceived threats to imperial authority.

Philosophy also mattered. Confucian ethics shaped Edo governance, emphasizing loyalty, harmony, and correct social roles. In the Meiji age, these ideas blended with Western theories like human rights or scientific rationalism. Tokyo's intellectual scene wrestled with questions of moral duty versus individual liberty, or how to integrate Darwinian evolution with Buddhist views of life. Philosophy clubs and reading circles sprouted among educated citizens. Translated works from Western thinkers—Locke, Rousseau, Mill—provoked lively discussion. The city's long tradition of learning under Confucian tutors now opened to a global spectrum of thought. This convergence made Tokyo a unique meeting ground for philosophies that might, in other contexts, have stood apart.

20.6 A City of Contrasts: Rich and Poor

Despite the grandeur of modernization, Tokyo did not escape inequality. Wealthy families resided in comfortable houses with partial Western décor, while poor laborers packed into tenements lacking basic sanitation. Samurai descendants with bureaucratic jobs enjoyed stable incomes, yet other ex-samurai languished in poverty. Merchants who rose to wealth sometimes showed off mansions and modern luxuries, while artisanal workshops struggled under pressure from mass-produced goods.

Workers in new industries toiled for long hours, earning barely enough for rent and food. Diseases raged in cramped neighborhoods, highlighting the gap between shining boulevards in central districts and squalor in the shadows. Social charities and philanthropic efforts stepped in, partly guided by Christian missions or local associations, but the scale of need outstripped relief. This dichotomy reminded the city that modernization could be dazzling on the surface—electric lights, paved roads, constitutional ceremonies—yet leave many behind.

Tokyo's leaders grappled with solutions. Some proposed stronger welfare measures or labor protections, but faced resistance from those who feared slower economic growth. Nevertheless, the conversation around poverty grew more intense, with newspapers exposing harsh conditions in factories, and small unions forming among workers. These seeds, planted in the late 19th century, would eventually push for broader social reforms. For now, the city's greatest achievements overshadowed but did not hide the struggles of its most vulnerable residents.

20.7 Echoes of the Past in Modern Culture

While forging into the future, Tokyo never fully severed ties to its pre-modern aesthetics and entertainment. Kabuki, with centuries of tradition, adapted to modern audiences by adding new plot elements—telegraphs, foreign visitors—yet preserved its dramatic poses and music. Noh, more formal and ancient, survived through imperial and aristocratic patronage, with occasional showcases for international guests. Rakugo storytellers reworked old Edo humor into comedic tales about modern confusion: a samurai's reaction to a steam train, or a merchant's bafflement at foreign table manners.

Traditional festivals continued to unify districts. People still danced in the streets carrying portable shrines, though overhead lines for telegraphs or street lamps might occasionally obstruct the procession. Fireworks colored the sky along the Sumida River, and families marked the changing seasons with special dishes—sakura mochi in spring or roasted chestnuts in autumn. Even the busiest factory worker found time to observe a local festival, reminding them that life was not just about production quotas but also about communal joy.

Tea ceremony masters, calligraphers, and ikebana experts maintained classes for those seeking Edo-era grace. Samurai heritage lived on in martial arts dojos teaching judo, kendo, or aikido. These arts re-envisioned fighting skills as spiritual discipline rather than battlefield prowess. Westerners in Tokyo often admired such cultural forms, while local participants found pride in preserving them. Thus, the city's vibrant tradition and modern impulse merged, ensuring that while machines, trains, and suits multiplied, the softer rhythms and refined arts of Edo did not vanish.

20.8 Embracing Global Influence While Shaping a Distinct Identity

In earlier chapters, we traced the influx of Western technology, governance, and cultural ideas. Tokyo's ability to integrate them so effectively stemmed from its robust internal culture, strong governance, and readiness to adapt. Foreign experts arrived, but local leaders always insisted on eventual Japanese control of projects. Western architecture might line main roads, but temples and shrines still anchored neighborhoods. English classes proliferated, yet Japanese language learning did not diminish; in fact, it grew more universal, courtesy of compulsory schooling.

The result was a self-confident capital, not cowed by foreign might, but using it as a catalyst. This stance kept foreigners from dominating Tokyo's destiny. Instead, each borrowed element was shaped to fit local tastes. Department stores sold Western hats alongside traditional hair ornaments. A tram conductor in a pressed Western uniform might chat with passengers about local sumo tournaments. The city's resilience and creative fusion encouraged travelers to call it a wonder of the East—an example of non-Western modernization.

20.9 Lessons from Pre-Modern History

Looking back, what lessons emerge for modern readers studying Tokyo's pre-20th-century story?

1. **Gradual Mergers**: Change did not happen overnight. Edo's policies, culture, and communal ties blended with Meiji reforms, forging a layered outcome rather than a total rupture.
2. **Local Agency**: Even when adopting Western techniques, Tokyo's leaders and citizens exercised choice, ensuring imported ideas served Japan's goals instead of simply imitating foreign powers.
3. **Unity in Diversity**: The city's new identity thrived on variety—samurai discipline meeting merchant enterprise, Confucian ideals mixing with Western liberalism, and advanced factories alongside centuries-old crafts.

4. **Continuing Struggle**: Modernization improved infrastructure and global status, but did not solve all issues. Labor exploitation, poverty, and class disparity cast long shadows, requiring future efforts.

These lessons highlight the complexity and determination behind Tokyo's evolution. Far from a simple success story, it is a narrative of negotiation—between old and new, local and global, progress and tradition.

20.10 Closing Thoughts: Preparing for the Modern Age

As the 19th century closed, Tokyo stood on the threshold of the 20th. Political reforms had established a constitutional monarchy, albeit limited. Economic growth surged, with banks, railways, and steamships weaving the nation together. The city, once dominantly wooden, now featured districts of brick buildings and electric lights. Public schooling spread knowledge widely, fueling a literate population. Women's roles, though constrained, were inching forward. Samurais had mostly merged into modern professions, merchants rose in prestige, and a new middle class formed, aspiring to modern comforts.

Yet deeper transformations lay ahead. The 20th century would bring global conflicts, further industrialization, mass movements for labor and women's rights, and a more intense interplay between Japan's traditions and Western globalization. The footprints of Edo shaped how Tokyo met these challenges, preserving a reverence for harmony, artistry, and communal ties even as the city faced the growing complexities of modern warfare, diplomacy, and economic booms or busts. In that sense, the city's pre-modern journey was not just a precursor but also a foundation—one that informed every later stage of Tokyo's ongoing life story.

Now, having concluded this exploration of Tokyo's complete history up to the late 19th century, we can see how deeply the city's pre-modern era influenced its growth. These pages have shown a robust tapestry of resilience, creativity, and cultural depth. Whether one focuses on ancient tribal groups, the bustling Edo metropolis, or the rush of Meiji-era reforms, the central theme remains the same: Tokyo's capacity to blend, adapt, and remain an ever-evolving home for millions—both then and now.

Help Us Share Your Thoughts!

Dear reader,

Thank you for spending your time with this book. We hope it brought you enjoyment and a few new ideas to think about. If there was anything that didn't work for you, or if you have suggestions on how we can improve, please let us know at **kontakt@skriuwer.com**. Your feedback means a lot to us and helps us make our books even better.

If you enjoyed this book, we would be very grateful if you left a review on the site where you purchased it. Your review not only helps other readers find our books, but also encourages us to keep creating more stories and materials that you'll love.

By choosing Skriuwer, you're also supporting **Frisian**—a minority language mainly spoken in the northern Netherlands. Although **Frisian** has a rich history, the number of speakers is shrinking, and it's at risk of dying out. Your purchase helps fund resources to preserve and promote this language, such as educational programs and learning tools. If you'd like to learn more about Frisian or even start learning it yourself, please visit **www.learnfrisian.com**.

Thank you for being part of our community. We look forward to sharing more books with you in the future.

Warm regards,
The Skriuwer Team